DOUBLE FEATURE OF THE LIVING DEAD: TWO ZOMBIE NOVELS IN ONE

BY RUSTY FISCHER

FEATURING...

USHERS, INC.

AND

PANTY RAID @ ZOMBIE HIGH

Decadent Publishing Company
www.decadentpublishing.com

Double Feature of the Living Dead: Two Zombie Novels in One
Copyright 2011 by Rusty Fischer
ISBN: 978-1-61333-159-0
Cover by Valerie Tibbs and Cribley Designs

Published by Decadent Publishing Company
www.decadentpublishing.com

Printed in the United States of America

~Author's Note~

Movies have always been a big – really big – part of my life. My earliest memories are of sitting in front of the TV, eating Little Debbie brownies rolled up into balls (don't ask me why) and watching "After school specials." They don't have those anymore, but most of you will know what I'm talking about: movies that played after school and taught you all kinds of values like don't drink and drive or have premarital sex or smoke marijuana, courtesy of the day's biggest stars aka Kristy McNichol and Scott Baio. (Google 'em, kids.)

Then we got HBO, and that was it; all the movies I wanted, right there on my TV. When I got a little older, "TV movies" lost some of their appeal thanks to one seminal trip to the local multiplex. I can vividly remember sitting in the theater for *Star Wars* and feeling my life change right in front of my eyes.

I was hooked on movie theaters after that. Big screens, popcorn, Twizzlers, cold soda, wide seats, no Mom telling you to turn it down after every shootout or explosion – what's not to love?

Only problem was: I was only nine at the time! Once I could ride my bike beyond junior high and back a few years later, I tried making it to our not-so-local mall – it was one town away and over a pretty hardcore bridge. I made it, watched something awesome (I'm sure), and promptly got hit by a car on the way home. That was it for my *Breaking Away* moment.

I had to depend on others for my movie moments after that; at least until I got my first car, a faded maroon Ford Zephyr (Jane Fonda drove a gold one in *The Electric Horseman*, for a frame of reference) and I was off to the races. Every chance I got, I haunted our local mall movie theater. Day, night, school or no school.

High school in the 80s – with a car – was prime movie time; Breakfast Club, Chopping Mall, Back to the Future, Top Gun, Fast Times at Ridgemont High, Poltergeist, Rocky 4 and too many more to count. I can vividly remember skipping school with a buddy to see Rambo 2 on opening day.

College, first job, second job, third job, every day off or semester break was spent catching up on movies. Once real life started, I often had to squeeze two in on one day just to fit them all in.

And that's when my love affair with double-features began, and continues to this day. Four hours of movies, thousands of calories in snacks, all for the price of a couple of tickets (or one, if I'm feeling larcenous). No email, no phone, no clients, no bills, no worries, no fuss; just pure movie heaven.

Fast forward to a few weeks ago when the forward-thinking folks at Decadent Publishing emailed me to say they were thinking of putting my two YA zombie books, Ushers, Inc. and Panty Raid at Zombie High in one brain-chomping volume.

Oh, and did they mention... it would come out in print?!?!?

Yowza, who says "no" to that, right? Don't get me wrong, I love my EBooks and it's been a real learning experience discovering new and unique ways to promote and share them with YA paranormal readers, but I have to admit being partial to print, so... double yowza, sign me up!

Trouble is, the book needed a catchy new title that would quickly and (hopefully) easily explain what was inside: two zombie books for the price of one. So... hmmm... how the heck do I do *that*?

Well, hold up now, one of these books is about four zombie-hunting movie ushers, right? And the other is about an abandoned hospital nicknamed Zombie High, yes? And there are two books, correct? So, how about... wait for it... *Double Feature of the Living Dead*?!?!

Nice one, I thought; luckily Lisa and Heather agreed!

And so here we are, however many weeks later and that is pretty much what you're getting: two zombie books in one convenient volume for the price of one. Kind of like a double feature, of books... with reanimated main characters!

Sounds good to me, and I hope you agree!

~ Rusty Fischer, 2011

USHERS, INC.

BY RUSTY FISCHER

PROLOGUE

"**A**bby!" Zach bellows over the sound of fresh corn sizzling in The Pop-U-Later 2470. "Someone's calling for an usher in Theater 12."

"So?" I snap, deeply busy cleaning off the completely grody half-frozen nozzles of the Sergeant Slushee machine. "You're an usher; hit the bricks and get to stepping."

"It's your *turn*," he whines (adorably), yanking over the giant gleaming steal popper and emptying it as pounds of fresh, hot, greasy, buttery corn dump into the nearly empty bin below.

The familiar fresh popcorn smell is such a big part of my life, like the cheap hand soap in the downstairs bathroom or my Gilded Lilac shampoo or Zach's dollar store imposter cologne that I barely even notice it anymore.

"It was my turn the *last* three turns." I wipe my hands with a limp dish rag and slide over the top of the candy counter with barely a push from my gray, cement-colored wrist.

I shake my head, prepared to storm past him without a backward glance when he gives me that pouty look with the fluttering butterfly eyelashes and simpering hazel eyes and pinched, plump lips.

"Hey, you know our rule; no going on missions without a goodbye kiss."

"Zach, dude, it's 9:30 on a Tuesday night, how dangerous could this 'mission' really be?"

He shakes his head and wags his finger. Wow, he must *really* be serious about this new rule of his.

Not that I'm complaining, mind you.

"Remember what happened *last* Thursday when you said that?"

I nod my head, but that's not good enough.

"*What* happened, Abby?"

I hang my head and repeat in a sing-song voice, like a fourth grader getting scolded for not cleaning up her lunch tray. "I stormed off without a goodbye kiss and nearly got cursed by that Mummy in Theater 4. Okay I feel you, but again, if any of you *other* ushers would take your stupid turns on the Undead Rotation, I wouldn't always be risking life and limb up in here."

"So where's my kiss?" he asks, unaffected by what I thought was a pretty persuasive argument. (Guess not.)

Great, now he's jinxed me.

I lean over the candy counter—purposefully smearing my hands all over the glass top because I know he just spent five minutes waxing it while the popcorn was popping—and plant one on those luscious lips.

It's always such a fine sensation; my cold, dead lips on his ruby red warm ones.

Although they're quite dead, too—stupid lucky vampire lips!

Usually I can't get enough of that sweet sensation, but the 9:45 show is starting soon and if I don't go take care of business, I won't have time to tear tickets and our new night manager—I won't tell you what happened to the "old" night manager—stupid Mr. Bagley will have a (nother) cow.

I sigh and peel myself away, although it's never easy.

I sneak a peek before turning around.

Now, just for the record, Flickers Cinemas has just about the all-time, mother-lovin', fugliest usher uniforms on the entire planet.

At least the new 24-theater place down at the mall has casual uniforms: khaki slacks, maroon shirts, black ball caps. And at the dollar cinema beachside, they literally get to wear jeans and T-shirts. Now *that's* class!

Maybe work wouldn't be such a drag if we could wear something casual like that.

But Zach?

Zach makes our fake half-tuxedo uniforms look *good*.

Maybe it's his height, his long arms and legs stretching the black pants and white sleeves out and making them look more dramatic, somehow.

Or perhaps it's those broad shoulders all hard and striking at the top, or the narrow waist, or the long, crooked fingers sticking out of his cuffs or the dirty blond curls falling over his forehead and collar.

Whatever it is, looking away from Zach has always been harder than looking *at* him, that's for sure; one reason I turn quickly to avoid getting drawn in once again.

8

I know he's watching me go but if I look back, I'll just fall under his spell again and, like I said, tick-tock, tick-tock.

Theater 12 is showing *Vampire Platoon 5* so it's not very crowded.

I slip in through the door, let my eyes adjust to the light, and poke my head around the corner.

A little old lady is waving her open cell phone at me, shining the eerie blue light in my face to get my attention.

I smile behind my hand and ease over to the third row, where she's sitting with her plump legs up on the seat in front of her (that's sooooo a Flickers Cinemas violation, but, business first).

"How can I help you, ma'am?" I whisper. Already I can smell the wet dog fur that can only mean one thing: a werewolf in the back row.

"Yes, well, that...creature...back there keeps growling at the scary parts, and do you smell that? I was around for the Great Werewolf Roundup of 2010, missy, and I'd know that scent anywhere. You've got a wolf in here somewhere! Now, what do you intend to do about it?"

If you only knew, I think.

Instead I pat her on the shoulder, sending up a cloud of that old lady makeup dust above her equally powdery hair and assure her, "I'll take care of it, ma'am. I'm an usher, remember?"

I lift my dead, stiff legs up the stairs, letting my nose guide me past the middle-aged man sitting amidst about a week's worth of junk food wrappers, past the young couple who can't keep their hands off each other, and straight to the lethal-looking punk in the back row.

He's in jeans and a leather jacket, which is a little odd because most werewolves know that whatever they're wearing when they morph won't be in such great shape once they turn back into a human, so they tend to wear baggy or cheap things—four dollar sweatpants and cheap T-shirts they get five to a pack and won't worry about leaving behind, in bloody tatters, as they run away from their latest victim.

His hair is longish, his eyes alive and alert, his scowl feral and onerous.

He starts right off with the attitude, hissing, "Out of my way, loser. I'm trying to watch the movie."

I stand politely just out of swiping range and whisper, "Yes, sir, so are the other patrons and well, frankly we've had...complaints."

"From who?" he asks.

"From *whom*," I correct, because there's nothing a werewolf hates more than being corrected, let me tell you. Well, aside from getting capped by a silver bullet, of course. "And that's confidential, but if you don't take the growling, hissing, and fang licking down a notch, I'm going to have to ask you to leave."

He smirks, because he knows he has me.

After all, according to the Living with the Living Dead Laws, you can't just toss suspected werewolves, vampires, mummies, or even zombies out on their ears just because you *suspect* they're one of the undead.

That is, unless you're one of them yourself.

Now, this guy doesn't *look* like a werewolf at the moment, but that's one of the joys of being a werewolf, looking like everybody else for twenty-seven days every month.

It's those last three you really have to watch out for.

Take my best friend, Tracy—werewolf through and through, and to look at her, you'd think "teen supermodel" not "vicious killer."

Still, get between her and some unlucky farm animal under a full moon, and you're lucky if you walk away with all your limbs intact.

If you walk away at all.

I'd checked my handy pocket calendar on the way into the theater just now (yes, I *do* have a handy pocket calendar, what of it?) and, sure enough, tonight's a full moon.

Hence the wet dog smell, which is all part of the transformation process.

If the old busybody down in aisle three hadn't reported it, we could have had a full-fledged werewolf convention in Theater 12 by the closing credits, and that wouldn't be good.

Not when I have that term paper in Sociology due tomorrow.

"Are you still here?" he snorts, wiping the customer service smile off my face. "You know you can't do anything to me, even if you *are* an usher."

I kind of smile at that.

Just a few weeks ago, before this whole thing started, there were few jobs less respected than being a lowly movie theater usher.

Now, thanks to Ushers, Inc., it's suddenly "cool" to be an usher again.

But that's getting a little ahead of ourselves, isn't it?

For now, I've got to eject this creep and do it legally, which means I have to prove he's a werewolf first, you know, *before* he tears the rest of the theater patrons limb from limb.

Fortunately, I've come prepared.

On each finger of my left hand is a simple ring; silver, of course.

I reach down and grab his forearm, gently, so gently, and instantly his arm…does…nothing.

"Told you," he sneers, looking past my head to a particularly scary part on the giant movie screen behind me. (You know, at least, for amateurs.)

"Why don't you check out those teenagers in the middle row? They've been going at it like dogs in heat ever since the previews. They're probably *both* werewolves. And even if they aren't, you should throw them out on principle alone."

I apologize and turn just in time to avoid the huge paw slashing the air two centimeters in front of my face.

I scramble backward as the werewolf advances on the long-haired dude in the back row.

He screams at me to help him and, as I unclasp the specially-made bowtie around my neck, that's just what I do.

Clasping one end in my hand I snap it out, watching a long, thin but strong silver chain uncoil until it's like the whip that old guy used in *Raiders of the Lost Ark*.

I snap it within inches of the werewolf's thick, impenetrable hide and he hisses, sniffs, and promptly ignores it.

Okay, okay, he wouldn't be the first.

I know it doesn't look like much, but it's not looks I'm worried about at the moment.

Leaping onto a chair, I snap the silver bowtie whip again, and this time it wraps expertly around the wolf's front paw, once, twice, three times, instantly searing the skin and bursting the thick gray coat into flames.

Suddenly the recognizable smell of a pure werewolf—a little sulfur, a lot of cat food and plenty of wet, low-down dirty dog fur—fills the arena as the young guy with long hair scrambles down the theater aisles and out to safety.

I turn to follow his progress and suddenly all the seats are empty.

Well, at least I'll be the only victim, if it turns out that way.

The wolf yelps and yanks its ruined paw from the whip, but I crack it again—over its big, burly head this time—and send it running, cornering it just under the still-flickering digital projection booth as I use my free hand to grab the silver toothpick I always keep wedged in my standard issue Flickers Cinemas cummerbund, for just such occasions.

The whip is losing its effectiveness now, the werewolf limping around in its corner, angling for its chance to strike the only target left around—me.

I put the whip down; the wolf makes its move—I'm ready.

With the palm of my hand, I hide the toothpick until just the last minute. When the wolf snarls and opens its jaws to strike, I roll just out of range and jab the sliver of silver straight into its armpit, where it sticks like a burr and, as the wolf rolls around trying to get it out, sinks in even deeper until none of the silver is visible and it's dead stuck—for good.

Suddenly the werewolf stops in mid-air and lands on me in a heap of gray hair and withered skin, and…and…old lady face powder?

It was the granny with her feet up in the third row, after all. That old coot!

So, you may be wondering, why do I use a silver toothpick—something so wimpy and minor—as opposed to, say, a silver stake or bullet?

Here's why: this way, grandma gets to wake up.

Too much silver and they're gone forever; just enough—like the silver bowtie and the tiny toothpick—and they get knocked down, but have the chance to get up again.

And when granny does, her face is a mask of pain and shame and grief and sadness and despair but, mostly, shame.

If I'd used something bigger, or more lethal, grandma would have just, well, gone to that great monster graveyard in the sky.

And why?

Just because some wolf bit her however long ago and she's been craving human flesh ever since.

It's not her fault, so why put her down when with a simple trick she can wake up—and stay—human?

No more fearing the full moon, no more chaining herself up in the cellar three nights a month, no more tricking plucky little ushers into putting her out of her misery.

"Did I hurt anybody, dear?" she asks as I cover her cold, quivering, naked body with a glittery pink hoodie one of the teenagers left behind when they deserted me during the werewolf's violent rumble.

"No ma'am," I whisper reassuringly, texting Zach a quick "911" code to alert the medics and get poor grandma some help now that her days as a carnivorous, fang-baring member of the Undead are over. "And thanks to that little burr in your side, you never will again."

She smiles. "Thank you, dear. When I heard this was the movie theater where the ushers worked—I mean *the* ushers—well, I could only hope *one* of you would help me. I'm sorry to scare you, dear, but I thank you for saving me."

I stand her up, pull the hoodie down nearly to her knees. "All in a night's work, ma'am."

It just goes to show, when it comes to werewolves, you just never know.

But, like I said, I'm getting ahead of myself.

Here, let's go back to the beginning and I'll tell you how Ushers, Inc. got its start.

CHAPTER ONE

Two Weeks Earlier

"**T**racy!"

My best friend hears the tone in my voice and follows my eyes to the thick line winding in front of the ticket booth, where chubby Cliff sits pleasantly spitting out tickets and giving unsolicited reviews of tonight's 7:30 showing of *Vampire Biker Chicks 3*.

"*Bloody Gore* magazine gives it two severed thumbs up," I hear him pleasantly telling a middle-age couple, who wince at his garish enthusiasm—but buy their tickets anyway.

"You won't want to miss the third act," he tells the burly college dudes next in line. "I hear one of the vampires gets staked through the heart by her own motorcycle's tail pipe. Nice, huh?"

They kind of snort appreciatively and hand over their bank cards.

Meanwhile Tracy stands by my side, two inches taller and several shades hotter.

Together we watch "the holy couple" in my line of vision cling to each other like the co-dependents they are, halfway through the slow-moving (thanks to Cliff's non-stop reviews) line.

"Hell *no!*" she hisses, holding up her broom in one hand and a dust tray in the other and literally backing away from my little ticket podium as if it were cursed. And, in moments like this one, she could be right. "Mia and Wyatt *already* treat me like the hired help at school. I'm not giving them even more ammunition."

I shake my head even as her tightly-woven dreadlocks rustle away atop the shoulders of her crisp, white usher shirt.

"You *owe* me, Tracy," I hiss between ripping tickets, growing desperate now and not caring who sees it.

"For *what?*" she snaps back, sweeping up a stray mustard packet from in front of the concession stand, where Zach happily hands out licorice vines and chocolate-covered raisins to hungry moviegoers with his adorably crooked smile.

"I *so* wrote your book report on *Moby Dick!*" I practically shout.

Zach and a few customers turn their heads.

She glares at me with her brown eyes. "You promised you wouldn't tell anybody that."

"And you promised you'd 'hit me back' when I needed it, remember Tracy? Well, I need it!"

"I *did* hit you back, girl," she reminds me, "by working your Saturday shift last week, remember?"

Suddenly I'm bested; she knows it, smiling triumphantly and waving her raggedy pint-sized broom in victory.

"No," I whimper as Mia Hopwood and Wyatt Winters inch forward in the ticket line, though from the looks of it they'd be just as happy nibbling on each other's model-worthy ears for the rest of the night as watching *Vampire Biker Chicks 3.*

"Well, I do," she snarks, strutting away with her long, limber, volleyball girl legs and making sure to be as far from the lobby as possible when high school royalty walks in.

Now, a few things about tearing tickets at the 7:30 show—it's lame.

Nobody ever looks at you except the kids from school, and they just want to make fun of your fake tuxedo and your crooked bowtie and your goofy cummerbund.

And, really, who can blame them?

They all know that you, a.) live in the Meriwether Home for Wayward Boys and Girls, b.) make a measly six bucks an hour, and c.) can't do anything back to them because a manager is always hovering around, and it's just, well, horrible.

What's worse, they literally treat you like part of the entertainment; like you're some bit actor who just walked off the screen they can goof and crack and hack on and it doesn't matter anyway, because you're just part of the scenery.

Normally, it doesn't get to me. That's the nice thing about working with friends.

But, I dunno. Just once it would be nice if someone, anyone, other than my fellow ushers saw me as anything even close to a real, live human being.

You know?

Fortunately, in any given shift—except on the weekends—I really only see a few dozen kids from school, and most of them are cool so it's a small price to pay for just about the best job in the world for a (monster) movie lover such as myself.

Mia and Wyatt are nearly up to Cliff's window by now, and I can see Wyatt sliding his long, elegant fingers into his back pocket to reach for his wallet.

Mia never pays; you have to give her that much.

Wyatt has on one of those jean jacket hoodies, though it's really not that cool out, and aviator shades that go well with his wavy black hair and five o'clock shadow.

The jacket hugs his broad shoulders and the hoodie makes him look even taller, though he doesn't need any help in that department, thanks very much.

Next to him Mia holds her own, a few inches shorter but no less regal in her black leggings and sleek, silver thigh-length sweater, big black belt with an even bigger shiny silver buckle over her freakishly non-existent stomach.

She has black sunglasses set high atop her straight black hair and even from inside the lobby, I can see she's rocking the Goth eye shadow look, which (naturally) only compliments her whole Queen of Sheba vibe.

The crowd is thinning down now, the previews almost starting, but as Wyatt pays for the tickets and hands them to Mia, they saunter along like a couple of models looking for the catwalk.

I silently fume, and not because they're jealous-inducing beautiful, either.

It's just...ugghh...if it was *me* going to see *Vampire Biker Chicks 3* for the first time, I sure wouldn't be sauntering anywhere but straight up to the back row a good five minutes before the previews started.

There's nothing I hate worse than casual moviegoers, am I right?

I mean, if you're not even going to make an effort to see the movie from reel-to-reel, then go ahead and rent it at home and only watch it with one eye, am I right?

Wyatt moseys along beside Mia, his long, elegant arm draped gracefully over her sturdy shoulder as she spots me with her dead, limp, thousand-yard stare.

Mia may have the most beautiful, intense, and vibrant emerald green eyes I've ever seen, but I swear there's something...missing...behind them.

She's not dumb, exactly, though at Cypress Cove High she's known for her beauty, not her brains.

No, she's just...simple.

Like, despite my humble upbringing, job, appearance, and even humbler living conditions, I'm known as a pretty funny gal at Cypress Cove High School.

Not funny enough to have gobs of adoring fans mobbing me in the halls or anything, mind you, but if you're looking for a quick one-liner to break a little classroom tension toward the end of the day, it's a pretty established fact that Abby Cooper is your go-to gal.

Mia Hopwood has never once laughed at any of my jokes. And not just because she has an absolute and totally strict "Ignore Abby Cooper at All Costs" policy, either.

I watched her once as the rest of our Biology class giggled, even Mr. Hicks—a notorious non-giggler, trust me—and it was almost as if I was speaking a different language; like she just didn't get it, you know?

I don't have a problem with Mean Girls, per se, but *Dumb* Mean Girls? Dude, that just...*bugs*...me.

"Hey guys," I bluff effusively as they finally shuffle-walk up to my scratched black ticket podium, the one with the little slit in top for the second half of the tickets I tear for seven hours straight, four nights a week. "Whatcha seein' tonight?"

Mia looks at me like I've just upchucked with those piercing green eyes of her, looks down at her tickets and, as she's handing them over to me, conveniently drops them onto the slick black and white tiles of the lobby floor.

My hand is outstretched, hers is outstretched, and I'm not moving a muscle.

Witch!

I know, you know, and *she* knows she just pulled that crap on purpose.

No way, I don't care if Mr. Fletcher fires me for gross-insubordination-of-the-most-asinine-teenage kind. I am not reaching for those tickets.

"Whoops," she coos, jerking her hand back.

"*Whoops*," I purr coolly, pulling mine back just as quickly.

"Mia," Wyatt scolds in a familiar way, bending to pick them up. "It's not like you to be so...clumsy."

"Don't, *Wyatt*," she hisses. "That's *her* job."

He pauses just a smidge, as if he's seriously thinking about obeying his main squeeze's orders, but then his tan fingers jut out, deftly snatch the tickets, and hand them to me without comment.

I can't read his eyes behind the kind of cool, kind of cheesy aviator shades, but I can read hers, and man is she ticked *off*.

Which could explain why I'm still smiling two whole hours later as folks start lining up for the 9:30 show.

CHAPTER TWO

I don't know why Mr. Fletcher is the only manager—okay, he's just an assistant manager, but still—who hangs out with the ushers on Thursday *Free* Preview Night.

Maybe it's because he's still in his twenties, or maybe because he's hip to the fact that the four of us are actually "fun" to be around, or maybe he just plain digs bad—usually *really* bad—monster movies.

Of course, it would be "unprofessional" of him to actually sit with us, so instead he sits a few seats over—and two rows back; just close enough to whisper snide comments about the bad parts and guffaw out loud over the really bad parts, but not close enough to look guilty should one of the "real" managers stumble in after midnight.

On tonight's viewing list is the sequel to last year's non-hit *Panty Raid at Zombie High*, called *Another Panty Raid at Zombie High*.

Yeah, real clever guys.

You've probably never heard of either of these movies; here's why—they don't play them at most big-name theaters.

But since little Flickers Cinemas only has fourteen measly screens and isn't owned by some big-name conglomerate Fortune 500 mega-corporation, we can happily choose whatever horrible, crappy, sad, and lonely little B and C-Grade horror flicks we want, even if only a few hundred people ever come in and see them.

Okay, so the managers stick them in Theater 14, the very last theater in the joint, with only one hundred and twenty-seats, but still, they make more money than sticking the twelveth week of *Mission Possible 27* in there so…why not?

Tracy is to my left while Zach is to my right, with Cliff cussing just above our heads as he queues up the digital camera from inside the cozy little projection booth.

He insists on leaving the house lights on until he "makes his entrance," as he calls it, so the whole time we're all squinting.

Since we can't preview our Thursday movie until after work, everyone is still in uniform, meaning Mr. Fletcher is wearing his standard grown-up penny loafers, camel-colored socks, pleated khakis, braided belt, powder blue button-down collar shirt, and yellow tie.

We ushers are still in gear, too: thick, black Value-Mart sneakers, cheap black socks, snug black slacks, loose black cummerbunds, stiff white shirts and, oh yeah, bow-ties—not the snap-on kind, either, but the wrap around your neck kind.

Yeah, I know. Don't get me started.

Hey, getting paid to work with your best friends, eat all the free popcorn you can stomach and watching really, really bad movies a day before everybody else gets to see them has to have *some* drawbacks, right?

Well, the bow-tie is definitely it.

Tracy offers me another cherry licorice vine but I've already had four, and if I have one more this cummerbund is going to fly off and tear the screen, probably, so I reluctantly beg off.

She winkles her pug brown nose and admires, "Such willpower" before chomping on her ninth or tenth.

On the other side of me, Zach sits quietly munching popcorn, his long legs stretched out over the seat in front of him, his cummerbund loose and crooked, his bow tie untied and the top two buttons of his starched white collar open.

He hates anything clinging to his neck, which would explain his penchant for V-neck T-shirts—he has one in every conceivable color—and strict "no necklaces" policy, which I actually don't mind because I've never quite understood the whole "necklaces on a guy" thing anyway.

He offers me his extra-large tub but he puts so much butter on it always makes me sick.

Still, I need something a little salty to counteract my licorice vine high, so I scoot around the tub until I find a dry kernel and pop it in my mouth.

"Picky, picky," he sighs, head so close to me his luscious dirty blond curls practically rub against my straight, limp brown bangs.

I watch as Zach picks through the kernels, finding the most buttery, drippy, grossly yellow kernels way at the bottom.

His fingers are long, pale, and sensitive.

I should know; I've been watching those fingers butter toast, button buttons, scribble down notes, turn the TV on and off and all sorts of other finger-needing things since he moved into the Meriwether Home for Wayward Boys and Girls way back in eighth grade.

I hadn't fallen in love with him back then, or even lust, but I'd absolutely adored him and still do, only…lately…the love and lust dragons are kicking my butt.

More and more often now I find myself staring at him, oddly, at all the wrong times in all the wrong places.

In our tiny breakfast nook, when I'm supposed to be studying and he's standing on a stepladder across the room to change out a bulb, when Tracy's talking to me and I should actually be paying attention, or Cliff's bugging me.

I just can't help myself.

Maybe it's inevitable. You put two adolescents in a group home setting and there's bound to be some friction eventually, you know?

I suppose it just makes sense—who knows me better than Zach, Tracy, and Cliff?

Still, his stupid fingers—to say nothing of his curly hair, caterpillar brown eyelashes, hazel eyes and praying mantis legs—are starting to seriously interfere with just about everything I hold dear.

The house lights suddenly go down as Cliff makes a grand entrance, all three hundred and twenty rippling pounds of him.

He's surprisingly agile for a big guy, parading all the way up to the back row like a ballerina in a really, really off-off-Broadway ballet.

Cliff sits on the other side of Zach just as the screen flickers to life with the opening credits of *Another Panty Raid at Zombie High*.

We clap dutifully, even Mr. Fletcher, who is half-asleep and I'm sure has better things to do at this ungodly hour.

For me, the best thing about Free Preview Thursday isn't the movie, so much, or even the (half-price, employee discount) snacks, but the running commentary by my fellow roomies, orphans, and ushers and the three biggest movie know-it-alls I know.

"Those headstones are totally fake," Tracy semi-whispers as a gray hand bursts through dark, loamy soil in some studio back lot cemetery. "Look, you can practically see the Styrofoam through the gray spray paint!"

Cliff snorts around his own handful of mushy, buttery, lemon-yellow popcorn. "You are sooooo right, Trace. In fact, I do believe that's the same frickin' graveyard from the first movie!"

"Language," says Mr. Fletcher ironically without looking our way, and we have to laugh.

There is a strict "no profanity" policy at Flickers Cinemas, one even the assistant managers can't stick to.

"Check out the makeup on Zombie number two," cracks Zach. "Can you say 'do it yourself'?"

We chuckle knowingly about the bad makeup, worse special effects, and totally non-scary storyline, but if the fire alarm went off right now you'd need a court order to peel us out of our seats.

CHAPTER THREE

It's nearly 2 a.m. when we finally roll out of Cliff's primer-coated big gray van in the driveway of the Meriwether Home for Wayward Boys and Girls.

For those of you who have never seen an orphanage, let alone lived in one, first: get over yourselves.

Second: they don't all look like that spooky house from *Psycho*.

Okay, so maybe the Meriwether Home for Wayward Boys and Girls does, but I've heard they all don't.

Seriously, the Home (as we residents like to call it) is really just your basic neighborhood two-story house, only five people live here and four of them no longer have parents.

It's okay, really. You can stop crying now!

I mean, my parents were in a car accident so long ago I barely know their names (so I lied, they were Jenna and Raymond).

I'm not trying to sound blithe or bitter, or like I'm blowing off the whole "I'm an orphan" thing, because really…I'm not.

Growing up without parents sucks epically, for sure, it's just when you grow up in foster homes your whole life, having one place to call home—it even has "home" in the title—isn't such a bad way to go.

Especially when you hit it off with your fellow housemates, which isn't always the case (trust me).

To me, now, these guys *are* my family.

Cliff pockets his keys and yawns as Zach shuffles up to the front door, which is unlocked, meaning Mrs. Meriwether is up (God love her).

Zach kind of rolls his eyes as he slowly turns the doorknob, even though he'd take a bullet for the old gal any day.

Still, we all know what he means. Now our time-to-bed ratio has just been upped by at least twenty-five minutes full of cookies and cocoa and non-stop reminiscing.

"Oh, thank heavens," we hear her crooning as Zach steps through the front door, so tall his dirty blond curls swish against the top of the doorjamb. "I always forget Thursday night is your late night. So, any good movies tonight?"

We are in the foyer now, all four of us—five if you count a seventy two year-old woman who can't weigh more than eighty pounds—and Zach bends down to hug her and explains, "Nothing you'd like, Mrs. Meriwether."

"Oh, I believe you there," she concurs, leading us all into the small but tidy kitchen around the corner. "The last good movie I saw was…."

"Ben Hur," Cliff mouths as I stifle a snort.

"And that was at the Clarion Theater in Chicago…" Tracy continues, moving her lustrous full lips silently.

"And poor Herbert snored through the whole thing…" I finish mouthing, all behind Mrs. Meriwether's back, of course.

Mrs. Meriwether is about five-foot-two inches tall, fond of petite housedresses in mint green with tan orthopedic shoes, which she wears up until the very minute she climbs into bed.

It's pretty convenient for us kids, though, because all the floors are hardwood and you can hear her coming from two rooms away, which is great when you're doing something you're not supposed to, which at the Home is just about everything but a.) praying, b.) eating, and c.) sleeping (in that order).

We gather around the breakfast nook and before Cliff can reach for his first cookie of the evening (and there will be many, trust me), Mrs. Meriwether slaps his hand, grabs it instead and insists, "Let us pray."

We roll our eyes and grab hands, bowing our heads as she prays, "Dear Lord, please watch over these lovely children, who I have come to know and love as my own. Reward each of their special talents with abundance and praise, and thank you for getting them home safely to me tonight. None of us are orphans in your eyes, Lord, and for this we thank you. Amen!"

After the last "amen" we nibble half-heartedly at a fresh plate of homemade sugar cookies—her specialty, although sometimes it's hard to tell the cookie from the plate (bad girl!)—and sip plastic cups of lukewarm cocoa, even though we can barely keep our eyes open.

We listen patiently while Mrs. Meriwether tells one of her patented "Herbert stories," Herbert being her late husband who passed away twenty plus years ago and, according to Mrs. Meriwether, singlehandedly won World War II.

Or was it WW I?

Once she scuttles off to bed, Tracy and I bag up the rest of the cookies and rinse out the cocoa cups so she won't have to do it tomorrow morning, then it's straight up to our rooms.

Zach and Cliff fight over the upstairs bathroom while Tracy lingers in my doorway as I change into my standard issue knee-length blue T-shirt, which is just sexy enough to entice Zach should he ever knock on my door in the middle of the night feeling randy (yeah, right), but just "mature" enough to pass Mrs. Meriwether's strict "no see-through nighties" rule.

"Some movie tonight, huh?" Tracy asks, her face tired and drawn from another long day.

I shrug. "Seen better, seen worse."

She winks and waits until Zach weasels his way into the bathroom before asking what she *really* wants to know, "Think he'll say 'goodnight' tonight?"

I smile.

"I dunno. He's in a pretty good mood."

Tracy and I have been keeping track of how many nights a week Zach says "goodnight" to me ever since I admitted to her that I had a minor (okay, teetering on major) crush on him during a weak moment last Christmas Eve.

So far the average is four nights a week, though one week over the summer he actually said "goodnight" every single night.

I dunno, must have been a full moon or something.

Anyway, so far this week he's only said "goodnight" once, so I guess you could say I'm due.

She yawns one last time and I groan, "Stop, girl, you know that's contagious!"

She laughs and saunters across the hall to her own room, which I can see from sitting on my bed is three kinds of messy and two degrees of cluttered.

I bide my time straightening the throw pillows from my bed on the pink chair in the corner until I hear the telltale squeaking of the warped floorboards outside my room.

I turn and pout, seeing Cliff leaning there in his size XXL all-white, mail-order, saved-up-for-three-months-to-afford-it Storm Trooper bathrobe.

"So," he asks with a yawn, and it's all I can do not to join him. "What'd you think of that movie tonight, huh?"

I roll my eyes.

"Is that what you're *really* standing in my doorway at 2 a.m. to ask me about, Cliff?" I tease him.

"Naw," he admits, looking over his shoulder at the still-closed bathroom door. "I just wanted to find out if Zach has said 'goodnight' yet!"

I toss a throw pillow at him and he scampers away playfully. He knows he's not to divulge the worst kept secret at the Home!

I can barely keep my eyes open and have shut off my bedside lamp and crawled under the covers by the time the long, lanky shadow fills my doorway.

"Abby?" he asks, voice husky with near-sleep, and I know he's smiling crookedly.

"Zach?" I ask, leaning up on one elbow and squinting against the light spilling in from the hallway. "You okay?"

"Yeah," he chuckles. "Cliff told me to come say 'goodnight'!"

He laughs all the way back to his room, but I take the little diary out from under my mattress and make a hash mark next to today's date just the same.

Hey, in my book, a goodnight's a goodnight!

CHAPTER FOUR

"**A**bby!" Cliff shouts a few days later, four chins wobbling as he rounds the corner into the concessions stand and smacks straight dab into the Raisinets window. "Throw me a roll of your pennies!"

I can feel his breath all the way across the candy counter, which is saying something since I'm currently wrestling with a four-ton bag full of tonight's leftover popcorn.

His hands are red and beefy on top of the glass candy counter, fogging them up with ham-size handprints.

"Uh, Cliff? Can't you see my hands are full?"

"Yeah, drop that and throw me a roll of pennies. *Now*, Abby! We've got a zombie uprising in theater—"

"What? I thought that uprising was up in Sunset Lakes? That's, like, forty minutes away from—"

"Pennies, Abby! *All* of them! *Now!*"

"Register's locked, Cliff! *All* of it! *Right* now!"

Sweat is pouring down Cliff's red, flushed face and I'm thinking, if the brain suckers don't get him tonight, a triple coronary just might.

"Well, who's got the keys? This is serious. They're going to be out here any minute."

As if on cue, we hear screaming coming from the long, empty row of theaters to the right.

I wince and hold my rolled up sleeping bag-size plastic sack of greasy yellow popcorn even tighter.

"Mr. Fletcher's got the keys, Cliff! You know I can't unlock the register drawer without them."

Cliff looks momentarily thankful, though we hear a groaning sound to the right and he literally begs, "Where *is* he, Abby? I need those pennies, *stat!*"

Yes, actually, Cliff *is* that dude who says things like "Stat," out loud, and not just when in his own living room watching *ER*.

I shrug, using the popcorn bag as a shield. "Last I heard he was in Theater 6 using the Gum Away on that nasty stain on Aisle 10. You know he said it's been there for nearly three months—"

Cliff rolls his eyes and interrupts, "Oh yeah? Theater 6? Really? Great, Abby, 'cause that's not, like, where the frickin' zombie outbreak is happening or anything! Way to go!"

"What, like it's *my* fault the brain suckers chose Theater 6, Cliff!"

"This isn't helping, Abby!" he shouts and then, as if I hadn't heard, adds, "*You're* not helping, Abby!"

Cliff's chest is heaving now, sweat drenching his forehead.

He's a practical joker but he's never physically forced sweat from his brow before, so this must really be for real this time.

I shake my head. "That can't be, Cliff! Isn't that a…chick flick…in there or something?"

Cliff is rumbling through his pockets now and looks up at me.

"Wow, that's not very empowering of you, Abs. I mean, ever heard of girl zombies?"

Just then Zach comes shambling out of the men's room, plastic gloves on his long, slender fingers and a hospital mask on his face.

Can you say "germ freak"?

"Zach!" Cliff shouts, still turning his pockets inside out. "Gimme your pennies!"

"What?" Zach asks, slowly peeling his fingers from his gloves and snapping his mask off. "Pennies? You know I only use plastic, dude."

Yeah, 'cause your debit card with seventeen dollars on it is sooooooooo suave, Zach!

More groaning and I drop the bag of popcorn into the giant gray trash can on wheels and start jingling through my own coinage, not that there's that much of it to begin with, mind you.

I see one quarter, two dimes, plenty of nickels and, of course, not one single penny.

I hear singing as Tracy backs out of the swinging double doors from the soda room, where four shelves full of boxes of cola formula hiss and slurp every time we pour a monster size refill.

She has the softest mocha skin and long, flowing dreadlocks in her hair and a wicked cool voice.

Usually I love to hear her singing old eighties love songs (Mrs. Meriwether's favorite, for whatever reason), but right now it's a little...creeping me out, you know?

"What's all the commotion—?" she starts before interrupting herself to announce, almost casually, "Hey, zombie!"

We turn and see a middle-aged woman in knee-high stockings and a blood-splattered church dress shamble out of Theater 6.

Her skin is so pale it's almost blue, with big black veins visible all up and down her cheeks and throat, her hair splattered with blood, her purse still dangling from the crook of her fleshy arm, a leg hanging from her mouth; well, not hanging so much as she's actively gnawing on it at the moment.

"Is that—?" blathers Tracy in a shocked whisper as she quivers behind me.

"Are those—?" gulps Cliff, miraculously hauling all three hundred plus pounds of himself up and over the candy counter with one—count 'em— one hairy wrist and ducking down beside us.

"Dude!" shouts Zach, leaping over the counter and tucking into a seamless roll onto the clean white tile floor before popping up right in front of the Sergeant Slushee machine where Tracy and I cling to each other like barnacles in a hurricane.

"Mr. Fletcher!" I scream, noticing his telltale polished loafers and crisp khaki cuffs as blood from his snatched-off leg drips onto the floor I'd just mopped!

The living dead housewife ignores us, which is a good thing because between us we have no pennies, no weapons, and not one single spine.

I'm trembling behind my bag o' popcorn, Tracy's trembling behind *me*, Cliff is bashing on a cash register as if it might magically open and Zach?

Zach holds the grody hot dog tongs in his trembling hands!

Church Dress Zombie kind of gnaws absentmindedly on Mr. Fletcher's bare calf as she circles the lobby, round and round on thick white nurse's shoes, not quite sure where to go or what to do when—and if—she gets there.

Suddenly, we hear more footsteps—shuffles, really—coming down the hall from Theater 6.

Two more zombies amble into the lobby to join their friend, two more undead single women clutching more of Mr. Fletcher's jagged, ragged, blood-gushing body parts.

"His hand!" I shout. "Cliff, look at his hand; he's still got his key bracelet on there!"

Good old predictable Mr. Fletcher, always hung his single master key—"Do Not Duplicate!" printed in all caps—dangling from a burgundy key bracelet from his wrist.

Now, all I have to do is pluck it gently from the gaping maw of some undead creature with a taste for human flesh.

"Yeah!" he shouts. "Good luck getting it."

I look around at my fellow ushers and it's clear nobody's helping me on this one.

Cliff has given up on busting the cash register open and now crouches on his size twelve Value Mart sneakers, peering into and out through the clear glass candy window to watch the zombie women from a safe distance.

Tracy has literally clawed her fingernails into the top of the gray rolling trash can and has made herself all but invisible behind the giant bag of popcorn that had once been my biggest challenge on this stupid Tuesday night.

"Zach?" I kind of mumble.

My knight in shining cummerbund shakes his head, his mop of curls shaking with the back and forth motion. "I'll back you up, Abby, but this is your call."

"How is it my call?" I blurt. "We need the keys to open the register, to get the pennies Cliff needs for God knows what, the zombie has the arm with poor Mr. Fletcher's keys on it, hey…where's she going?"

"She's heading for the door!" shouts Cliff, suddenly popping up—if not over—the candy counter. "Stop her, Abby, before she gets out in public and starts another uprising!"

"What? Me? Why? *You're* the one who wants the stupid pennies, Cliff!"

"*You're* the one working front register, Abby. You're the only one who can *technically* ask Mr. Fletcher for the key!"

I look to see Mr. Fletcher's blood-drenched key dangling from his severed wrist. "Uh, Cliff, when said manager's wrist is no longer attached to the rest of his body, I think the chain of command pretty much flies out the window!"

Cliff isn't hearing my arguments; he's using his pre-paid convenience store cell phone.

"Who are you calling?" I shriek, emotions getting the best of me.

He barely notices as he answers, "The cops, duh? And then the reporters. I mean, how often do you get trapped in a movie theater with three crazy zombie broads, right?"

Good old Cliff, always the frustrated screenwriter.

I sigh, and resign myself to doing battle with the living dead.

But…with *what*?

I look left and see only flat, unused popcorn bags and mustard packets. I look right and, wait…mustard?!?!

"Doesn't mustard, like, make you barf?" I ask of the group of ushers as a whole. "I mean, if you eat too much of it?"

Tracy whimpers, "That's what Mrs. Meriwether used last time I swallowed one of her buttons."

"Please tell me that was when you were like, six, Tracy?" Cliff slanders, but I'm already reaching under the counter for the giant mustard jug we use when we run out of single serving packets which is like, every other week.

God love him, but Mr. Fletcher wasn't exactly the best assistant manager on the planet, if you went just by his mustard ordering abilities, that is.

I'm already screwing off the top as I leap over the counter.

The zombie with Mr. Fletcher's arm in her mouth is ambling for the front door, not quite sure what it is, but ambling toward it just the same—and we can't have that.

One hungry zombie in the crowded Cypress Cove Galleria—even at this late hour—and she'd be biting rich housewives and mall cops and shiftless sk8tr boyz and bored shop clerks by the dozen.

My slimy sneakers squeak against the once polished floor, now awash with my assistant manager's blood.

I kind of retch and beat the stupid, shuffling zombie to the door.

She is in a pantsuit, that was once upon a time maybe, possibly cute, but now looks torn, possibly from fighting the other zombie women watching the chick flick in Theater 6 over Mr. Fletcher's body parts.

Gawd, I hope not!

Her skin, like the others, is pale blue and veiny, like the Z-disease is already filling every cell in her body.

Pantsuit Zombie looks at me, blinks twice, and lowers Mr. Fletcher's arm for the slightest moment.

I make my move, shoving the mustard jar over her mouth like one of Zach's beloved Michael Jackson face masks and tipping it up, up, up, watching the mustard pour into her open, shocked, simple gullet as she drops Mr. Fletcher's forearm to the floor. It lands with a sickening, thickening "thwat-splat-thwump" sound as it bounces once, and then rolls…just out of reach.

I can hear the single shiny master key clattering on the slick tile floor.

I abandon the mustard jar just as Pantsuit Zombie retches, filling the lobby floor with gallons and gallons of green, slimy, bilious gore.

It smells putrid, like sixteen-day-old dumpster drool on crack and I retch again, like I do whenever it's my week for garbage day at the Home, bending low to reach Mr. Fletcher's arm.

I grab it, apologizing to the poor guy in eighteen different languages—dude, he was only in his twenties!—but when I reach up to grab the key the first zombie, Church Dress Zombie Lady, and the third one, a kind of youngish, college age Hipster Zombie in an ironic pink baby doll T-shirt with a fuzzy black kitten in the middle under a slim silver hoodie are angling on me.

"Toss it here!" Cliff shouts, just as Zach finally leaps to my rescue.

He knocks down Church Dress Zombie but she's strong (as the undead tend to be), and grabs his sneakers as if her very afterlife depended on it. He yelps and starts running the other way, dragging her with him.

Some rescue.

But, hey, let's look on the bright side; at least he's gotten rid of one of the zombies for me, so…there's that, right?

Now Pantsuit Zombie is drying her lips with the back of her arm like a cowboy after wetting his whistle in some old-timey saloon and heading my way.

Suddenly, I'm cornered.

I can't leave my post or the zombies will literally bolt out the front door and start turning good old Cypress Cove into an all-you-can-scarf brain buffet, and I can't get to the candy counter and open the register.

Cliff is literally jumping up and down on the candy counter now, his massive man-boobs jiggling like some X-rated theater usher peep show that is sooooo not turning me on in the slightest.

He's waving his massive arms, like a receiver in the end zone.

I decide to play quarterback, grab the key bracelet, and toss it across the brightly-lit lobby.

Then, suddenly, all is zombie—zombie arms, zombie breath, zombie claws, zombie stank.

I shove my back against the door as they crowd me, catching Zach dragging Church Dress Zombie toward the water fountains outside the B-wing bathrooms as he screams—*screams*—for help.

I manage to keep my body parts out of reach (one bite and goodbye Abby Cooper, hello Zombie Usher), but…for how long?

Suddenly Hipster Hottie Zombie smells fresh meat, drops Mr. Fletcher's ankle like a forgotten dog bone and licks her lips, angling for my bare throat.

"Cliff!" I shout, kicking her back momentarily. "Whatever you're going to do with those stupid pennies, hurry up and do it with the quickness!"

And just as Hipster Hottie Zombie is reaching in for a bite, and while Pantsuit Zombie is clacking her empty teeth next to my ear, making room for more fresh human flesh, I feel a rain of copper pennies splatter my forehead and shoulders and the glass doors behind me and...suddenly...all is calm.

All...is...quiet.

As if they were vacuums and someone has just pulled their plugs, the zombie women fall to the floor; their heads hit the slick, bloody tiles with a hard, heavy splat.

Behind them Cliff stands triumphantly, half a roll of pennies still clutched in his grubby little mitts.

"Cliff!" I shout, leaping over the Ladies of the Living Dead to hug him. "How did you *do* that?"

He looks at me like I've just turned in my very first usher application. "Duh, Abby, don't you remember that scene from Zombie Wedding 4, where the groom has the copper cuff links and when the zombie bites his arm, he passes out? It's copper, Abby; it conducts electricity, and the zombies can't handle it. But it's only temporary, if we don't silence them permanently, they'll be up and running in a matter of—"

As if on cue, Hipster Zombie kind of grunts and flickers her eyes open.

Cliff takes a single penny and, gingerly, as if touching a hot stove, sticks it in the middle of her forehead.

She blinks and lies there, totally out of it.

I hear sifting behind me, a kind of powdery, sandy noise and turn to find Tracy—little, mousy, sing-song Tracy—pouring a whole jug of popcorn salt in Pantsuit Zombie's gaping mouth.

I'm thinking it's some kind of jinx or superstition, but she looks deadly serious.

Before our eyes, the undead woman's head shrinks to half its size, like...instant shrunken head!

"Tracy!" I shout as she repeats the formula on Hipster Silver Hoodie Zombie. "Way to go!"

As the second zombie's head literally shrinks in front of our eyes, Tracy tosses the empty salt shakers over her shoulder, shakes her dreads like a lion getting ready to roar, and squeaks in her mousy little voice instead, "I saw that in *Zombie Autopsy 6*, remember? That creepy coroner guy mistakenly dumps the salt shaker on the zombie's hand and it shrinks to half its size. Something to do with drying out the cells or whatnot. I never thought it would work in real life!"

Cliff shakes his head in amazement as the two women continue withering before our very eyes, like fuses burning out until it looks like their necks end in baseballs instead of heads.

Just then I hear gurgling and remember, "Zach!"

We turn as if one, first Tracy, then Cliff, then me—like a barber shop quartet looking for its fourth man—and Zach literally has Church Dress Zombie's head jammed over a water fountain and is filling her with water.

Seriously.

Her ankles and thighs have doubled, maybe even tripled in size.

"*Zombie Grave Robbers 2!*" he shouts triumphantly. "The cells of the living dead can't process water anymore; their cells literally flood and, with enough water in them—"

As if on cue, the lower half of the zombie's body literally explodes from inside out, splashing all over the walls like a human water balloon.

"—that happens!" Zach concludes triumphantly, stepping over wet gore as he returns to the lobby.

And so we're standing there, all four of us, our black and white usher uniforms bloody and wet, our hair a mess, faces drenched with sweat, mustard, gore, salt, and water flooding the lobby tiles like some impressionist painting when the tapping starts on the glass lobby doors.

We turn as one just as the flashing starts.

I figure it's the cops, waving flashlights or something.

It's not. It's the news crews, maybe three or four of them, the lights are on top of camcorders as five reporters poke their heads into the lobby and start peppering us with questions.

Before they can, the rest of the zombie audience from the chick flick pours into the lobby, handbags dragging from the crooks of their arms, soft worn flats shuffling across the grody tiles, body parts hanging from their mouths.

Cliff hands us each a handful of pennies, I grab up the last of the mustard, Tracy hoists a box of salt and we go to town; suddenly it's like Food Fight of the Living Dead up in here!

In less than three minutes, the Flickers Cinema uprising, such as it were, is over.

Up and down the hallways, all over the lobby, zombie corpses lie motionless with copper pennies on their foreheads or, if Tracy's gotten to them with her canister of mysterious shrinking salt, no forehead at all!

We turn, sweatier and bloodier now, and a reporter asks, "How did you do it?"

Another explains, "The cops in Sunset Lakes are overrun! How did you kids know what to do?"

Before we can answer one more stutters, "You guys are…are…heroes. What do you call yourselves?"

I'm stammering, more concerned with how my hair looks than what he's just said—or how it's going to affect the next two weeks of my life.

But Cliff knows.

Somehow, Cliff knows what we've done; he's the first one to grasp what the reporters are saying, what it means for society at large and how to spin it so he can get something out of it at some point.

"Who are we?" he asks dramatically, spreading his feet a little and putting his plump fists on the side of his waist, Superman style. "We're Ushers, Inc.!"

And, as if naming us something isn't enough (you know, when there really isn't an "us" to begin with), Cliff has to go and add a tag line: "Where fear takes a backseat!"

CHAPTER FIVE

"**W**hat are you guys *talking* about?" Cliff asks, bent over his laptop the next morning, which rests on his ample belly, blotting out his third size XXL Yoda T-shirt this week. "'Where fear takes a backseat' is an *awesome* tag line!"

"Well, it sounds cool. I guess," hems Tracy around a bite of burnt raisin toast as we cluster around the breakfast nook at the Meriwether Home for Wayward Boys and Girls. "But 'backseat' makes me think of a used car lot, you know? How about, 'Where Fear Takes the Back Row,' huh? I mean, if we're using usher lingo."

Cliff sighs and I can tell by the pink in his cheeks—even before he shakes his scruffy head—that he's not having it. "No, that doesn't flow at all. I still think 'backseat' works best."

Zach shakes his head, his adorable dirty blond curls rustling atop his hazel eyes as he wipes the crumbs from a generic Pop-Tart off his plain white T-shirt. "She's right, Grove. Nobody calls it a 'backseat' in a theater; they call it the back *row*."

I roll my eyes and sigh, blowing the steam off a fresh cup of microwave hot chocolate (Mrs. Meriwether won't let us have coffee).

"Seriously?" I bark. "You guys, we put down *one* zombie outbreak, and now you've got us launching the next Fortune 500 company? Need I remind you mid-semester exams are coming up, to say nothing of the, ahem, Fall Formal?"

I bat my eyes at Zach, who blushes cluelessly.

For two straight weeks now I've been steadily campaigning for Zach to ask me to the Fall Formal, and for two straight weeks he's smiled, blushed…and clammed up like a…a…well, like a zombie with a mouth full of salt!

It started with the little Sticky Note Campaign I waged last week, where every day I'd come to work and post a new note on his employee locker: "29 Days to the Fall Formal, wink-wink," or "27 Days to the Fall Formal, nudge-nudge," never signing them, of course, but seriously?

I've been doing the dude's homework since freshman year so...he *knows* how I dot my i's (with a smiley face, not one of those cheesy hearts like Mia Hopwood does) and cross my t's (with a little upward slant to the left), so I'm pretty sure he knows it's me.

That didn't work, so this week I shifted my focus to outright bribes: "Free dinner to the lucky guy who asks Abby Cooper to the Fall Formal" I'd left in his locker or "I'll buy my own dang corsage, you cheapskate!"

I know, I know...desperate much?

But the thing is, I'm already a junior and I only have two more chances to go to the Fall Formal before I graduate and I have a feeling that if I don't snatch Zach off the market before senior year starts, some other girl at school is going to realize what an absolute catch he is and, okay...okay...what were we talking about?

Oh yeah, Ushers, Inc.

Please.

As if.

Cliff looks at me as if I've just bitten the head off a chicken. "Fall Formal, Abby? Fall *Formal?*" he shakes his woolly head, sideburns and all, spins his laptop around onto the tiny breakfast nook we're clamored around and pushes play on an open video window. "Watch this, Abby, and tell me you're not going to have to clear your social schedule for the next, oh, I dunno...forty years or so!"

I roll my eyes and do as I'm told.

It's early, he's loud...what else am I gonna do?

It's another TV spot, this one running the same footage of the four of us there in our usher uniforms—black shoes, black socks, black pants, black cummerbund, crisp white shirts and black bowties—standing in the Flickers Cinema lobby talking about our "exploits" with a friendly reporter.

"I've seen this—" I begin before Cliff cuts me off with a single beefy hand, seeing his mouth is full of the second half of Zach's uneaten pop tart.

"Keep watching," he gloats good-naturedly around toaster pastry and artificial blueberry filling, but only because he's so busy gloating.

I sigh and watch as the reporter signs off and sends the story back to the news desk, where an anchorman informs us, "Kids these days. Amazing, aren't they? If you are a local resident experiencing an unprecedented influx of the living dead, be it zombies, vampires or werewolves, heck, I guess they could even handle mummies, don't hesitate to call the four kids from Ushers, Inc., at 1-900-USHERS! Thanks for watching, folks, and have a great—and a safe—night."

"What?" I ask, literally shoving the laptop back at Cliff because I know that he is a.) right and b.) that he knows he is right and c.) that there will be no Fall Formal for me—again—this year!

"1-900-USHERS?" Zach asks, cocking an eyebrow. "Where'd they get *that?*"

"I gave it to 'em, moron," Cliff sighs, shutting his laptop and sliding it into his Chewbacca backpack in preparation of another long day at Cypress Cove High.

"When?" Tracy asks, scratching the side of her nose. "How? I was right there with you the whole time."

Cliff shrugs all nonchalant like. "I followed him back to the news van after the interview was over and casually mentioned the number. He thought it was a great idea. Don't you guys?"

"No," Zach groans. "I think between work and school I'm busy enough these days and, in case you forgot, I. Almost. Got. Killed. By. A. Zombie. Last. Night!"

Tracy and I laugh and Cliff just shakes his head. "I had your back, bro! I was two pennies away from saving your hide before you aced that brain-chomper like a big old zombie water balloon."

Zach gives me a can-you-believe-this-guy look but I'm too busy grieving the Fall Formal that never was to face the future that will never be.

"You can't just incorporate yourself, Cliff," Tracy lectures in her grown-up voice, cleaning up her raisin toast crumbs and putting her empty plate in the dishwasher. "There are legal, grownup things you have to do and…."

"Did 'em all last night, Tracy. The paperwork should be here by the end of the week but it's already official. And don't make any plans for after work tonight; some tipster already called the 900-number to report a rash of missing livestock over in Catfish Cove. I checked. It's a full moon, we'll have to head over there right after work."

CHAPTER SIX

School starts crazy and never quite lets up.

Cliff's big, gray, wheezing van—he calls it "the Millennium Falcon," if you're keeping track of that kind of thing—chugs into the student parking lot and while we're normally ignored like the oddly-sized, mismatched, rundown, runoff, misplaced orphans we are, today it's like someone spray-painted "stare at me" on the side of the van 'cause that's what everybody is busy doing.

It's not quite Hollywood perfect, 'cause kids still don't know what to say to the four of us in public, but it's not an entirely...*bad*...feeling to see smiles attached to the faces watching us everywhere we go for a change.

"What's happening?" Tracy asks as we alight from the van together, clutching our schoolbooks protectively to our chests as if this is all some potential prank involving prom dresses and plastic tiaras and buckets of blood overhead.

"Is someone famous behind us?" I crane my neck and see only Zach and Cliff stepping stoically out of the van.

Cypress Cove High is like a big sunny square with palm trees on all sides and an open quad full of benches and vending machines and little half-walls surrounded by plants where everybody, who isn't a geeked out orphan zombie killing usher, sits and chats all morning.

It's never looked particularly pretty to me until today, when everyone is smiling at us as opposed to, you know, pelting us with stuff.

The halls are crowded and a tad more friendly all of a sudden, with kids actually coming up to us on the way to our lockers with cries of "Ushers Rule" and "Zombie Killers" and one who blurts, "Ushers are hot," but none of us know *quite* who he's talking to.

Kids we've known for years—or, at least, known of—are suddenly patting our backs, smiling, and following us. All because of Cliff and his stupid "Ushers, Inc." bluster at the end of one goofy zombie outbreak in front of a few rolling news cameras.

There's Jergen, the foreign exchange student, giving us thumbs up from a bench in the quad.

And Camille Brogan, who won that Song Search contest last year, smiling and waving as we walk by her locker.

Cliff leans against his locker—he carries all his books in his Gigantor Chewbacca backpack anyway—and gloats, "*Still* think giving out our number last night was a bad idea? Who knows, Abby, you might just get a date to the Fall Formal yet."

I have to admit, it's all kind of…intoxicating.

Tracy and I have homeroom together, and she kind of clings to me the whole way there, like someone's going to suddenly yank out the popularity rug from beneath our feet and she wants a big, roomy peasant blouse to hold onto when it happens.

But it doesn't, and she gasps when we walk into homeroom and Mrs. Arnsburger leads a—get this—standing ovation.

In.

Our.

Honor.

I look at Tracy and she looks at me and as we're walking to our desks in the back of the room (natch) Mrs. A announces, "Class, thank you for helping me honor these two young heroines into our midst this morning. As you know, ever since the Great Werewolf Roundup of 2010, monsters have come out of the closet, so to speak, and unfortunately we humans are their favorite snack. Now, seven years later, to think that two of our own are leading the charge to take our lives back from the living dead, well, it's just…touching to see."

As she sits sobbing into her grade book a warm, buttery voice from two desks over whispers, "Hey, Abby, nice job!"

I can't look. I…just…can't.

Tracy whispers, "Abby, he's *talking* to you."

I'm frozen. I can't respond.

"Pssstt," the voice continues as Mrs. A finally controls herself and gets back to the 8,000-page romance novel she's been reading since school started up a few months ago. "Way to go last night, Abby. That was awesome!"

Finally Tracy jabs me in the elbow and I turn to look and see Wyatt Winters—Wyatt *Winters*—smiling across the aisle at me.

"T-t-thanks, Wyatt," I stammer, sounding absolutely petrified, which is only half as terrified as I actually feel. "T-t-thanks a lot."

He kind of slides his chair over a smidge and insists, "No, I really mean it. My dad and I were watching the news last night and, when he saw it, the first thing he said to me was, 'Those kids are going to need a publicist before they know it.' First thing, that's what he said."

I nod, thinking he's out of his skull but also thinking, well, if anybody would know, his dad would.

After all, Wyatt Winters Senior is the head of the Winter's Words PR agency, who does the advertising for everybody from The Cypress Cove Bar & Grille to the chain of Roxy's Rocks rock climbing gyms.

I kind of steal glances as he explains the finer points of PR to Tracy, who's a willing student, if only to watch Wyatt's straight white teeth move as he blathers on about "social media" this and "keyword rich" that.

Wyatt is a soccer stud, not quite star of the team but definitely what Tracy and I like to call "MVP," or Most Valuable Piece.

His skin is perpetually tanned, his teeth gleaming white, his black hair oil slick shiny and perfectly coiffed, his clothes Italian and fitted, like today's jeans, which are so thin and snug they might as well be a second skin, to say nothing of his white cashmere sweater and sockless loafers.

He's definitely a standout at Cypress Cove.

Unfortunately, so is his girlfriend Mia Hopwood, who is sitting in the very next chair fuming—fuming, I tell you—as he chats up Tracy.

Mia is, in a word, flawless.

Long black hair, perfectly straight, Cleopatra bangs, dark eye shadow to offset her Roman nose and thick lips, slathered today in just enough glossy mauve lipstick, but never too much.

Her cheekbones are sharp but not severe, giving her beautiful face an almost predatory look like, well…like a werewolf under the full moon.

Her eyes are a luminous green; Zach calls them emerald green.

At least, he does until he sees my nostrils flare with jealousy, then he quickly adds, "You know, if you like that kind of thing."

Today she's in all white—white heels, white mini skirt topping her long, slender legs, white tank under a short white leather jacket zipped down to her navel but with a stylish stiff collar that sticks up instead of lies down.

She does that, Mia does; sticks with one color and does it to death.

Sweet, beautiful death.

Like the other night in line at the movies, gray on gray.

And today, all white.

And then she'll have her red day—red heels, red pencil skirt, red jacket.

Every once in awhile, she'll slip in a brown under a tan, or mix a black with a white, but she tends to stick with solid colors, and always the classics: black, red, white, silver, and gold.

She catches my eyes as they're lingering nervously on the swell of Wyatt's closest thigh and grins, "I'm sure any PR firm could handle *your* needs."

I nod, again, with the deer frozen in the headlights look.

After all, this is the first time Mia's ever spoken to me in homeroom.

Well, I mean, without getting a demerit for, now, what did Mrs. Arnsburger write on the referral slip that day?

Oh, that's right, "Derogatory, foul, and unspeakable language of the highest caliber!"

"I dunno," I manage to squeak. "Winter's Words is the best agency in town, don't ya think?"

I mean, I'm pretty much lobbing her a softball she can knock back while talking up her boyfriend's Dad's company, you know?

No dice; instead she clucks a barbed tongue and runs a perfectly manicured index finger over a perfectly tweezed brow.

"Like you losers can afford him anyway," she slithers.

I shrug.

Maybe it's all the fans in the hall, or the 1-900 number, or Cliff's confidence in us, or the foreign exchange student giving us the thumbs up in the quad this morning or the fact that I shoved a vat of mustard down a zombie's throat the night before just to get the master key and stop the living dead from infesting all of Cypress Cove, but *something* makes me say, "How would *you* know anyway, Mia? We've got our first gig tonight and I'm sure they'll pay at least—"

"Tonight?" asks Wyatt, eavesdropping and cutting me off from my grand slam of his gorgeous girlfriend. "Great news!" he continues, oblivious; all business. "Listen, be sure to let me know how it goes tomorrow. I'll want to work it into some kind of press release for the local newspaper, maybe even feed it to the networks, you know?"

Tracy's eyes get wide as she twists a dreadlock around her finger nervously and asks, "You mean, you'd really work with us?"

"Would I?" Wyatt practically shouts, ignoring Mia's emerald green laser beam eyes of death. "I'd love to. My only account so far has been the soccer team, and we hardly need advertising when we're state champions and all. This would be a really great opportunity for me."

"Look at her, Wyatt," spits Mia, noticing my hesitance but now rather than sounding superior, there is an almost...pleading...tone to her voice. "Abby is obviously weighing offers from other firms."

I go to answer her, to say something stupid like "What firms?" or "What offers?" when Wyatt blurts, "I'll give you half off my usual rate!"

"Done!" I snap, and Wyatt's smile lights up the room.

Too bad I'm so busy staring daggers at Mia I hardly have time to enjoy it.

CHAPTER SEVEN

"**W**yatt *Winters*?" Zach snaps on the way to work that night. "What'd you have to go and ask *him* for?"

"She didn't," Tracy insists since I'm still so tongue-tied from the encounter I can't quite defend myself—yet. "*He* asked *her*. Went out of his way to ask her, in fact."

She nudges me with a soft elbow in that "we'll make him jealous yet" way of hers, but I just shrug kind of helplessly and try to catch up with myself.

Everything is just happening so...*fast*.

I mean, what was I thinking, asking Wyatt to help us like that?

I knew it would upset Zach, and I did it anyway.

It would be like him asking Mia to design the costumes for Ushers, Inc., or something, you know?

But then I think, "Abby, you've been stalking this guy since you both reached puberty, he's never made a move, *ever*, won't ask you to Fall Formal and, so, what are *you* worried about *his* feelings for?"

Zach eyes me suspiciously; like he's still unconvinced I didn't purposefully flash Wyatt or something just to get him to do our stupid PR for half-price.

"I think that's great, Abby," huffs Cliff proudly as we pull into the employee parking lot behind Flickers Cinemas. "And weird, too, because just this morning you were so...reluctant...to be a part of Ushers, Inc."

"I never said that," I snap, and now it's like I'm suddenly...afraid...to get kicked out of the group.

I mean, why would Wyatt ever talk to me then?

He smiles knowingly. "No, but your eyes did. I'm just glad to hear

47

you're on board. I think Wyatt and I will make great collaborators."

"Whatever," grumbles Zach, arms folded across his chest as he rides shotgun. It's his turn all week. "He's still not going on any missions with us."

I kind of pout, but even Cliff says, "Agreed. He doesn't quite seem the 'Usher' type, know what I mean?"

Tracy kind of snorts. "Yeah, horror movies aren't exactly his bag."

Zach corrects her while staring daggers at me, "Sure they are, Trace. He's the kind of horror movie poser who brings a chick just so he can cop a feel when she gets all scared and needy like."

Tracy nods as she and Zach spill out of the van, all long arms and long legs and happy faces.

It's so nice for them, just being friends, without all this "does he like me, does he hate me?" baggage I've been lugging around for the past few years.

I remember when Zach first came to the Meriwether Home in eighth grade and I knew we'd become instant friends when I saw the T-shirt he wore getting out of the short white county van that dropped him off from his latest foster home: *Zombies Are After Your Brains—Relax, You're in No Danger.*

He was nervous and shy—for about four whole minutes.

Then he heard Cliff playing a video game upstairs—the whooping and hollering and applause and standing ovations were hard to miss. Cliff never let playing alone stop him from enjoying himself—and disappeared into the big guy's bedroom for the next, oh, fifteen hours!

After that he came down, hungry as a bear, and sat across from me at the breakfast nook, stealing my graham crackers and smothering them in crunchy peanut butter without even asking if he could use my knife.

He said, "I've never seen a girl eat crunchy peanut butter before."

I said, "I've never seen a guy have to cover all four corners of his cracker before eating it before."

He blushed, slugged me lightly on the shoulder and that was that; we were fast friends.

Eighth grade was awesome after that; Cliff had a buddy to play video games with, and I had Zach for just about everything else.

He didn't mind chores, and would often trade with Cliff just so we could do them together.

We'd weed the lawn together, and take turns mowing it while the other laid out in the driveway on Mrs. Meriwether's creaky fold up lawn chair.

We liked the same junk food, were both vegetarians, read the same comics and, of course, loved the same movies.

And, long before we worked there, Flickers Cinemas was our home away from home.

Mrs. Meriwether gave us each an allowance every week: thirty-five dollars, provided by the state.

We were supposed to use it for lunches, textbooks, lab fees and stuff like that, but since we were wards of the state, we got everything at school pretty much for free, so we'd use it all—I'm talking every last cent—on movies.

There was a drug store on the way to Flickers, where Cliff, Zach, and I—Tracy didn't move in until later that year—would go in, buy our snacks there on the cheap, and sneak them in.

We'd always make sure to get there right after school on Thursday, to catch whatever movies we'd missed over the weekend, and of course Friday, when the new movies came out, and pretty much all day Sunday.

If something really good was playing, like *Bikini Zombies 4* or *Werewolf Wedding 2*, we'd see it three or four times.

If something really *bad* was playing, like *Vampire Surgeon 3* or *Zombie Autopsy 9*, we'd see it five or six times.

Lots of times Cliff would get pulled into some Power Kong or Battlestar Galaxy challenge or something with a kid in the game room in the lobby, and he'd be so into it he'd let Zach and I watch a movie—or two— by ourselves.

We always put a seat in between us, I dunno; back then I still thought guys were "gross" and he wasn't quite ready for lady love yet either, you know?

It was stupid, really, because the best part about seeing a movie with Zach, or even Cliff and Zach together, was talking about the cheesy parts, and we always had to lean over the seats to do it.

Life was great for awhile, until he got that growth spurt halfway through freshman year, and suddenly I started noticing his deep hazel eyes, and those bushy brown eyebrows, and he stopped straightening his hair and he started wearing those boxer shorts to bed. Every once in awhile, we'd bump into each other in the halls coming in or out of the upstairs bathroom in the middle of the night and…hubba-hubba.

Ever since then there's been something between us. Sometimes it's great, other times, like right now, not so great.

So I kind of linger near the van, gathering up my backpack at zombie shuffle speed as Tracy and Zach saunter their way into the back entrance of the theater, and when I close the side door and look up, Cliff is standing there with the most understanding expression on his round, ruddy face.

"You know he's just giving you the business 'cause he's jealous, right?"

Now it's my turn to snort. "Yeah, right."

I kind of make a move to walk away, figuring he'll follow me right away like he always does, but he doesn't, so I turn and he's looking at me almost…sympathetically.

"You guys are crazy, you know that right?"

"Yeah, so?"

"Why don't you just give up the whole 'I love him so much I hate him' act and just fall in love already?"

"Love?" I ask, making a face I already know is ugly.

"Or, at least, a lot of like."

"How can he 'a lot of like' me, Cliff, when he won't even ask me to the Fall Formal?"

Cliff snorts and I watch his chins move.

He tries to hide them with three-day old stubble, but his facial hair doesn't grow that fast.

"What is this, 1783?"

"What does *that* mean?"

"It means you're liberated, Abby. Ask him to the stupid Fall Formal already."

I shake my head. "That's not right. The guy should ask the girl. Besides, if I did ask him, you know Zach, he'd only say 'yes' to avoid hurting my feelings."

"Is that such a bad thing?" Cliff asks.

Suddenly, I'm too choked up to answer.

I think of all I've gone without in my life.

I mean, not that I'm into pity parties and as Mrs. Meriwether is always saying, we all have so much to be grateful for but…really?

No parents, no home of my own, not even a bathroom of my own, and is it too much to ask the one guy I really care about to ask me to some stupid dance already?

Cliff opens his mouth, to crack wise, probably, but he sees me having what he calls "a feminine moment" and thinks twice.

Eventually, he doesn't say anything at all.

He just lopes a big, beefy arm on my shoulder as we stroll across the parking lot and into the back door of the theater.

Cliff isn't so bad a guy, he just tries too hard, you know?

Like, it would be bad enough if he was just an orphan, or hairy, or over three hundred pounds or just loved all things Star Wars, but to be all of those in one unhappy bundle just paints a big bull's eye on his back.

So instead of laying down and rolling over, like I do most days, or Tracy does half as often, or even Zach if he's outnumbered, Cliff just acts like the whole world's out to get him and so instead he's got to get them first.

Sometimes, the attitude spills over onto his three friends—his *only* three friends.

But not today. Today he's being "good Cliff," and that's the way I like him best.

I clock in and find Tracy in the girls' room, tying her lush dreadlocks back with a simple black hair tie and smiling back at me with her soft, brown eyes.

"Lots of drama going on up in here lately," she sighs as I straighten my bow tie, which is always too tight.

I shrug. "I think I just added some."

"You sure did." She laughs in her crinkly way, the way that makes her face look like a bowl of cinnamon frosted mini-wheats. "But, you know what, Abby? Sometimes that's good."

Another shrug. "I guess."

She nods. "Between you, me and the werewolves, honey, I don't think either of us is going to have much time for romance this week."

Tracy's usually right.

Not this time.

I can't tell if that's good or bad.

CHAPTER EIGHT

The moon is full as Cliff's van races toward Catfish Cove, a little fishing village less than twenty minutes away.

It's nearly midnight already but we couldn't help it. With one assistant manager already mauled by zombies, the management staff at Flickers Cinemas was shorthanded, so we all had to pull double-duty on cleanup after the last 9:30 show let out for the night.

Pulling up to a mini-mart, we stock up on supplies we should have had hours ago.

"Is this how you're going to run your company, Cliff?" Zach is asking as he undoes his bowtie on the way into the tiny Traffic Town convenience store. "Grabbing stuff on the fly? I mean, this is a real werewolf we're supposed to be stopping, right? Or is this all just some big publicity stunt to get Ushers, Inc., off the ground?"

"Uh, it's *our* company, Zach, and who had any spare time? Between our regularly hated duties and then trying to clean up that mess we all made during the Zombie Invasion of Theater 6 last night, we were all pulling double duty tonight. Besides, once we get our first few missions under our belt, we'll have all the supplies we need."

Zach looks doubtful. For the first time in the last twenty-four hours, we're finally in agreement.

With time running out, we split up and race down the aisles, looking for anything silver.

It's not easy.

Have you ever looked for silver in a convenience store?

There is no silverware aisle, no silver jewelry, to say nothing of…silver bullets!

The best we can come up with is four rolls of tin foil, three packages of instant film circa ten whole years ago, five digital watches and, well, that's pretty much it.

As we're ringing it all up, I hear an old eighties song on the radio and notice a beat-up old AM/FM set high on a counter behind the clerk's head.

"Is that for sale?" I ask the clerk, a plump woman in a pink housecoat with blue umbrellas all over it.

She smiles and explains, "Everything's got a price, dear."

Cliff grunts, "Name yours."

"Fifty dollars," she replies smoothly, as if she's just told us it might rain.

"Fifty bucks?" Zach shouts. "For that old thing? You probably only paid five bucks for it back in the day."

"Maybe, young man, but that was then and this is now, so—"

"Sold!" Cliff quickly hands over four fresh $20 bills for everything on the counter before Miss Bargain Hunter can haggle us out of any more.

On the way back to the van, Tracy asks, "Where'd you get all that money, Cliff?"

As Cliff goes to open his mouth to make some excuse, Zach huffs, "And don't tell me you've been saving up your allowance, either, because we each get the same thirty-five bucks from Mrs. Meriwether every Sunday and I know for a fact you spent yours on the new Boba Fett trading card."

Cliff blushes and fesses up. "Okay, so maybe one of the reporters paid me for an exclusive interview. It was only two hundred. I was gonna tell you guys, honest!"

"When?" I ask, sliding into the backseat. "After the werewolf chewed us up and spit us out, and you could keep it all for yourself?"

We peel out and head toward the remote farm address left by Cliff's werewolf tipster, while Tracy rips open the faded, dusty Polaroid boxes and starts peeling apart the instant film sheets.

"I can't believe they still sell those things," Zach remarks, turning around in the front seat as he winds tin foil around his wrists and calves. "I thought they stopped making that stuff years ago."

"You remember that movie. What was it?" yammers Tracy, sliding sheets of film in every possible pocket before handing us the rest. "*Moon Night 7*, I think, the one with the sorority girl werewolves?"

Zach snorts. "I think they called them 'were women' or something stupid, right?"

He and Tracy share a laugh and she adds, "Right, well, the

photographer for the college newspaper got wise, and followed them around, and they all trapped him in some old shed and there was absolutely nothing around and—"

"He choked them with rolls of film because they still use silver in instant camera film!" Cliff barks from the driver's seat, stealing Tracy's thunder—again!

She kind of pouts but it's cut off by a violent, thunderous roar.

It's the werewolf, and he's not happy!

CHAPTER NINE

We see why right away: the cops are shooting at him!

Cliff pulls up behind a series of boxy black and white squad cars straight out of some cheesy 1970s cop show, red and blue lights flashing, lined up side by side to block off the werewolf.

Yeah, like he couldn't leap over all four of them in a single bound, lopping off heads as he goes.

Putting the van in park with a nasty little jerk, Cliff murmurs, "Amateurs. You just know they don't have any silver bullets in those guns."

I don't know what he's squawking about; it's not like we've come any better prepared or anything.

My pockets are lined with film strips, but that's about it.

Zach rushes out of the van and hands me the dusty radio Cliff bought for fifty dollars.

"I never had time to open it and Cliff doesn't have any tools so…."

"Well," I sigh, a little exasperated as I look at the ancient, boxy thing with lots of "WTF" face going on over here.

It's like at the theater last night when he hid behind the counter while I went to battle Church Lady Zombie for Mr. Fletcher's keys.

"What do you want *me* to do with it?"

He cocks his head and smiles. "They use silver to solder down the wires, Abby. It's full of the stuff. Just, in case of emergency, break it open and…and…."

"And what?" I ask, sliding it into my black backpack purse. "And what, Zach?"

But he's already rushing away with Cliff to talk boy talk with the cops.

Tracy sidles up by my side and asks, "What now?"

Just then the werewolf roars and we cling to each other, B-movie actress style, screaming into each other's ears.

Yes, werewolves are four-hundred percent more common this year than they were, say, ten years ago.

Yes, they've been photographed, catalogued, and even recognized by *International Geographic* magazine, but that doesn't mean we've actually been within spitting distance of one!

And let me tell you, that sucker is *loud*!

Tracy and I kind of part and don't look at each other.

"Some superheroes, huh?" she asks, looking at her squeaky clean black sneakers.

"Hey, Cliff called us that. Not me!"

Just then I hear the pop-pop-pop of gunfire, and we instinctively crouch behind a ragged old oak tree; its roots dry and dusty, its branches long since leaf-free—the perfect horror movie oak tree.

Above us the moon is high and bright and oh, so, full.

The werewolf roars again, causing even the police officers to crouch behind their battered cruisers.

From the looks of it, they've been at this for some time now.

"We better get in this," Tracy blurts, watching Cliff talk to the cops, "before our two heroes try to make it on their own."

"Yeah, right," I grumble, following her lead.

The cops are cussing, reloading, and shoving Cliff away as he offers his help.

"But we got a tip," he whines uselessly, sounding exactly like what he is at this very moment: a whiny high school kid. "We were asked to be here."

"Kid," grunts a scruffy sergeant in a graying flat-top, his gravelly voice pitch perfect, "I don't care who called you, even if it was the dang werewolf himself, we can't have you here. Can't you see we've set up a perimeter here? Now back up to that tree line or I'll take time off from firing at this beast and arrest you myself."

"But sir," Zach cautions, "those bullets won't do anything unless they're silver."

"Silver!" barks the sergeant. "I can barely keep my men in polyester pants and copper-tipped bullets. Silver! You hear that, Rufus?" he asks, turning to his partner.

They talk amongst themselves, but Zach waves us back to the leafless oak tree.

"Guys, he's clueless. We have to help him."

"But how, Zach?" Tracy asks, itching to yank some instant camera film from her pockets. "They've got the place roped off."

We turn to where she is pointing and see the sagging yellow police tape in front of the dented cop cars, tattered in places, waving free and flapping in the breeze.

But that's not all; there is fresh blood on the ground in front of an old farmhouse.

The windows are smashed, curtains torn, as the werewolf dashes first behind a window, then the door.

You can hear smashing and crashing, each one causing Ushers, Inc., to flinch here by our little tree.

"There's got to be a way around," Zach insists, craning his neck before pointing one long, bony finger. "There," he says, "that shed. It's behind the yellow lines, but look behind it; it's got a clear shot to the house."

"Let's go," Tracy urges eagerly, but Zach holds her back.

"Let's split up instead," I offer, grabbing Zach and yanking him with me. "You two stay here in case the werewolf gets through the police lines, and we'll circle around the back and try to stop him."

Cliff smiles and Tracy frowns.

Zach and I crunch quietly across the spotty lawn to the abandoned shed, which is leaning and moldy and all kinds of stank.

"Great idea," he groans, following me to the back of the shed, which has a leaning door hanging off rusty broken hinges.

"You know Cliff didn't want to come, anyway," I point out. "And this way Tracy can watch over him in case something does happen."

"So what about us?" he asks, breath hot on the back of my neck as he leans behind me, peering out through the crack between the warped, moldy slats in the shed door.

I turn to peer up at his rugged chin and quip, "Us us, or werewolf-killing us?"

He smirks. "I guess both, but for right now…werewolf-killing us."

I jab him in the ribs with the back of my elbow and sigh. "Okay, well, I guess we kick out this door and run for the house, that what you're thinking?"

"I'm thinking about going home and eating a bowl of mac 'n cheese, that's what I'm thinking. But your deal sounds good, too, I guess."

The werewolf roars again, literally shaking the shed with its power and I feel Zach's hands on my shoulders, squeezing tight.

Ah, he does care if I get torn limb from limb by a blood-crazed werewolf. How sweet!

"Just…be careful, okay. This is crazy, I know, but the cops are dumb and can't stop this thing so, I dunno, maybe Cliff's right after all."

I shrug, he lets his hands slide off my shoulders, and I sigh a little before counting to three and then kicking the door open with my tidy black sneakers.

It swings open and promptly swings right back on its hinges, knocking both Zach and me on our butts!

I hear something crack in my backpack and hope it's not my iPod!

"Nice," he snorts, lifting me up and scrubbing off his pants legs.

"We suck at this," I confess, edging the door open this time and quietly creeping out.

"Maybe by the time someone tips us to a vampire coven," he sighs, looking at me before leading me. "We'll be better."

"That's if we live that long," I joke, but as we stay low, inching across the grass, it suddenly hits me—we are hunting a werewolf.

I clutch the little squares of instant film in my pockets; they're about the size of a slice of American cheese and just as slimy.

I can smell the chemicals from here and suddenly I think, *How am I going to get the silver from the film on, let alone in, an 8-foot tall, screaming, slashing, claw-having, fang-biting werewolf?*

"When the cops see us," Zach huffs, all the exertion of running across an open field toward the back of the house getting to him, "just keep running. I'll divert them."

"What?" I snap, racing to keep up with his long, bony gazelle legs. "You'll divert them so, what…I can kill the werewolf?"

He shrugs casually, like we're talking about me using my fake ID (not that I have one, of course) and he's talking about distracting the sales clerk with his third nipple (not that he has one of those, either!).

"Hey," he reminds, already peeling away as a bullhorn squawks to life, "it worked pretty well last night. Besides, I already gave you the radio!"

Just then the sergeant's voice barks, "Warning! Stay away from the werewolf or we will be forced to apprehend and arrest you."

I look to where the voice is coming from and it's just on the other side of the yellow crime scene tape.

Yeah, as if they're going to risk crossing their own police line to cuff me when a big, bad werewolf could—

A giant, ear-splitting roar interrupts my reverie.

I fall to the ground, crouching just shy of a tricycle that's been tipped on its side.

The yard is full of junk—bikes, balls, shovels, a sandbox—and as the werewolf continues trashing the ground floor, I creep from junk heap to play pen until the porch is just out of reach.

The yard has grown eerily still now, and I peek from behind a half-inflated beach ball to see the cops waving me back, to see Zach trying desperately to outrun a younger deputy who is chasing him behind the yellow tape, gun drawn.

Great, so Team Zach is on the run. No help there.

I look to the giant oak tree, hoping against hope reinforcements have crept in but, no, even though Tracy is chomping at the bit Cliff has her in a giant headlock and I know for a fact this is one of his non-shower days so she must be about ready to pass out from the ripeness right about now.

I kneel there behind the ball, calculating the steps to the front porch.

I'm figuring two, three tops.

I swing my backpack purse so it's in front of me, like I sometimes do in the halls when I don't have time to go to my locker, and I root around in there as I walk.

It looks like one of those baby slings but if I need to grab something inside, another few strips of instant film, maybe, or Zach's stupid radio, it'll be within reach.

I sigh, and steady my trembling hands, and stand just as the werewolf literally bolts through the side of the house in a smashing of old wood and musty wallpaper.

He is gigantic as he soars over me. My eyes so close to his underbelly, I can count the hairs between his leg joint and his chest.

He smells like wet dog, hot cat, baby slobber, and fresh blood, and I glance toward the hole he's ripped in the wall and see a bloody leg gushing from a tear in worn overalls. Probably the poor farmer who tipped off Cliff about his missing farm animals.

The werewolf hits the ground in a flurry of torn grass and ripped dirt and spins with his backside, facing me as his big, bushy tail wags toward the cops, just behind him and over beyond the yellow tape.

They fire a round of volleys and the porch behind me erupts in a patchwork of splinters and explosions, like something out of a Hollywood special effects shot.

The wolf yelps but stands his ground as I hear Zach shouting to the police, "She's human, stupid! Quit firing!"

Well, at least the coward cares enough to heckle the cops from the sidelines.

The wet dog smell is almost overpowering as I creep on my backside toward the porch, making retching sounds like that one time Cliff found a dead rat and put it in the trash can and forget to tell anybody about it for a week!

With every inch I crawl back the werewolf creeps forward, closer now, crushing a plastic golf club under one of its massive paws and tearing the earth with each step.

It walks on all fours and is huge; eight feet, nothing, ten feet, maybe even twelve feet long from his quivering, drooling snout to the tip of his bushy, wagging tail.

I dunno, the biggest live animal I've ever seen was a crocodile in a zoo once and it was nine feet, and this is at least three feet bigger.

Its coat is a deep rich brown, like grizzly bear brown, it's snout drooly and bloody, its teeth the size of matchbox cars.

I see all this even as I'm creeping backward, my heart pounding as I forget all my lofty plans about film strips and radio connections and kung-fu moves.

This is no B-movie; this is a real-life werewolf and I know it: I'm going to die.

Any minute now this thing is going to slash at me and there goes my throat, my head dropping to my shoulder like an apple rolling off the display in some grocery store produce aisle.

I reach for a sheet of film, but my hands are trembling so badly I can't get my hand in my pocket, let alone grab one square sheet.

The werewolf advances steadily, its eyes an even, cold, angry blue, its muzzle vibrating with each throaty growl as it moves step by step.

Just then I hear the megaphone; so does the wolf.

It turns with a snarl and growls, then howls, and I use the distraction to clatter onto the porch, my back to the house, still trying to monitor the wolf's activities with one eye while I beat a hasty retreat with the other.

Suddenly the wolf is startled and yelps, distracted by the sound of running feet; so am I.

It's Zach, shouting into the megaphone, two cops on his tail, guns at the ready.

Zach is four paces out front when the wolf turns, rises up on two feet and leaps in his direction.

"Zach!" I shout as the werewolf opens its mouth to bite him in the arm.

Zach yanks his hand back but the werewolf digs in just around his wrist, then quickly aborts, yelping like a wet kitten and scrambling back on all fours like something out of a bad cartoon.

Its hair lays down on his back as it scampers and I see Zach go down, blood dripping.

A cop lifts up his white tux sleeve, now red at the cuff, and I see the tin foil wrapped all around Zach's arm with two fresh tooth marks.

I sigh; stupid tin foil.

There must be just enough silver derivatives in there to spook off a werewolf.

But not stop him.

Now the wolf is mad—embarrassed and mad.

He's facing me again, ignoring the shouts of the officers on the grass.

I've found some film strips and am tossing them at him, strip by strip.

Most fall short and he snorts an almost human laugh until one strikes his backside and sizzles to life and he squeals like a werewoman, scooting on his backside to put the fire out.

But now I'm out of film strips and

He.

Is.

Pissed!

He leaps from the ground, onto the porch, his huge claws digging out slashes in the old wood as I scramble back against the wall.

Suddenly I'm helpless, no camera, no film, no weapons, no silver left.

I try to get in the window and climb inside, but he barks and I stop, turning toward him.

He is inches away now, his teeth bloody, his breath rank, his eyes alive and evil.

No, not evil—just…empty.

I close my eyes but he roars again until I open them, then his muzzle erupts in a smile as he springs forward, mouth open, lunging for my chest.

The force of his attack knocks me clear through the window and into the living room.

He lands on me with all his weight, nearly crushing the breath from my lungs.

He is all claws and teeth, teeth and claws, and I know that no matter how many movies I've seen, none could have prepared me for the overpowering wet dog smell, the acid drool, the fiery eyes, or the razor sharp claws of this massive beast.

He is all sharp edges and hairy joints, claws reaching for my face but tearing up the floorboards beneath me as I manage to zig just when he zags; zag when he zigs.

But I know I can't keep it up forever.

He is too strong, too powerful, too heavy on my chest, and I'm already too weak from fear and dread.

I try to roll over so that when he finally lands a blow, when his teeth finally hit their mark, he'll get my shoulders instead of my chest; my skull instead of my face!

He's fighting me, though, and won't let me do it.

Every time I try to turn away he yanks me back, like some giant cat with a toy.

I can feel his weight crushing me as I struggle on my back, splinters digging in, his claws tearing my skin, his smile growing impatient.

He roars, teeth wide, as I try to hold my hands up and block his inevitable attack. He knocks them away with hairy fists and lunges, jaws open wide, aiming squarely for my chest.

I shut my eyes, feeling the weight of his muzzle digging in.

And then...and then...nothing!

Suddenly I'm fighting myself; the wolf is nowhere to be seen.

Standing, scrambling toward the window, I see the wolf lying limp on the porch, my backpack in his mouth—no, that's not quite right, either.

The backpack is torn and shredded, so is Cliff's stupid fifty-dollar radio.

In front of my eyes the wolf's muzzle slithers and melts into the porch wood, teeth falling out one by one to reveal the shiny silver specks soldered inside the radio, holding red and blue wires in place.

In moments the werewolf turns into a human. But it's no man, it's a woman.

A middle-aged woman, naked and shivering on the floor, her mouth scarred and toothless, one eye seared shut but...alive!

Chapter Ten

"**M**abel Redbone," grunts one of the cops, stepping on the porch hesitantly as his partner covers the poor woman with his jacket. "She owns this farm, along with her husband Rolf. The werewolf must have bit her, and she turned into one."

When the werewolf turned back into a woman, her snout shrunk and now the radio is lying on its side on the deck, its front smashed in, silver scattered throughout the hull, bits of teeth and bone fused to the plastic.

The cops kind of look the other way as Zach, Cliff, and Tracy climb onto the porch.

Tracy hugs me and asks, "You okay, girl?"

I nod but suddenly I'm trembling, and she holds me closer. "I wasn't sure I'd make it this time, Tracy."

"Me either," she admits, pulling me close before letting me go. "From where we were sitting, it looked like you were a goner. Which is why," she explains more loudly, looking at Cliff, "Ushers, Inc. has a new rule—no more splitting up. 'In for a penny, in for a pound' as my auntie used to say."

Zach murmurs meekly, "I agree," before pulling two of the digital watches out of his pocket.

"What are those for?" I ask, drawing near, if only to be closer to his side.

I think back to the quiet minutes in the shed, joking around, but it was no joke; those really could have been our last few moments together.

If I hadn't turned my backpack around for easy access, if that werewolf had bitten into my chest instead of that old radio...who knows where I'd be right now.

He seems to sense it, looks at me in the eyes and says, "The watch batteries still use silver. You remember *Moon Lake 2*? To make sure the wolf people didn't turn back into werewolves, the tracker shoved watch batteries down their throats."

"Oh yeah," remembers Tracy, eyes wide with the memory. "That way they had just enough silver inside of them to be human, but not too much to hurt 'em."

"That'll really work?" asks one of the cops, bending down as Zach uses his house key to open the back of the digital watch before prying out the dime size battery inside.

"You mean, she'll never turn into a werewolf again?" asks the other cop.

"We're about to find out," Zach points out, opening the woman's mouth and sliding the battery over her tongue and down her throat.

Some air escapes, rancid and coppery with the scent of fresh blood, but he pulls his hand back and wipes it on his black pants.

We wait as her gullet swallows, almost reflexively, watching the little silver disc move through her throat like water moving slowly through a hose.

Suddenly she gasps, burps, blinks her one good eye and howls herself awake.

"Mabel," whispers the younger officer gently, reaching out a hand to comfort her broad, naked shoulder. "It's Jimmy Oslin, from on up the road. We're here; you're safe."

"Did I hurt anybody, Jimmy?" she asks with a trembling voice, vocal chords permanently scarred by the silver down her throat and her missing teeth.

"No, Mabel," he lies, looking over our heads at the shattered wall and her hubby's bloody legs.

As we leave the two police officers to comfort her and step quietly away, Cliff groans, "The husband's next."

We look through the wolf-sized hole in the side of the wall and see a middle-aged farmer in shredded overalls lying in a pool of his own blood.

I know what he's saying; if we were to leave him be, he'd only be one more werewolf come tomorrow's full moon.

Zach goes to kneel next to the poor man, but I grab the watch from his fingers and hand it to Cliff.

"Your turn," I growl with just a hint of menace in my voice. "What did Tracy say the new rule is? All for one, one for all? So far you've done exactly *squat* on these missions but toss a few pennies and give us a ride. You open the watch, you open his mouth, and you shove the battery in and make sure this poor guy wakes up human instead of hairy, 'kay?"

"Or what?" he asks, beefy arms crossing over his big belly.

"Or you'll be looking for three new monster killing ushers at school tomorrow," snaps Tracy, sliding up beside me in solidarity.

"Fine," he huffs, prying off the back of the watch and digging out the battery just as Farmer Joe starts to grow hair from the middle of his stomach.

We hear bones crunching as his legs distend, then his arms, his entire torso lengthening in a shuddering display of curving muscle and snapping bones.

It looks painful and permanent, but just as quickly as his legs get longer they kind of, I dunno, flicker and then shrink back to his normal size.

Cliff quivers but we shove him forward.

"Now, Cliff!" we all shout.

The werewolf is trying to take over again.

We all watch as overalls tear at the seams and fall away as skin becomes hide and hide becomes hair.

Claws peel from large, weather beaten hands, as teeth—huge, drooling fangs—spring from a healthy pink gum line.

The wolf is still on his back, legs stretching, cracking as paws spring claws and the floor tears away beneath his curved, bony fingernails.

Soon he turns over, circles around like a dog chasing his tail and spots us—sniffs us, is more like it.

Cliff stands paralyzed, watch battery in his fingertips like a chew toy.

The wolf sniffs once more, drools at the scent of human flesh and stands on both legs, howling into the night, his mouth wide open, big enough to swallow a full-grown pig.

Behind us poor Mabel screams as the cops pull their guns, ready to unload on her husband any second.

Not that it will do anything but make them feel better, of course.

"Now, Cliff!" I shout, afraid to nudge him or the battery will drop and then we'll all be screwed.

At last Cliff emerges from his trance and, like flipping a penny into a wishing well, tosses the watch battery right into the werewolf's throat.

The wolf howls for moment then coughs, sputtering up fiery phlegm and flinging drool but...no watch battery.

Then all is still.

He howls again, louder, more violent, thrashing his giant, massive, hairy head, and I'm thinking, *Not enough silver. There wasn't enough silver in that stupid, tiny thing and now we've just ticked him off and he's going to rip us—*

But all of a sudden patches of hair start to disappear as skin returns.

A once huge head shrinks, bubbles, then boils into human skin; weathered and middle aged and suntanned.

Claws turn to nails turn to fingers and, at last, the farmer returns, naked and curled into a fetal position on the hardwood floors, claw marks still scratched there from his momentary transformation.

He doesn't open his eyes, or blink, or give us a shaky thumbs-up, but we can see his chest breathing in, breathing out and know he's going to be okay.

At least, according to legend.

"How did you kids know to *do* that?" asks the youngish cop, Billy What's-his-name, literally scratching his head under his plain black ball cap.

And, with pride, Cliff pivots on his plump black sneakers, spreads his legs, hands on hips and announces, as if he'd rehearsed it in the mirror back at the Home, "We watch movies, sir. Lots and lots of movies. After all, that's what Ushers do."

And only then do I turn to follow his smiling gaze and find pretty much the same news crews from last night, flooding us with lights from their cameras.

"Great, Cliff," blathers one reporter, shaking Cliff's hand.

Cliff smiles and asks, "Did you get it, guys?"

Another reporter, this one a woman, a blonde, smiles back and sidles up to Cliff. "Every minute of it, kid. Thanks for the tip. Our ratings are going to go through the roof when folks see this."

I blush and creep into the background, joining Tracy and Zach as Cliff does another round of face-to-face interviews.

"You think the kids at school will see this?" asks Zach as we walk to the van.

I shrug, thinking it wouldn't hurt a bit if rich witch Mia Hopwood saw what I could to a werewolf.

Or, for that matter, Wyatt Winters.

But it's Tracy who's really thinking ahead.

"Forget the kids at school," she murmurs, face as troubled as the moonlit night. "What if the monsters see it?"

Chapter Eleven

"**Y**ou guys were great last night," Wyatt informs us in homeroom the next morning.

His hair is a little less glimmering this morning, and I notice he's had it cut since yesterday.

I like it shorter, with less goop glamming it up.

It makes him look, I dunno, more…real?

"Really?" Tracy asks.

"Oh, man, when Cliff tossed that battery into the werewolf's mouth, it was golden. Seriously. Better be wearing something fireproof, girls, because Ushers, Inc., is about to blow *up*!"

Sitting next to Wyatt, her head so close, her black hair is attracted to his rough fisherman's sweater with static electricity, Mia does one massive eye roll and hisses, "Chill, dude, it's not like they're American Idols or anything."

"No," Wyatt brags, ignoring her, "they're bigger. Show me the Idol who can defeat a couple hungry werewolves with an old radio and two watch batteries."

She slumps down in her chair, her shimmery gold top showing more skin than a werewolf with a mouth full of silver.

I look down at my wheat-colored chords and ratty sneakers and, not for the first time wonder, *How exactly does one become a Mia Hopwood*?

But it doesn't help being Mia this morning, and she knows it.

Wyatt is saying, "—all four of you need head shots, I'm thinking black and white. It will set off the usher uniforms. We'll use Dad's favorite photographer. His studio's convenient and he always makes time for us. Is tomorrow afternoon okay?"

"We're working," I hear myself blurt, even as Tracy jabs me in the ribs.

"We lost our best assistant manager in that first zombie outbreak," I explain, ignoring her painful interruption technique. "So until they replace him, we're all just kind of pulling double duty."

Wyatt cocks his head, fixes me with those deep blue eyes and smiles.

"Even better! We'll take them right there at the theater, you know, a darkened theater, backs to the movie screen, those classic old movie chairs, it's perfect. Great thinking, Abby!"

Mia groans and settles in for a long homeroom.

After head shots and photo shoots and biographies for us all, Wyatt is still talking as the bell rings.

Tracy and I get up to leave and Wyatt follows; we both look at each other.

This is, like, first period sacrilege or something.

I mean, Wyatt and Mia *always* walk out of homeroom together.

Now she's still sitting, and he's halfway across the room.

Tracy has to turn right, toward first period gym, but I keep walking and Wyatt follows.

"Aren't you forgetting someone?" I ask, looking at Mia still fuming in the classroom.

He doesn't even glance back. "She'll get over it. Business is business, right?"

I shrug and walk a little more slowly.

He is half-a-head taller than I am, but insists on talking up close and personal, so his face is right next to mine the whole way there.

His skin is warm, I can tell from a few inches away, his breath fresh, not minty, more like…cinnamon or vanilla, maybe both.

I catch the half-dissolved breath mint in the middle of his tongue as he finishes lecturing me on my "good side" for the photo shoot and wonder, *When did he have time to pop that little sucker in?*

I spot Zach at our locker, but Wyatt all but ignores him as he asks, "So, I mean, what do you do after work?"

Zach turns and slides a book out of his locker before quickly slinking away.

"Who, me? Or…all of us?"

Wyatt moves quickly to lean on Zach's empty locker. "You, obviously."

I shrug, watching Zach lurch away toward our next class together, Home Ec.

"We're kind of a package deal, we ushers."

He doesn't flinch. "Sure, I get that. I mean, I know you live at the Meriwether Home together but…you must have some outside, uh, interests, you know?"

His long, tanned fingers fiddle with Zach's lock in a kind of proprietary way that ticks me off just more than a little.

"I do have outside interests," I insist. "Seeing movies and saving my job, that's about all I have time for."

He smirks. "All work and no play makes Abby a dull girl," he recites in a sing-song way that would be annoying if he didn't look so darn dashing doing it.

I snort. "Look, Wyatt, if it's all the same to you, I'd rather not get a knife in the back from your crazy-eyed girlfriend, okay?"

"Mia?" he asks, waving his long, elegant hands in the universal "pshaw" gesture. "We're cool."

"Dude, I saw her face after homeroom. You are definitely *not* cool."

He shrugs, smiles a little more. "I'll buy her a Diet Lemon Twist from the soda machine on the way to Calculus and we'll be good to go."

"Hmm, something tells me a girl like Mia Hopwood isn't so easily bribed."

"She is when I'm the one doing the bribing."

He leans close, flashes that smile and, you know, he could just be right.

I hear the sound of silence and look up to see the halls almost empty, and I haven't even opened my locker yet.

Halfway through deciphering my combination—it's a little hard with a Greek God leaning two inches away from me—the final bell rings.

"Wyatt!" I shout. "Now I'm late."

"Big deal," he brags, shoving off the locker and following me toward Home Ec. "I'm late all the time."

I snort, clutching my recipe folder to my chest as we double-time through the empty halls. "Yeah, well, you're Wyatt Winters, Wyatt. I'm stupid Abby Cooper and no one cuts me slack, least of all Mr. Freschetti."

"So tell him you were with me," he offers, just before peeling off toward his next class in D-wing. "And I meant what I said about going out sometime after work. I'd like to get to know you better."

I smirk, blush and have to wait outside the Home Ec door until I'm through smirking and blushing, making me even more late.

When I open the door, Mr. Freschetti is interrogating Zach, my lab partner.

"There she is," he intones in his oh-so-dramatic voice. "Thank you for favoring us with your presence, Abby. I suppose now that you're on the news every night, you can pop in and out of class any time you want, huh?"

"N-n-no, Mr. Freschetti," I stammer, aware the whole class is looking at me and my stupid broken shoelaces. "I'm sorry, it won't happen again."

"Indeed," he proclaims with that superior tone, "it better not. I know Mrs. Meriwether has a zero tolerance policy at the Home. What would happen if you got Detention for being late, Abby? Let's think about the consequences of our behavior from now on, shall we?"

"Nice!" Zach hisses once Freschetti has gone back to his roll book in the back of the room. "You're already on thin ice with this creep and you're risking a Detention over stupid Wyatt!"

I shrug, because he's right and I'm too tired to fight it.

Still, would I do it all over again?

Sure would, but he doesn't need to know that.

I ignore him for as long as I can, then tap his forearm, watching to see if he winces; he does, just a little.

Without comment, I slide the sleeve of his one good rugby shirt up a little and see the bandage there.

It's white and pristine, and I arch my eyebrows and he rolls his sleeve down and insists, "Abby, seriously, the fangs never got through the tin foil, honest."

His eyes are sincere and, maybe, just a tad bit...frightful.

"You sure?" I whisper as Freschetti stalks the room handing out recipe cards for today's assignment. "I don't want to have to shove a watch battery down your throat in the middle of the night."

"Just try it," he murmurs, reaching over to cover my hand gently.

And I think, *Whoa, that's never happened before!*

Then: *Is he just doing that because he thinks Wyatt is interested?*

And, finally, this: *Who the hell cares?!*

CHAPTER TWELVE

I'm tearing tickets for the 7:45 showing of *Vampire Vixens 4* in Theater 9 when I see Mia and Wyatt canoodling in the back of the line for the second time in one week.

I kind of flinch mid-ticket, the older man with the wiry white beard in front of me whining impatiently until I snap back to life and smile, announcing, "Enjoy the show" brightly although I'm pretty sure he won't.

Wyatt is in snug black jeans, a crisp white V-neck T-shirt, an appropriately distressed leather jacket, while Mia's in all red; clunky red heels (her specialty), tight red leather pants, darker red tank top covering her pale white chest, tiny red leather jacket, red sunglasses snug atop her straight black hair.

I snort and shred tickets until they saunter up, two posers on the red carpet.

Whose idea was it, I wonder, to show up at the movies on the very night Wyatt dissed her in homeroom?

Hers?

Or his?

Anyone?

"Tickets please," I ramble anonymously even though Wyatt tries ESP-ing me "I'm sorry" looks with his adorable baby blue eyes.

Wyatt stands there helplessly as Mia roots through her so fab little black cocktail purse.

"I am *so* sorry," she sighs insincerely. "They were just here a second ago."

"They had to be," I mumble.

"What's that?" she asks, stopping her rummaging to eye-spank me.

I've never noticed but her eyes are more than just green. They're shiny, like little green Christmas lights.

Or, at least, they are when she's eye-spanking you.

"Nothing," I keep mumbling, "it's just, you bought them thirty seconds ago so. How lost could they be, right?"

She sneers and peels them from a front pocket so tight she can only snatch them loose with her manicured fingernails.

"Here they are!" she cries, eliciting cheers from the crowd of eight to ten anxious moviegoers behind her.

I tear them and freeze a smile on my face as I utter, "Theater 9 is on your left and down the hall. Enjoy the show!"

She ignores me and lets Wyatt grab the tickets. He tries to get all touchy-feely as he grabs them but, remembering the look, the feel of Zach's hands covering mine in Home Ec, I let him have them quickly with no funny business.

I can feel that my face is hot and pink as I rip the next few customers' tickets, and after the mad rush to get in before the previews, I turn from my empty ticket stand and see them still lingering at the cash register, talking to Cliff intently as Mia takes slow, halting bites of popcorn one single kernel at a time, like she's rationing them out or something.

I look at my cheap digital watch—one of the extra's from last night's raid since mine broke months ago—and see it's well past preview time.

Don't these fools even think about wanting to see the opening credits?

As Mia nods soberly at something Cliff has just said—and I can see the flop sweat peeking through Cliff's tight white tux shirt from all the way across the lobby—Wyatt kind of looks at me and winks.

I frown and turn around, but then I spend the next five minutes thinking, *Way to go, Abby, your butt only looks Ha-Yuge in these black usher pants!*

Finally the buzz of low talking ends, the last of the prime time movies have started and I leave my post, sauntering over to Cliff as Tracy starts wiping down the Sergeant Slushee machine as one of her closing duties.

"What was that all about, Cliff?" I ask suspiciously as he cleans the top of the candy counter with a slimy disposable wipe.

"Waddya mean?" he asks, avoiding my eyes as I pick up some stray popcorn kernels from my side of the counter.

And you just know Mia dropped them there on purpose!

"Cliff, don't, just...don't even. Mia. Wyatt. What were you guys talking about for so long?"

"So long? Abby, it was only a couple of minutes."

"Cliff, they were, like, ten minutes late for the starting of *Vampire Vixens 4*! I had half a mind to give them their money back. That's just…wrong."

He snorts, because deep down I know he feels the same way.

"I know, I kept telling them the beginning is the best part, but between you and me, Abs, our newest team members aren't exactly fans of the genre, if you know what I me—"

"Back up, rewind, hold *up*! What newest 'team members' are you talking about, clown?"

"Why, Wyatt and Mia, of course."

"Oh, hell no!" Tracy shouts from the Slushee nozzles. "Wyatt was one thing, but Mia? No flippin' way, no how."

Cliff shrugs. "Hey, she said it was a package deal or Wyatt would have to bow out, so…."

"So let him!" I snap. "What has he done for us anyway, Cliff?"

Cliff's eyes get as big as malted milk balls in the microwave. "What has he done? Abby, we already have three bookings for next week, and he hasn't even officially started yet."

"Why does he need to?" Tracy asks, leaning one cash register over and waving her dirty Slushee rag for emphasis. "We're on the news every other night. You think that might have something to do with next week's gigs?"

"Maybe," Cliff admits, "but I'm telling you, having two, you know, people who look like, you know…*them*…won't hurt things in the marketing department, okay?"

Tracy and I give each other the "did he just say what we think he just said?" eye roll and she asks, "What do 'people who look like them' look like, exactly, Cliff?"

"Come on you g-g-guys," he stammers, more flop sweat rolling down his broad, unlined forehead. "You know what I mean."

"I don't, Cliff. Tracy, do you?"

"I sure don't Abby, do *you*?"

I wrinkle my nose and offer, "I know what I think he means, which is that we're not, not…pretty…enough to be in Ushers, Inc."

"Exactly!" Cliff snaps, then instantly backpedals *again*. "No, not exactly, I just mean, you know, we all look like character actors and, well, let's face it, Mia and Wyatt look like stars. We need A-Listers if we're really going to bust out. I mean, at least, that's what they said."

"I bet they did," Tracy mumbles as she shakes her head and shuffles back to the Slurpee grinder.

"And who cares what the PR people look like anyway, Cliff?" I ask.

"They're behind the scenes anyway, so…. Cliff, why aren't you looking at me? They *are* still behind the scenes, right?"

He shrugs and looks intently at a box of Raisin Clusters.

"Cliff, look at me and tell me they are still behind the scenes."

He doesn't.

So I warn menacingly, "Cliff, look at me and tell me they are still behind the scenes or I will rip your head off your neck and try to shove it in my ticket box before this shift is over!"

He looks up and whines, "Look, Abby, you don't understand. Business is…complicated. I told them they could be on the team, and Mia just ran with it. Suddenly she's talking about getting fitted costumes and having superhero names and—"

"You can stop right there," I snap. "Because I'll tell you right here, right now, and I don't care who hears it, if Mia Hopwood steps one tiny, perfectly-shaped, French manicured toe in one of our big black sneakers, you can find another zombie, werewolf, and vampire killer because I'll be flipping burgers at the Shake Shack by the end of the week. You can count on that."

When I pivot to return to my ticket box in front of the glass double doors, Zach is silently sweeping a pile of popcorn kernels behind the life-size lobby statue of Count Victus from the upcoming *Caped Casket Stealers* sequel.

I can't be sure, but it looks like he's finally, finally…smiling.

CHAPTER THIRTEEN

Mia is all sugar and spice and (almost) nice to me the next morning in homeroom, which makes me all kinds of sick, terrifically suspicious and, okay, just the slightest bit…star struck.

I mean, she's so frickin' beautiful, how can she be *all* bad, you know?

Tracy makes clucking noises from one seat over but Mia ignores them; so do I.

"I love your…peasant blouse," Mia coos with a bittersweet look on her face, and just the fact that this major priss is uttering "love" and "peasant" in the same sentence is enough to make me smile.

"Thanks, Mia," I sigh. "I love your Hermes shades."

Mia kind of nods.

Then there is this dreadfully awkward silence before she leans over conspiratorially as if Wyatt might hear, which of course he can because the two are always glued to each other's superficial sides and oozes, "I *really* wanted to thank you."

I whisper back, "Thank me for what?"

She smiles wickedly and explains, "Well, Cliff says the rest of the ushers were really reluctant to let Wyatt and me join the team, and that you were the last holdout, and when you gave in, well, everyone else caved."

I gulp and grip Tracy's wrist so she doesn't brain Mia with her forty-two pound Chemistry book.

"Did he now?" I manage to sputter through clenched teeth. "Is *that* what Cliff said?"

Mia nods quietly, her straight black hair shimmering around her clean, pale face.

"I'm taking the second half of my day off to get my costume tailored, that's how important it is to me."

"Costume?"

"You know, black pants, white top, Cliff already gave us one, courtesy of Flickers Cinemas, but there's nothing in the rule book that says we can't...alter...them a little, right honey?"

Wyatt smiles but it doesn't quite reach his eyes, which look to me almost...*almost*...apologetically.

"Well," he hems nervously, "we probably shouldn't try to look too different from the other ushers, you know Mia? I mean, it is a team and all that."

Tracy can't help but butt in, literally sliding her desk over to hiss, "We all wear the same thing, Mia. Period. It's not about standing out; it's about backing each other up."

Mia sneers. "Well, it's all well and good if you *can't* stand out, but if you can, why not take advantage of it?"

Tracy starts to snap something off but I kind of step on her foot and ask, "Do you watch a lot of movies, Mia?"

She shrugs. "Sure, I guess."

"Monster movies?"

She wrinkles her nose. "Heavens no, why would I?"

Tracy snorts. I promptly inform Mia, "Well, the reason we've been so successful at knocking off a few zombies and werewolves lately is because we do. Tracy, Zach, Cliff and I, together we've seen just about every cheesy monster movie Hollywood's put out in the last thirty years."

Mia looks bored.

I told you she was simple.

She puts up a bejeweled hand and ponders, "What does this have to do with me and my tailor?"

I lean in for the kill shot. "Don't you know, Mia? The pretty girl always gets killed first."

I hear snorts in stereo and see Tracy and Wyatt both covering their smiling mouths.

Mia huffs and snaps, "Yes, well, Cliff said we're mainly on the team for moral support and backup, so—"

"Oh no," explains Tracy with a great sense of gravity. "Everybody on the team goes on every mission, no matter how just oh-so-cute they are."

The bell rings just then and Mia rises elegantly, her pencil skirt barely creased as her bare midriff stretches like the washboard that it is.

She huffs off, unconvinced, and Wyatt barely has time to make the universal "sorry she's such a witch" shrug over his shoulder before she literally yanks him by her side.

Tracy and I are up and at 'em, too, sprinting into the halls and spotting Cliff lavishing in the attention of a group of geek girls on one of the cement planters bordering the quad.

We approach stealthily, but he's not the unofficial head of Ushers, Inc., by accident; he spots us halfway there.

He runs as fast as he can in the opposite direction.

That's the good thing about Cliff; he's not too hard to catch up with.

CHAPTER FOURTEEN

The break room is tiny and claustrophobic and three times as loud because there's just nowhere for the sound to go as Cliff calls us all to order later that night.

It's during the last show of the night and the few remaining managers have long since gone home—and wisely so.

But this is the only time we could reserve the break room without making them suspicious, so I resign myself to another sleepless night.

It's not like any of us have anything to go home to anyway, right?

"I'd like to welcome the two newest members of our team," Cliff announces, pointing to Mia and Wyatt sitting, Barbie and Ken-like on the far side of the double-wide picnic table in their identically tailored fake tux uniforms.

Tracy smirks and I catch it out of the corner of my eye, but wisely don't return the favor because I know Cliff would see and draw attention to it and then it would get ugly and it's *sooooooo* not worth the drama.

Because, clearly, Mia and Wyatt are meant to be the poster children of Ushers, Inc.

No ifs, ands, or buts.

I mean, it's obvious from just their uniforms.

Mia sure wasn't kidding about going to a tailor, and it looks like she dragged Wyatt along with her.

While our uniforms are stiff and bland, and snug in places where they shouldn't be and tight in places where they *also* shouldn't be, there is not a wrong seam or a missed tug in either of their outfits.

Wyatt looks like he should have a cigar in one hand and a brandy snifter in the other; his half-tux looks so snug and tight and smooth and…careful,

Abby.

Take it down a notch before you spontaneously combust from the navel down!

And Mia?

Mia?

How should I put this?

Uhhm, how about this: tramp, much?

I just—I've never seen a tux shirt look quite like the one she has on.

It's, well, she's somehow managed to make the sleeves just before the snug cuffs around her wrists puffier and the waist more narrow.

She had to let the chest out, for obvious reasons, and has somehow made the button down collar a banded collar, with a big gap in front of her throat that pretty much extends to her navel. And the bow tie, well, the bow tie is now in her hair and I know I'm not doing this justice but, there it is just the same.

Mia is one hot Ushers, Inc., tramp mess.

And she knows it, and she loves it.

And so, apparently, does Zach.

If he stared any harder, he'd sprain a retina or something.

"Down boy," I lean over and whisper at one point, and he literally flinches like I've just brought him back to earth.

He blushes, smirks…and blushes some more.

"Now," Cliff continues, standing next to Mia and Wyatt on the other side of the double picnic table from Tracy, Zach, and me, "as I was saying, Wyatt here has really ramped up the marketing blitz. We'll have stories in both the Cypress Cove *Bugle* and the Catfish Cove *Classifieds* tomorrow, and it looks like the papers in Orlando, Miami, and Tallahassee will all be picking up the story as well.

"Uhhm, what else? Oh yeah, Wyatt and his dad have worked up an awesome website that should go live by end of the week and feature both YouTube hits from our first two missions—well, the first thirty seconds anyway, after that viewers can pay to see the extended cut."

Zach and I exchange our best "WTF" faces and he asks, "Cliff, why would anyone pay to watch either of those clips when they're all over the web for free?"

Cliff looks at Zach as if he's wearing a coonskin cap and bluffs, in his adult voice, which he usually only uses around Mr. Fletcher (you know, before he was ripped apart, that is) or one of the other managers, "Good question, Zach. Wyatt here has used some of his Dad's video editing tools to clean up the picture, bring it back in focus, take out the harsh news camera lighting and just generally enhance the quality of the film two hundred percent."

Wyatt puffs out his chest a little and takes it from there with a cocky tone as he adds, "I've also added a soundtrack and extended the tapes by four minutes each, you know, by repeating the good stuff at the end. It really adds value for the end user, and $9.99 isn't a bad price to pay for—"

"Ten bucks?" Tracy interrupts. "Bad enough they have to pay at all but…ten bucks? I know I'm just some lowly orphan but that sure seems like a lot to me."

"That's because it *is* a lot," I snap. "Cliff, what gives?"

"Hey," he snaps back, "gas and digital watches and instant camera film don't come cheap, Abby."

"Yeah, Cliff, they do, remember? We started this because people need our help and the cops don't know all our little secrets. We didn't start this to jack up the price on some ten-minute video of us doing what we do."

"Yeah," Zach adds, "that's totally cheesy and I don't want any part of it."

Cliff smiles a sleazy little smile. "Really, Zach? What are you going to do about it?"

"Hey," Tracy answers for him, "it's our pictures in those videos. I mean, what right do you have to make money off them anyway?"

"The news crews took those pictures, Tracy, and we were in a public place, in plain view, when they took them. I can do anything I want to them, and I have, and I will, and there's nothing you guys can do about it, so just…get used to it."

"Why wouldn't you guys *want* to make money?" asks Mia with her 'it's un-American not to rip people off' face. "I mean, I'm pretty sure you guys can use it."

"What Mia means to say," Wyatt interjects quickly before any of us can reach over the table and yank the bow tie out of her long black hair and shove it down her elegant, porcelain throat, "is that no one's going to complain about spending ten bucks to see you guys in action."

I shake my head and focus on Cliff. "All people need is a number to call, Cliff. That's it. When they're in trouble, when they need help, when bullets and machine guns won't stop whatever's chasing them, all they need is to call that 1-900 number, period. Everything else is just profit, dude, and that's wrong."

"Why is it wrong, Abby? We're putting our lives on the line out there—"

"Correction, Cliff," huffs Tracy, "*we're* putting our lives on the line out there. So far you haven't put down a single monster, and I know for damn sure these two pretty people here don't know the first thing about monster killing, so if you think—"

"That's not entirely true," Wyatt rationalizes. "I mean, Mia and I know plenty about killing monsters, don't we dear?"

She huffs but avoids my eyes because I already know she doesn't know jack.

"Really?" sneers Zach, eager for the chance to take Wyatt down a peg or two. "So tell me, Wyatt, which works better on a vampire: cloves or minced?"

"Cloves or minced what?" Wyatt sneers, and when he sneers, his hotness dampens by about twenty degrees.

"Garlic, Wyatt. So, which is it: cloves or minced garlic?"

Wyatt looks unsure but answers quickly anyway. "Cloves, I imagine."

Zach makes that game show "wrong answer" sound and busts him with a blunt, "Wrong, dude. Minced garlic quails on cloves."

Wyatt cocks his head and asks, "I'm not sure that's entirely true."

"It *is* true," argues Tracy. "Cloves still have the skin, the peel, and the real garlic oil is clustered in the center; minced garlic has none of that and almost all center, so it's the closest you can get to pure garlic oil without squeezing it yourself."

"Okay, great, well like Mia said this morning, we're here for support so that kind of stuff should come in handy on a mission, right Cliff?"

Cliff's about to reply with one of his kiss butt answers when I point out, "Yeah, Wyatt, but what happens if you and Mia here get separated? How will you know what to do to fight your way out of a really nasty situation?"

When he doesn't answer right away, I lower my tone a notch and declare, "I know you guys think we're just marking our territory here, but really…it's for your own protection."

"I'm sure it is," Mia snaps, soothing her boyfriend's arm with one long, slender hand.

Just as Cliff goes to mend fences by opening his big, fat mouth there is a sudden knock at the back door and Tracy, Zach, and I literally jump about three feet.

"Oh, good," Cliff announces, cluelessly, completely un-ironically. "The photographer's here."

Chapter Fifteen

The girls' locker room is empty and dark when I step in, using the light from Mia's text to guide me in.

I look down to read it one last time, one foot in the locker room, one foot in the gym; it says, "Locker room; midnight, don't tell anyone else—super secret sexy spy stuff!"

I should have ignored it when the text buzzed in my pocket on the way home from our meeting-slash-photo-shoot tonight, should have known it for the trap it most certainly is, but there's just something so intriguing about Mia I can't resist.

Besides, she weighs as much as Mrs. Meriwether and I've already put down two monster uprisings this week so…what's to fear, right?

The text came in just as we pulled into the Home driveway, and Cliff's not really generous about loaning out his van, but I guess he feels a little guilty about turning Ushers, Inc., into a big, fat money-making joke, so he doesn't even flinch when I tell him I forgot my purse in my locker.

He just yawns, hands me the keys and gloats, "More sugar cookies and cocoa for me."

Tracy looks at me funny—she knows I'm hiding my little clutch purse behind my back—but before she can say anything, I give her the universal "I'll tell you about it later, girlfriend" look and she just kind of shrugs and follows the boys inside.

I'm nearly to the van when Zach races back with a gleam in his eye.

I turn and he's grinning that goofy grin and explains, "I thought you might like some company?"

The question is in his eyes, not his voice, and my first reaction is to say

"No," to leave him hanging.

Because Mia texted *me*, right?

Not Tracy, not Cliff, not Zach—me.

Then I think Zach's been pouting something fierce lately what with this whole Wyatt thing, and I know how much I hate it when he drools over Mia, and he can't be feeling too confident right about now, and by the time I process this, he's already snatched the keys and is starting up the engine!

It's a short drive back to the theaters but before we get there I confess, "I lied, Zach" and slide him over the text from Mia.

His face looks seriously handsome in the shiny blue glow from my cheap convenience store cell phone, and he frowns as he hands it back.

"What do you think she wants?" he asks, making the turnoff for school instead.

I shrug, sliding sideways in the shotgun seat just a little during his hairpin turn.

"I don't know," I admit. "I don't even know why I'm running when she says jump, you know?"

He shrugs. "Beautiful people always get what they want, Abby. You should know that by now. I mean, Wyatt makes you late for Home Ec, he doesn't care that Mr. Freschetti is going to rag on you, he just knew he wasn't going to get in trouble so, big whoop. Mia bats her eyes at Cliff and, boom, she's an Usher. Now she texts you and, boom, you come running. I'm not judging; I'd do the same thing."

"You would?" I ask, not sure if I'm disappointed that he'd be as easily duped as me, or glad that I'm not the only fool in Cliff's van tonight.

"I already am, remember."

"Yeah," I smirk, "but I lured you in under false pretenses."

He doesn't look at me when he says, quietly, "Like I said, Abby; pretty people always get what they want."

I snort, but he doesn't crack a smile.

The student parking lot is deserted, and he steers past the Driver's Ed circle and around the back to the indoor pool and gym door.

He goes to get out and I touch his arm, gently.

"I should do this alone, you know, just in case it's something totally innocent."

He looks at me gravely and croaks, "I have a feeling it's not going to be anything close to totally innocent."

"Me, too," I admit, sliding out of my seat as he dutifully stays put. "So let's do it this way; if I'm not back in ten minutes, come running."

He smiles. "If you're not back in five, Abby, I'm calling the cavalry, then running."

I open my mouth to argue but he's already futzing with the radio and, who am I kidding?

This is Zach we're talking about here; stubborn is his middle name.

Come to think of it, I've known the kid since eighth grade and have no idea *what* his middle name is.

Mia hadn't said how I was supposed to get into the girls' locker room before the school janitor showed up for his rounds at 6:30 in the morning, but I'm not entirely surprised to see the chain that normally winds twice around the outside gym doors unwound and lying at my feet.

I try the door and it opens.

The gym is quiet and dark, lit only by a few dim, red "Exit" signs over the doors in the back and front.

My work shoes squeak on the shiny gym floor as I take a few brave steps in.

My heart is pounding in my chest, my breath heavy, my palms clammy, and I call myself "stupid" in about two hundred different languages.

This is ridiculous. I've killed zombies and put down two werewolves this week—what am I afraid of?

Then the volleyball hits me in the back and shoves me to the floor.

I go down with a shuddering "oomph" and slide three feet toward the cinderblock wall at the back of the gym.

I sit up and look just in time to dodge the second ball, but I'm not so lucky with the third; it slams into my shoulder and slides me another four feet across the floor.

What is *happening*?

Covering my head with my arms, I peek through and see dark, shadowy figures leaping down the bleachers one by one.

They are tossing thick white balls as they go, one after the other; most sail past my head at blinding speeds, a few land solidly until I'm literally curled up in a ball under the basketball net.

There is squeaking on the floor and I look up to see three of Tracy's teammates stalking me silently.

"Jill?" I ask of the buxom blonde in the middle. "Amy? Julie?"

I don't know the girls well, but Tracy sure does and enough years in the stands of this very gym have taught me their first names, if not their last.

But volleyball season hasn't even started yet and what the heck are these girls doing in the gym, at midnight, trying to kill me with…oh, that's why.

The first pair of fangs glistens as Jill passes under an "Exit" sign, the dim red light catching the drool-covered fangs as they quiver in the middle of her upper jaw.

"Jill!" I shout, hoping it will be loud enough for Zach to hear, but God knows he's got the radio turned up to his favorite speed metal station for at least the next four minutes; more than long enough for these chicks to tear me to shreds. "Amy! Julie! Stop, it's me, Abby; Tracy's friend!"

They don't stop and now I get up, scrambling, but it's not easy because there are volleyballs everywhere and I've got about three simultaneous concussions going on from their first barrage.

I slip and tumble and they snicker over their fangs; they must be pretty new, though, because the girls don't look too comfortable with them.

I pick up a spare ball and toss it back as hard as it will go, but I'm only human and it doesn't go very far; but still far enough to get stuck on Jill's fangs!

She looks like a giant jack o' lantern for about 6 seconds, before she yanks off the ball with a horrible hiss of moldy inflated air.

Jill tosses it back to the ground where it lies like a limp piece of squash.

I scramble until I find myself pressed up against the girls' locker room door and that's when it hits me: Mrs. Wannamaker, our PE coach-slash-nutritionist, is a total health nut and is always popping garlic pills from her bottom desk drawer as we shower after class.

I yank open the door and slam it shut just before the three girls reach me.

There is a long wooden bench just behind me and before they can shove open the door I use all my (not) considerable muscle to shove it against the door and wedge it up against the closest row of lockers.

It's not exactly a tight fit, but tight enough to buy me some time.

Mrs. Wannamaker's office is a little glass cubicle in the front wall of the locker room, and of course the door is shut.

I try punching the large, glass window from which she watches us change each day (not like that, you perv) but nothing; it doesn't even budge.

The girls are slamming into the locker room door now and they'll be through it soon, one way or the other.

My heart is pounding and my mind is racing, but not the way you think.

Instead of escape routes and defense moves and karate kicks I'm thinking, *What the hell? Did Zack tag along tonight because he was finally going to ask me to that stupid dance or what?*

It's not my life flashing before my eyes as death comes knocking; it's my social life!

Or lack thereof!

Then I stop and think, *Screw this. I'm not dying until I go to that moronic Fall Formal*!

With a new reason to live—even if it is the lamest reason *ever*—I run to my locker, open up the combination, miss it twice, and finally snap it open.

The door is wedging open, inch by inch, the Volleyball Vampires hissing, drooling openly on the locker room floor.

I ignore them as best I can—which is hard when your heart is pounding like a drum—take the lock off and literally hurl it through the big plate glass window.

Finally it shatters and I leap over it and onto Mrs. Wannamaker's desk, scattering a big paper blotter onto the floor.

Her bottom drawer contains about two dozen vitamin bottles and of course I have to go through every letter (A, B, B6, B12, C, and D) before I finally spot the Gigantor size of garlic capsules she thinks reduces her blood pressure.

I break three of the gooey, mushy golden capsules open and smear them on my throat, just so none of the girls will get any bright ideas about noshing on my neck, then shove as many capsules as I can in every single available pocket.

Suddenly the door bursts open and Jill literally crawls through the shattered remains like a hound dog cornering its prey.

I back away from Coach Wannamaker's desk, and that's when I run smack dab into the bow and arrow sets from last week's archery lesson.

I load up one bow and scatter a quiver of arrows on top of Coach's desk, like I'm preparing for some kind of final showdown or something.

The minute Jill comes into focus, I shoot her with an arrow.

Okay, so it only hits her shoulder but man does she *wail*!

The other two girls don't know what to do and lurk around the window's perimeter, but I manage to squeeze a few shots off at them, too, only…with no luck.

Now all I've done is tick them off, and they make short work of climbing into Coach's office with me.

They smell something awful but come anyway, their nostrils wide, their fangs long, their claws longer.

Before they can do too much damage I launch myself at Jill, shoving my throat all up in her grill and feeling the steam rise from her cheeks as her skin comes in contact with the pure garlic oil I've slathered all over myself.

The other two shrink back and as Jill howls, mouth wide open in pain, I toss two capsules down her throat, like feeding a monkey at the zoo.

She gargles a rich, red, bloody foam and claws at her neck as the other two scramble to get out of the room.

Now they're the ones who are trapped and I torture them by tossing garlic pellets at every piece of exposed skin, which is pretty plentiful since for some odd reason they are wearing their brown and orange volleyball uniforms (why????).

Their skin sizzles and it doesn't hurt that I squeeze each capsule first just to get the garlic nice and oozy before I toss them at several strategically fleshy locations.

The room is full of the stench of fresh garlic and searing flesh and now the girls are howling in pain as Zach finally jumps through the crashed open door and says, "Abby, enough! Get out of there!"

He yanks me through the office window as the girls clutch and claw, but their eyes are teary from the garlic fumes and their melting faces and I'm so happy to see him I literally defy gravity to leap into his arms.

The girls are squealing, mewling, steaming, parts of them melting as we stand outside the window, looking at each other.

"We've got to...finish...them," he blurts.

"I can't, Zach. They're just...girls."

"Those zombies the other night were just ladies, Abby. Those werewolves were just a couple of nice, old farmers. I mean, we didn't make these chicks vampires, we're just stopping them from making *other* chicks vampires, you know? We can't leave them like this, Abby. We can't let them get out into the world like this."

Even as I shake my head, I know he's right.

"We'll come back with Tracy and Cliff," I argue, bartering for, begging for more time. "We'll...we'll...all do this together."

But Jill is already crawling through the window, eyes blind with red steam and gargling with rage.

As she stumbles across the floor hands out, trying to feel for me, he insists, "There's no time for that, Abby."

I see the rack of jump ropes hanging near the door and grab a handful.

"Fine," I relent. "We'll tie them up and strap them to the shower poles, then turn on the water."

"What good will that do?"

I snort, tossing a jump rope around Jill's arms and yanking it into a tight knot behind her back. "That's what you get for ignoring the *Vampire Gym Teacher* series, Zach."

"That series was so lame," he disses, yanking Amy out of Coach's office and hog-tying her as if he's done this before.

I finish off Julie, the last girl, and we drag them into the shower area.

"I've never been in here before," he manages to joke. "It feels kind of…kinky!"

"Down boy," I sigh, adding, "If you had watched any of those three wonderful films, you would have caught *Vampire Gym Teacher # 2: Back to Cruel*, where the vampire hunter ties a vampire chick to the shower and tortures her by turning on the water. They can't stand water, even if it's *not* holy water."

"Will it kill 'em?" he asks, yanking the knot tight behind Amy's back as he ties her to one of the eight stainless steel shower towers.

"No, but it will keep 'em put, that's for sure. At least until we can drag Tracy and Cliff back here with some fresh stakes and put these three out of their misery."

When we've tied the three to the towers they are a sore sight, scarred and broken, burned and bent, too weak to put up much of a fight—or snap their heavy tethered jump rope bonds.

I turn all four spigots on in each shower tower, and immediately they are wet and soaking and steaming and angry, but docile and beaten.

They're not going anywhere; at least, not until someone turns off that water and sets them free.

Just to make sure, I reach into my pockets and dump the last of the garlic capsules onto the shower floor, the water quickly dissolving them and forming a kind of garlic water soup at the girls' feet.

Then Zach yanks me out through the door, into the gym, and out the back door, where the fresh air fills my pores and I drink it in with huge, gushing gulps.

He tosses me in the passenger seat, starts the van up, and peels out.

Zach doesn't comment on what's in my lap until we're halfway home.

"Souvenir?" he asks with that crooked smile.

I look down at the spare jump rope in my hand and whisper, "Lasso."

He shakes his head and keeps driving.

CHAPTER SIXTEEN

I knew I wasn't done with vampires yet.

I just knew it.

Case in point: there is something hovering outside my window. Something not...quite...human.

It's nearly 2 a.m., but I can't sleep.

I mean, first zombies, then werewolves, now...now...volleyball vampires!

It's enough to make any Usher freak.

While I'm waiting for Zach to carve up some fresh stakes and wake the others, I study the jump rope in front of me.

On our way in from Operation Hit the Showers, I'd grabbed a jar of minced garlic in the kitchen—Mrs. Meriwether only uses it for her six-layer lasagna and since we had it last week she won't make it again until next month—and headed back to my room to change and get down to business.

Now the whole jump rope is smeared in garlic paste, the once pink and blue threads already a kind of greenish-yellow from instantly coming in contact with the rich garlic oils which, according to about two thousand, one hundred, and seventy-four vampire movies is like kryptonite for vampires.

I'm thinking I'll hang it up in my closet until we leave, let it marinate until we go to finish off the Volleyball Vamps and then, bam, instant garlic lasso!

Wait'll Cliff sees it; he'll freak.

So that's where I'm headed, straight to my closet, garlic lasso in hand, when I see the figure floating outside my second story window.

I duck instantly by the wall just to the side of the window, where the floating shape can't see me.

My heart is pounding as I lean back against the wall, mere inches from the thin glass pane.

In case you've never lived in an orphanage, and I'm guessing you haven't, windows, especially those on the second story, aren't exactly a priority.

I mean, forget birds flying through the glass; a big enough mosquito could break through if he was going fast enough!

And if a person, shape, or thing can hover fourteen feet above the ground, I'm figuring he, she, or it isn't going to have too much trouble shattering some dime store glass orphanage window.

I look around the room for a weapon, but Cliff has all the crucifixes in his room because now that we're officially Ushers, Inc., he wants to put our initials on the back of each one so we don't get them confused.

And Zach has the holy water because he's got the biggest squirt gun collection known to man, so naturally it's his job to fill them all.

Of course, he hasn't quite started yet but, Zach's good like that; he might take awhile, but once he gets started, he'll stay up all night to fill those holy water squirt guns if necessary.

And since Tracy's in the room with bunk beds—but no roommate—it naturally fell on her to turn that spare bed into a few dozen stakes.

Now, I've yet to hear her carving away on anything so far, but she's like Zach; give her time and—

Wait, shut up, Abby; what's...*that*?

Scratching, more like scritching, on the window pane closest to my ear; so loud I flinch and move away, if only for a second.

It doesn't stop, but instead kind of gets louder; it's a wonder the whole house isn't awake.

No, wait, it does stop, but then something else sounds even louder; like glass falling out of glass.

Suddenly a square pane of glass drops to my feet and shatters into a dozen pieces.

The scritching-scratching starts up again and, a few seconds later, another pane of glass falls onto the first.

I try to remember how many panes of glass are in my bedroom window but it's not one of those things I ever stopped to count, you know?

I can feel the cold October air rush in through the two open panes, but something more—the rustling of clothes.

And...hair.

Long hair.

So either the Shape outside my window (no name yet so I'm calling him, her, it the Shape) is a guy with long hair or, more likely…a girl.

I think I have eight panes in my glass; suddenly, I feel pretty confident that I have eight.

That gives me some time, even as the third pane falls and I panic.

I'd call for help, but I don't want whatever's coming after me to start knocking off my friends as well, to say nothing of poor old Mrs. Meriwether.

With no time for the closet, I loop the foul-smelling, grease-slimy garlic jump rope around my shoulders and hustle along the wall up to my nightstand, where I grab the gloves I only ever use on the first and last day of winter—the two coldest days of the year, in my experience—and slide them on.

I want some shoes on, some sneakers, in case the Shape floats away and I have to run downstairs and out into the street, but all my shoes are on the other side of the room.

I settle for some slip-ons I keep near my bed for when I get up in the middle of the night and don't want to feel the cold, hardwood floors beneath my bare feet.

So, dressed like a fool, eyes tearing up from all the garlic, I inch back to just shy of the window and find, five, maybe six panes of glass crunching underfoot.

The wind is really rustling now, some homework papers scattering across my desk and onto the floor and bunching up in the far corner of the room.

I crouch as the last pane topples to the floor, watching it land in one piece as the other shards break its fall.

Suddenly a long, pale, white hand pokes in to open the latch and, without even knowing it will work, I yank the garlic lasso from my neck and toss it up, over and around the wrist, pulling it tight into a nice crisp loop around the shape's wrist as shrieking cuts through the night.

I stand up, yanking on the rope, tighter and tighter as I try to get some traction in my slip-on shoes.

Suddenly, steam starts to rise from the lassoed wrist.

It yanks back, violently, but I yank back too, looping the jump rope around the sleeve of the thin white homework hoodie I've managed to change into as I tug, and tug, and tug until there's no slack.

Now I am face to face with the shape, its dark face a mask of pain in the shadows as the long black sleeve beneath the jump rope falls away in tatters and the skin beneath turns a hot, bright, bubbling pink.

Like reeling in a fish, I yank on the rope and the Shape's arm slides through the window and across cut glass, blood dripping onto the floor as the Shape howls.

I yank harder, sensing a weakness, until the Shape's face is pressed against the remaining glass.

"Mia!" I shout, and in my anger, rage, fear, shock, and shame, I yank so hard on the garlic jump rope that Mia Hopwood comes flying through the window and right onto my bedroom floor.

She writhes in broken glass, hissing in a black leather jumpsuit and long, black hooded cape, and even as she writhes, I take one look at her chunky black boots and think, *Those are actually wicked cool!*

Tracy and Zach come running, eager to see what all the screaming and glass shattering is about.

Tracy is still rubbing the sleep out of her eyes and forgot to slip a robe on to cover her tiny yellow nightgown.

Without blinking, Zach says, "Cliff's missing!" not even asking why I have Mia writhing in a garlic-smeared lasso.

CHAPTER SEVENTEEN

"**W**hat do you mean Cliff's missing?" I ask, yanking Mia down the hall toward Cliff's room.

His walls are painted black, and I don't know why he bothered because they are also covered, inch-by-inch, by free movie posters from the video rental place down the street.

I see a half-eaten snack cake dropped in the middle of his Gamma Man bed sheets and know it's true; Cliff would *never* leave a snack cake half-eaten unless he'd been literally snatched mid-bite.

I yank on the lasso until Mia is kneeling in front of Cliff's smelly, lumpy desk chair and snap it tight before asking her, "Where is he, *Mia*?"

"How should I know?" she rasps as steam continues to rise from her shoulders where the slimy lasso keeps her subdued.

"Oh, I dunno," I snap ironically, yanking on the lasso for emphasis. "What are the odds you show up floating outside my window for the first time on the same night Cliff goes missing?"

"Floating?" asks Zach, inching back. "Huh?"

"Yeah," I snap without looking over my shoulder at him.

Tracy covers her décolletage and crosses her knees before waving two fingers in front of her nose and asking, "What's that smell?"

I tug on one pink plastic handle of the jump rope and confess, "I was trying out my new garlic lasso when I caught Mia here hovering outside my window."

"Oh great," Tracy groans, grabbing Cliff's Gigantor bathrobe and slipping into it. "Now the bad guys are coming to *us*?"

Mia *tssks* and hisses, "What'd you think would happen, morons? You can't just go around killing off zombies and werewolves without there being, you know, repercussions."

"Repercussions from *whom*?" I ask, yanking her up.

"Get this thing *off* of me," she hisses, her eyes a putrid black now, her face a feral mask of anger and pain, "and I'll be happy to tell you."

I look at Zach and Tracy, and they shake their heads.

"How about a compromise?" I ask without asking, shoving her back first into Cliff's desk chair and, before she can react, yanking the jump rope out from around her throat and winding it through and around both hands.

She squeals and kicks but looks grateful to not have the garlic around her face anymore.

As we watch, her shoulders begin to steam less and less and kind of...glow...even more.

The torn parts of her cape kind of fall away to reveal the puckering, zippery rough skin of her pink garlic scars.

"Wicked," gushes Zach, voice full of awe and admiration. "So you *can* repair yourself."

"What would *you* know about it, geek?" she spits, wrists steaming like she's washing her hands with one of those hot white napkins at a sushi bar.

Zach kind of frowns (no snappy comeback, dude? *weak*) and I yank the chair around so she's looking at me.

"Focus, Mia. Who are you, really, and where is Cliff?"

She sighs, tests her hands, finds them lashed tight to thick armrests and tosses her long, straight hair back from her luminous, pale face.

"I am Mia Hopwood; that's my real name. I haven't changed since I transferred here freshman year—"

"You mean, aside from becoming a vampire and all?" Tracy jousts.

Mia merely blinks, twice. "No, I've always been a vampire, the whole time. You turds were just too busy watching imported DVDs of vampires and zombies and werewolves to notice you were sitting right next to one. A vampire, I mean; those other Undeads are losers."

I snort. "Why would a vampire go to school, though? I've never understood that."

Tracy and Zach kind of nod their heads.

"I mean, why not just go have fun and travel and see the world?"

"Because LAD pays me to go to school, morons! You think I'd hang out with a bunch of turds like you and date that creep Wyatt Winters if I wasn't getting paid for it! Please, give me some credit."

"LAD?" asks Tracy, winding one long dreadlock around one long finger nervously.

Mia sighs, looking at us like we're kindergartners at a Homecoming pep rally. "The League of Associated Undead, or 'LAD' for short. They're like, how should I put this? I dunno, the United Nations of Monsters. Run by a vampire, a zombie, and a werewolf, they make sure there is at least one immortal at every high school in the country, just to keep things...*even*."

"So, what?" Zach asks. "You guys are...good...monsters?"

Mia snorts. "No, tool, we're bad monsters; really bad, but we monsters do have rules and the rules state that no side can cause an infestation without permission from the other side, so...that's why LAD exists and that's why I'm here."

"That still doesn't explain where Cliff is, Mia," I point out.

"With LAD, duh! Why do you think I was floating outside of your window, dufus? For the fun of it? I floated out there while LAD snuck in here and dragged Cliff out of bed. Now you've got me, they've got him, and we're all set for a nice little tradeoff."

I look at Zach, who looks at Tracy, who looks at me.

I shake my head. "Fine, Mia, where?"

She shakes her head and sighs, "You guys really are clueless, aren't you? Flickers Cinemas, of course!"

CHAPTER EIGHTEEN

We wrap the garlic lasso around Mia's ample chest and shove her in Cliff's closet, sliding his massive desk chair under the doorknob so she can't break free.

From the other side of the door, we can hear her muffled cries as she complains, "Hurry up, dorks! It smells like twelve days worth of anchovy pizza farts in here!"

I stand guard while Zach runs into my room and gets my usher uniform and Tracy grabs hers—and his.

We lay them out on Cliff's messy single bed and stare at them intently.

"You know they're going to frisk us before the tradeoff," I whisper as Mia mewls in the closet.

Zach shooshes me and holds up his cummerbund, turns it over and slides his finger into a fold that sort of looks like a hidden pocket; Tracy and I inspect ours and we have the same thing.

He keeps his finger in front of his mouth and roots around Cliff's desk, looking for something; then he finds a drawer full of liquid candy inside plastic test tubes—they're called, "Gobbling Blue Goo!"

He dumps the contents from three tubes in an old bowl of popcorn and refills each tube with holy water from one of his bigger plastic containers.

We each slide one inside the back of our cummerbund.

Then he holds up our bow ties and puts his finger to his head, like a kindergarten teacher making "thinking" faces to his class.

I roll my eyes and dig into the bag of cheap digital watches Cliff picked up on the way home from school the day before.

We snap them open with a jelly encrusted knife from Cliff's desk, dig out the silver batteries and slide one on each side of the bow tie; they weigh them down a little, but not too much.

There are five watches left and he makes us put them on our wrist, as backup, I suppose; or…decoys…for the creeps from LAD.

Finally, he peels off a long sheet of duct tape from a roll in Cliff's bottom desk drawer and covers it with half a roll of pennies, then wraps it around his left calf muscle, leaving two sticky ends to seal it tight.

He hoists his leg and they stay put; we do the same.

We turn, and dress, and look at each other, straightening bow ties, tightening cummerbunds or loosening them so the plastic tube doesn't stick out.

More loudly, because I figure it's the first place they'll look anyway, I point out, "We should all wear silver earrings, you know, in case the werewolves show up."

I nod my head at the closet, where for the first time Mia has finally quit complaining; suddenly, all is quiet as she totally eavesdrops.

"Here, Zach," I proclaim dramatically, handing him a simple clip-on stud. "This looks pretty masculine."

Tracy gets the hint and announces, even *more* dramatically, as if auditioning for some kind of cheesy soap opera on the Bad Actors Channel, "Definitely, and we should hide these little crucifixes in our back pockets; they'll never look there."

Zach takes one, smiles, then takes one more; it's metal and jointed in three places, and he looks at it funny.

Then, as if forgetting them, he blurts, "I forgot deodorant in my room," and he dashes off.

When he comes back, both crucifixes are gone.

At last we look at the clock on Cliff's nightstand—it reads 3:45 in the morning.

"We better get going if we're going to make it to Flickers by 4:30," I urge, reaching for the closet door and yanking Mia out unceremoniously.

Just as I expected, there's a knowing smile on her face and a gloating look in her eyes.

Hey, at least one of us is confident.

CHAPTER NINETEEN

Wyatt literally falls into the doorway as we're storming out of the front door at 4 a.m.

"What the—?" Zach blurts as he helps the pretty boy up.

He's holding a single yellow rose, or at least what's left of it; half the stem is still poking out of the door handle.

Wyatt kind of shoves Zach's hand away before wiping his crisp white linen slacks. "My, you all rise early, don't you?"

I kind of creep to the front of the line and whisper, with only half of my mouth, like middle-aged women do in sitcoms, "Wyatt, what are you doing here?"

He presents me with the bud part of the yellow rose and gushes, as if it's not the middle of the night and he's not in front of an orphanage, "I was coming to apologize for Mia's dreadful behavior last night at your theater. I mean, what a cow! If she was here right now, I'd tell her just what I thought of her and…oh, hi, Mia, I didn't see you standing there and are those, Abby, does she have…*fangs*?"

I snort. "Only when she's really, really ticked off, Wyatt. Congrats, you must have done the trick!"

Mia is still bound by the garlic lasso, and not looking so hot.

I'm not really sure if her fangs are out because she's mad at Wyatt, though it sounded good at the time.

She is crying blood tears, and the skin around her arms and chest where she'd been tied in the closet looks beyond repair.

I almost, *almost* feel bad as we shove her into the back of Cliff's van and peel away from the Meriwether Home for Wayward Boys and Girls.

Behind her, Wyatt still grumbles from the backseat, where Zach and Tracy shoved *him*.

There are three limos idling outside the back of Flickers Cinemas as we pull up and park in the nearest handicapped spot.

Hey, if the local cops don't nab us for fighting vampires, werewolves, and zombies in the middle of a deserted theater at five in the morning, what are the odds they'll ticket us for parking in a handicapped spot?

Our usher uniforms are stiff, and we are stiffer as we sit in our seats.

Mia is still steaming, literally, while Wyatt is merely fuming beside her.

"I don't know why I'm getting dragged into all of this," Wyatt pouts, arms across his lovely chest like some big baby.

Zach stares daggers before quipping, "Because you had to go and be fake romantic and stalk Abby at our front door just as we were yanking a vampire out to go and fight the, what is it, Mia? LAD? Sorry Wyatt, but try to keep up; that stands for the League of Associated Undead."

Wyatt's eyes cloud over as he asks, "Uhhm, stop me if I'm over thinking this a tad, but…shouldn't that stand for LAU? I mean, technically, its initials spell—"

"LAD sounds better!" Mia spits in between waves of garlic-inspired unconsciousness.

"Whatever," he whimpers. "I w-w-won't tell anybody either way."

"Famous last words," murmurs Tracy, adjusting her cummerbund one last time.

"What's that burning smell?" he asks, even as steam rises from Mia in the backseat.

"Dude, that's your girlfriend," Zach huffs. "And, while we're on the subject, how could you not know she was a vampire this whole time?"

Wyatt shrugs. "I just figured she was into…biting."

The comment sends shockwaves through the van until Mia sits up and, above a waist full of steam manages to roll her eyes one last time and grunt, "Don't worry; the last thing we need is another vampire creep! Check him out, he's clean as a whistle," before passing out.

I look at her, but there's no checking her pulse because…undead, much?

Meanwhile, Tracy yanks open Wyatt's collar and looks for any bite marks.

"What?" he shouts, jerking back. "You think I'm…I'm…one of *them*?"

Tracy shrugs and I grab him by the arm, "Not really, Wyatt, but just to make sure why don't you come along and help us out? I think Cliff always keeps a spare uniform in here somewhere, doesn't he, Zach?"

CHAPTER TWENTY

T alk about a motley crew!

Wyatt is absolutely swimming in Cliff's spare uniform, but with some creative tucking in the back and notching up Cliff's belt a few extra notches, nothing is dangerously drooping as we slouch across the parking lot to the awaiting limousines.

But then there's Mia, who we drag along like a stuck pig to the campfire, her skin still steaming, blood tear stains dried on her pale, deadly cheeks.

She still looks radiant in the pre-dawn moonlight, her skin an almost translucent pale.

"I've seen white people before," Tracy whispers as we pass the empty limousines, "but this girl's almost see-through."

In another life, I might have chuckled.

In another life, she might have expected me to.

The back door is open, light spilling into the parking lot as we approach cautiously.

A burly man in a gray suit holds one of those metal detector wands, like Dean Winters uses on students as we stream into pep rallies on Fall Fridays.

Tracy is in the front so he checks her out first, scanning her body from neck to ankles before putting the wand down on top of the time clock and frisking her thoroughly.

He finds the crucifix in her back pocket, all according to plan, and scowls at her while yanking it out, roughly, so that the white lining from inside pokes out, and tossing it on the floor.

He stomps on it, smiles as if he's accomplished something, and is getting ready to shove her into the employee break room when Mia musters the energy to tattle on us.

"Her ears," she gurgles, blood and saliva mixing against her quivering fangs. "They snuck in silver earrings, all of them, to fool you guys and use on the werewolves. I heard them when they had me tied up in a closet!"

She looks triumphant and, to sell the story, I fume and kick the ground and offer up my earrings before Mr. Bodyguard wands and frisks me.

He finds my crucifix, too.

I hear it crushing as he shoves me into the employee break room, where three old men sit around the fold up picnic table that still has crumbs from Mr. Fletcher's wake the other day.

I stand next to Tracy, against the wall, as far away from the three men as possible.

When we're all through being frisked and Zach stands next to us, quivering, and the bodyguard finally unwinds the jump rope from around Mia, she slumps into a chair next to one of the old guys and steams no more.

One of them, the old guy in the middle, stands and proclaims, "Allow me to introduce myself. I am Count Imperialis, Head of the League of Associated Undead and representing the vampire race. To my right is Chancellor Elroy, head of the Greater Werewolf Coven of the United States. And on my left is Elder Stephan, he of the League of Unified Zombies. We are grateful for the return of our employee, Ms. Mia here."

"Hold up," Tracy points to Elder Stephan. "You're here to tell me this guy is a…a…zombie?"

Count Imperialis cocks his head and looks at Elder Stephan, a dignified if withered elder statesman looking dude in a blue prom tux (why do zombies always *wear* those?) and a fake gray wig.

"Of course," the Count boasts. "We have worked alongside each other for over six centuries, my dear. Does that…*surprise*…you?"

"Well, a little," she confesses. "I mean, no offense, sir, but most zombies we encounter—"

"End up dead again?" Elder Stephan croaks in a withered, but somewhat charming voice.

Tracy kind of hangs her head and murmurs, "Well, that, too," before looking up and adding, "But, what I meant to say was, most zombies we run across look like…gross…for lack of a better term."

Elder Stephan nods and announces, "I wholeheartedly agree, young lady. Which is why what you saw the other night—and who we watched you quickly dispatch on the evening news, by the way—were not technically 'zombies.' Yes, they were the living dead but a true zombie needs time to eat his first serving of brains, to let the electricity work through his system and then, you see, he'll wind up looking like, well…like me!"

Zach cocks his head and asks, "You mean there are zombies like you? Out in the world?"

"Of course, young man. There are thousands of us everywhere, living daily lives, working jobs, going to school, just like your vampires and werewolves."

"But where, exactly?" I ask.

Elder Stephan makes that whole "old person lips sealed shut, turn the key" move and reiterates, "My lips are sealed, young lady. But survive our little…test…tonight and you may just find out for yourself."

"Test?" I ask.

"Yes, dear," answers Count Imperialis. "Now that our little Q & A is over, and you've given us back our Mia, it's time for us to return the favor."

"B-b-but he said 'test' just now," Zach stammers.

"Well, of course. We can't have four young punks running around creation killing us every time we color outside the lines, now can we?"

"But that wasn't the deal," I shout, my voice growing louder in this tiny room. "We brought you Mia, you give us our Cliff back."

"And we have," Chancellor Elroy, head of the Greater Werewolf Coven of the United States, explains cryptically. "Just with a few…embellishments."

The men rise and, without another word, begin filing out of the room one after the other in a very dignified manner.

"Like what type of embellishments?" Zach asks of their giant, distinguished looking backs.

On his way out of the room, Chancellor Elroy turns and replies, "You'll see."

I watch them file into the outer vestibule just outside the break room and inside the back door and point to Mia, "Aren't you guys forgetting something?"

Count Imperialis blanches in a most unpleasant way and sneers, "Heavens no, child. She's useless to us now."

I cut Mia a quick glance and watch her face fall, if only for a second; I think it's the most "human" thing I've ever seen her do, even before I found out she was a vampire!

"So what did we have to trade her for?" I ask, turning back to the old, really old, men.

He smiles. "You didn't; we just wanted to lure you back here, naturally."

"Naturally," Tracy fumes as the lords and masters of the undead file out the back door and into their respective limousines.

In moments they are gone, and Mia sits, limp and lifeless, in a molded plastic chair inside the break room.

Wyatt cowers in a corner next to her, completely clueless.

He barely looks up as we leave.

Zach shuts the door and locks it with one of the employee master keys we were all given after our ninety-day performance review.

Then he turns to us and urges, "Let's go find Cliff."

CHAPTER TWENTY-ONE

Turns out, we needn't have worried; Cliff finds us.

We start in Theater 1, the three of us—me, Tracy and Zack—inching along, back to back to back, kind of like spokes in an ever-turning wheel.

There aren't that many places for a three-hundred and twenty pound kidnap victim to hide in an empty theater, so we make quick work of one, then two, then three auditoriums.

The minute we walk into Theater 4, though, everything changes.

Cliff is leaning way against the back wall, just under the digital projection booth, still decked out in his usher's uniform.

"Cliff!" I shout, leaping up two steps at a time.

He stops me before I reach the fifth row by bellowing, "Silence, Usher! That was my mortal name. The immortals have given me a new name, befitting my new status: Harrington Rathbone the Third."

Tracy snorts. "That's even more made up than…than…Wyatt Winters!"

"Yeah, Cliff, seriously, come on down so we can go home," sighs Zach, loosening his tie now that the Elders have left the building.

"Home?" Cliff asks, taking a tentative step toward us. "Where do you think I've been, children? Mortals? Humans? I have been supping with the Immortals."

"Supping?" I ask.

"Eating," he barks, impatiently, and is it me or did his neck just…bulge…when he said that?

"And they, thankfully, have been dining on yours truly."

"Gross, Cliff. Seriously, that's rude."

"What's rude about living forever, Zach? What's gross about facing the rest of eternity with more power than any mere mortal can possess?"

"Are you quoting one of your cheesy graphic novels again, Cliff, because this is—?"

Before Tracy can finish her sentence, Cliff has literally leapt the entire length of the theater.

By the time he reaches the ground floor, he has morphed into a living, breathing, furry, muscle bound...*werewolf*!

Werewolf Cliff grabs onto Tracy's forearm and yanks her around like a rag doll; she doesn't even have time to break out any of her hidden weapons!

I hear a few bones break and watch blood spurt and shout, "Cliff! Stop! What are you doing to her?"

He ignores me, and the only thing that saves Tracy is her bow tie, which she manages to unwrap from around her neck and slap at Cliff with.

The silver batteries inside slash at his skin, drawing blood and yanking hair from his tough, leather hide.

Cliff yelps like a beat pup and scampers away as we rush to Tracy and drag her from the theater.

I yank off a sleeve and wrap it just above her wounds, slowing the blood loss but not stopping it completely.

Her skin looks pale and ashen, gray and lifeless.

She is trembling as we toss her into the manager's office next to the concession stand, where Zach locks her in for her own safety.

And eventually, I suppose, ours.

"We have to get her help, Zach, or she's a goner."

Zach looks at me, then down at the blood on his hands and croaks, "Abby, she's a goner anyway."

CHAPTER TWENTY-TWO

Wₑ hear a roar in Theater 4, as both of us turn our backs to the office door and yank off our bowties, prepared to do battle with the werewolf known as Cliff.

Sorry, Sir Harrington Radcliffe Dorkus Frankincense the Fifth, or whatever his new name is.

"So that's it," Zach gasps as we scramble to catch our breath. "*This* is the test. The werewolf lord or whatever must have bitten Cliff, figuring we'd be too scared to kill him since he's our friend."

"Yeah, well, after what he's done to Tracy, I'll gladly eat Werewolf Cliff burgers for the rest of the month!"

It's not a werewolf that roars around the corner, but a half-naked Cliff in the tattered remains of his stiff white usher shirt and slashed black pants.

He looks like he's lost a good hundred pounds and then put on another forty—of pure muscle.

I see cheekbones where there never were any before, and…what's this: razor stubble?

He seems taller, too, his eyes bigger and darker and set off by the sudden, dramatic hollows in his cheeks and the firm, square jaw.

"Now what?" Zach rasps, peeling away from the door.

I join him as Cliff advances on us, all sinew and bone, saunter and strut.

Suddenly he bursts forth in a blinding flash and shoves Zach all the way back into the manager's office!

The door literally flies off its hinges and crashes into the small work desk where Tracy has been busily knitting her hands.

She leaps, and yelps, catching Zach just as he continues to fly through the far wall.

I jump on Cliff's back, slashing at him with the battery end of my bowtie but he just laughs and tosses me off like a piece of lint from his favorite jacket.

I land on the lobby floor and slide across on my butt, landing in a heap against the front of the candy counter.

My pants leg rolls up in the process, and suddenly I remember the duct tape and pennies trick.

I rip them off, turn them around so the pennies are facing out and wind the two sticky pieces of tape together in a kind of penny bracelet.

Whatever Cliff is, he's no longer a werewolf, so maybe he's something…else.

I race across the squeaky clean black and white tiles just as Cliff is zeroing in on Zach, leap through the doorway and onto his back.

As he gets ready to buck me off, I slide my penny bracelet arm around his throat and give a not-so-gentle tug.

Beneath me I feel the life go out of him, instantly.

It's like someone's just pulled the Cliff plug!

We fall to the floor like partners in a potato sack race and I yank off the bracelet, wrapping it around his wrist, penny side down this time.

"That should keep him!" I shout as I yank Zach to his feet and Tracy follows us out of the shattered office and into the lobby.

"Now what?" she asks, already scratching at the deep gouges on her forearm.

I'm selfishly thinking what might happen if my friend Tracy turns into Werewolf Tracy when I yell, impulsively, "Let's split up!"

CHAPTER TWENTY-THREE

"**B**ut Tracy said we should never split up, Abby," Zach observes.

"Yeah, well, that was before Cliff turned into Superbad Monster Guy and there were three of us and one of him. The harder he has to look for one of us, the better chances the other two have of making it out of here alive."

Tracy looks at the glass walls of the theater lobby and points out, "If you just want to get out of here alive, Abby, we could all leave right now."

As if to prove it, she reaches for the keys in her pocket.

I nod. "We need to stop Cliff first, then run!"

"Wait, what?" Zack asks. "I mean, isn't that what we just did?"

He looks over at zonked out Cliff for emphasis.

I bite my lower lip and frown. "I don't think Cliff's a straight-up zombie, guys, so...I'm not sure how long that bracelet's going to last before he comes after us again. And we want him to come after us again, right? So we can be sure before we...well...take care of him?"

Tracy nods and agrees, "Okay, so we split up then, hide and wait for him to come find one of us. When he does, the other two come running and, splat, we finish him off once and for all. Me first!"

And off she goes, racing for the far end of the theater.

I follow Zach right, down the second hall that has Theaters 7-14 in them.

"Don't tell me where you're going, okay?" I insist.

He doesn't; instead, goes me one better.

While I'm looking up at Theater 8, thinking it might be a good choice, Zach leans down from on high and literally snatches me into his arms.

His lips are warm against mine, soft yet firm, with just the slightest taste of abject fear on his tongue.

I grunt, sigh, then push him away, making sure Cliff is still passed out in the manager's office.

"What was *that* for?" I gasp, slapping him on the (surprisingly firm) chest.

"Everybody knows the hero and heroine kiss just before the final battle in the scary movies," he proclaims proudly.

"Yeah, right before one of them gets hideously slaughtered in some ghastly way."

"Okay, sure, but…those are just movies."

"You jerk!" I shout, slapping him again.

"What?" he asks. "I thought…I thought…you liked me."

"I do, you jerk."

"So why are you so mad at me for kissing you?"

"Because you took too long. If you'd done that, say, three years ago, we wouldn't have only had one kiss before we both get horribly mutilated."

We hear groaning and scamper.

I'm so scared I don't even look over my shoulder to see which theater Zach is hiding in.

Chapter Twenty-Four

I skip the theaters altogether, and leap over the mini-concession counter at the end of the back hallway, crouching low to the ground as my heart pounds in my ears.

There is a small front counter, with one cash register on top and loaded down below with jelly beans, licorice vines, penny candy, and all kinds of sugary treats.

This way I can peak past the bags through the window beyond and watch Cliff shuffle out of the manager's office.

Wait...what?

He's up already?!

I watch in horror as he looks down at the penny bracelet, smirks and...throws it right off.

What, do zombies get immune to the copper or something after awhile?

Or, wait...maybe there's enough werewolf in him to make the copper trick only half as effective?

Then I notice something...odd...sticking out of Cliff's mouth as he shuffles onto the carpet of our hallway, looking left and right as he considers which theaters we might have scampered into.

But no, they're not odd at all; not after this night.

What they are...are...fangs!

Big and sharp, and nearly twice as long as Mia's.

And suddenly it hits me; that's what that old werewolf had meant about this being a "test."

They hadn't just turned Cliff into a werewolf.

Or a zombie.

They'd turned him into a vampire, too.

No, no, they'd turned him into...all three.

Not just one of the Elders had bitten him, or two, but they all had.

So what does that make Cliff?

If he is part werewolf, part zombie, and part vampire, is he a...vambiewolf?

A wombire?

A vombolf?

Wampire?

Werezompire?

No, no, he must be a...Werevombie!

I shake my head as he disappears into Theater 7, looking around the tiny space I've hidden in for something to use against a Werevombie.

CHAPTER TWENTY-FIVE

By the time Zach comes screaming out of Theater 10, his usher shirt torn open, a long gash across his pale white chest, I'm ready for him; ready for them.

I rise up, waving Zach over.

He smiles, then leaps over the counter, his face slathered in sweat as we embrace, crouching on the floor.

I shove him away and look at his chest.

"What happened?" I ask.

"No time," he gasps. "Now what?"

"Now," comes a voice from the other side of the counter. "Now we dance!"

I scream, and yank Zach up and back into the tiny stock room next to the mini concession stand.

"He totally stole that line from *Zombie Ballroom 3*!" Zach hisses cattily as I shove salt shakers down his pockets.

"Really?" I ask as I hear glass shattering atop the candy counter. "I thought it was from *Vampire Dance Academy 2*

He shrugs and whispers, "Let's not fight, dear."

Together we shove the stainless steel shelving in front of the door, leaning against it as I bark, "Give me your holy water!"

He opens his mouth to argue, then hands it over.

I take it, pop off the top, and pour it into the open end of an empty "Sweetheart Syringe," one of those god awful candy toys the kids love so much.

The theory is they take the protective red cap off the pointy end of the plastic syringe and then gently squeeze the candy into their mouths all movie long by carefully applying pressure to the giant plunger top.

Yeah, right!

What really happens is that they yank out the plunger immediately, turn it upside down over their mouths and let the liquid candy slide into their mouths in one giant gloop-plop, which immediately makes them bounce off the walls for the next twenty minutes until they thankfully crash—and promptly pass out (preferably for the rest of the flick).

I'd emptied out the blue raspberry goop just a few minutes earlier all over the floor in hopes that Cliff would eat it when he ran toward the door.

Now I pour the holy water in, followed by a generous amount of salt from an open shaker and both silver watch batteries from my bow tie.

I shove the syringe cap on and shake it up, watching the holy water and salt dissolve the battery like an antacid at the bottom of one of Mrs. Meriweather's famous retro juice glasses.

"Will that work?" Zach asks as Vampire Cliff starts banging against the stock room door.

"I have no idea," I admit as I hide it in my cummerbund. "But it's better than nothing."

He smiles.

"Not quite nothing," he admits, taking off his left shoe.

There, shoved in between the tread on the very bottom, are the three pieces of the double-jointed metal crucifix from the Meriwether Home.

"So *that's* where that went?" I shout over Cliff's incessant banging. "I knew you were up to something when you went skedaddling out of our room with two of those and only came back with one!"

He shrugs, kind of proudly, quickly putting the metal crucifix back together and clutching it protectively against his chest.

"I figured with all our other decoys, the watches and earrings and back pockets, they wouldn't check our shoes. I was right!"

Just then Cliff bursts through the stock room door, shoving us over and away from each other and into opposite corners of the room.

Cliff fills the room with his evil presence, his once gentle eyes hard and cold, his once flabby body broken and bent and shaped into something false and oddly...beautiful.

He barks, screams, and laughs; the three monsters inside of him battling to get out first.

We watch as patches of hair gurgle to the surface of his dead pale arm, then just as quickly disappear, only to reappear in the middle of his formerly hairless chest or on the side of his left thigh, exposed between the tatters of his torn and barely-there tux pants.

His fangs are like flippers in a pinball machine; pushing forward, sucking back, seemingly at will.

"You can't control yourself!" Zach accuses, clutching the crucifix at his side.

"You're wrong," Cliff corrects, inching forward. "I'm like a monster slot machine. You never know what will come up next. For instance," he begins, only to have his entire head morph into a giant werewolf face, his howls filling the little room as we cower at the sheer awesome power of his voice.

Just as quickly the hair, the jutting jaw, the snarling snout of Werewolf Cliff recedes and it's Zombie Cliff, back again, his face suddenly fish belly white and going gray, the black veins beneath his skin drying up before our very eyes.

Then it's back to Vampire Cliff, fangs jutting, quivering, drooling and suddenly Zach leaps forward, shoving the crucifix so far into Cliff's mouth one of his fangs breaks off.

Vampire Cliff screams, howls, and tears at his throat, until Werewolf Cliff takes over and spits the crucifix out like a chicken leg at a family cookout.

The rest of his body follows, and the second his arms are topped with fierce, jagged claws Cliff lashes out at Zach, sending him flying up and over his side into the mini-concession stand beyond the tiny stock room.

I hear more glass shatter, tinkle and the wince of someone discovering something broken.

I stroke the plastic syringe in my cummerbund with trembling fingers as I cower in the stockroom corner.

Werewolf Cliff morphs again, this time into Vampire Cliff.

He shakes himself off like a wet dog, licks his fangs and purrs in a throaty voice, "I much prefer myself this way, Abby, don't you?"

"Actually, Cliff, I much prefer you the old way, you know?"

His eyes look almost…sad…as he pauses midway across the room.

He explains, "It's no fun being the fat guy, Abby, trust me. The goof-off, the nerd, the geek, the laughable guy who makes fun of himself so nobody else can get there first. You never looked at me twice, Abby, not like you did Zach. Not that you're my type, exactly, but…nobody likes to be invisible."

"You're not invisible anymore, Cliff," I blurt through clenched teeth. "So go on, get out of here and go have your fun. You don't have to kill us to be the big, bad monster you already are."

"Of course I do, Abby," he points out, inching forward.

My fist clenches around the open syringe.

I feel moistness against my belly button and realize, too late, the little plastic stopper at the tip must have gotten dislodged as I scampered away.

I hope his speech is short, because I don't have much time now.

"I can't have Ushers, Inc. running around anymore, killing off my kind. Without you three, Abby, I'll be unstoppable."

He's close now, within striking distance, and suddenly the holy water and salt and silver against my skin is cold and tingly, like electric lemonade.

"Only if I don't stop you first!" I shout, raising the syringe and plunging it into his neck.

But even as I push the plunger I see it's empty, and as he swats me away with one hand I yelp.

He rushes to hover over me and now my whole mid-section is drenched with the contents of the tube, giving me one last idea.

He leaps for me, ready to take me out, and I zig-zag just at the right time; he spills onto the cold tile floor and I leap into his back, grinding my stomach into his back and feeling his skin bubble on contact.

He screams and tries to buck me off, but I hold fast, in the biggest reverse bear hug ever.

I can feel bone beneath my belly by the time he finally casts me off, his body morphing into all three monsters at will now, first zombie, then vampire, then werewolf and back again.

He thrashes on the floor, all teeth and fangs and fingers and claws and, at one point as I try to scramble away, he reaches out and gnaws on my ankle.

I scream and scamper, and run into long, shapely calves.

The *hell?*

I look up to see Mia standing above me, looking resplendently vampirific.

"Perv much?" she snorts as I cling to her ankle and stare up at her tight leather pants.

She kicks me off like a dog will a mouse and flies at Cliff, launching her quivering white fangs into his soft, thick throat, both of them screaming through the gurgling, bubbling blood.

CHAPTER TWENTY-SIX

"**H**oney," sighs Mia, wiping her bloody fangs off on the tattered sleeve of her once radiant and flowing black cloak. "As we rehearsed."

Dutifully, Wyatt raises one of the legs from the break room table and plunges it into Double Vampire Cliff's chest.

We hear the thick, juicy splooge of his heart imploding and then the thick, grating sound of metal against floor tile as the improvised stake rushes through Cliff's back and into the floor beneath.

I look at Wyatt admiringly until I realize, no human could be that strong.

I look and, sure enough, there are two clear pinpoints on my side of Wyatt's neck; the blood long dried.

"Trust me," Mia explains, catching me looking, "he's twice as cool as a vampire."

He looks at her adoringly and she clutches his arm to her side, "Besides, he's kind of cute without a heartbeat."

I hear a sizzling and turn to watch Cliff's ashes go from red-hot to thick black to gray white in an instant.

"But how?" I ask as the air conditioning kicks on overhead and scatters Werevombie Cliff to all four corners of the room. "How could a stake through the heart kill him if he was part zombie, vampire, and werewolf?"

"Once I bit him," Mia brags, "he was more vampire than anything, so…whatever. Try not to look a gift horse in the mouth, Abby."

I rush past her, pushing Wyatt to the side, only to find Zach weak and unresponsive on the concession stand floor.

His head is bent at an odd angle, his arm snapped behind his back, his eyes rolled back in his head.

I whimper as I straighten his body, peppering his dry as a bone forehead with soft, tender kisses.

"Move aside," Mia barks as she bends to Zach's face.

She puts two fingers beneath his nose and doesn't look happy.

"Yep," she sighs, still crouched by his side. "He's a goner. Unless...."

"Honey, no," sighs Wyatt from the doorway. "Three in one day is just too much."

"Unless what?" I ask, ignoring the world's newest vampire.

"Nothing," Mia says coyly. "It's just, he's a goner unless I do...you know...what I did to Wyatt, and now Cliff."

I gasp and lean back against the shattered candy counter, a fresh bag of torn jelly beans running down my leg.

"But then he'll be...like...you," I sigh.

She nods.

"He'll also be alive. You know, sort of."

"Do it," I groan, looking away. "Anything, just so he's...*alive*."

I can hear her fangs slipping into the soft white flesh of his neck, but even when Zach gasps and calls my name, I can't look.

Not just now.

Not just yet.

EPILOGUE

Thursday night, 12:01 a.m. and not a manager in sight.

They never like these first showings, or so they say.

I just think they don't like watching first showings with us lowly usher riff-raff but, what are you gonna do?

We sit way in the back, all the way, as the credits start and *Werewolves of the Open Plains 4* washes over the giant screen a football field away.

Zach sits next to me, his skin warm, his eyes cold in the flickering light.

His Slushee cup is full of fresh Type-O, as are the cups of our two new ushers: Mia and Wyatt.

Tracy is the only one of us who can still eat human food, a little known perk of being a werewolf—sorry, she prefers the term "werewoman"—none of us knew about until Werewolf Cliff bit her on the arm and "turned" her.

She steals a glance my way as she settles in.

Her skin is a radiant brown, her hair straight now, no more dreadlocks, and oh-so-long.

She doesn't look wild, exactly, more like…exotic.

The guys at school have noticed, too, and now she spends more time in the stands at school watching this new boyfriend or that than she does at the Meriwether Home or, for that matter, at Flickers Cinemas, where she's gone down to part-time hours.

I'm glad for her.

As monsters go, being a werewolf definitely rules.

Twenty-seven normal days a month and three measly nights of howling at the moon and stalking wild rabbits over in an abandoned field in Catfish Cove.

Not a bad way to spend eternity.

Much better than Zach and his vampire friends, Mia and Wyatt.

Man, do the movies have it wrong; being a vampire *sucks*.

And I'm totally not just being cute right now.

The constant need for blood, trying to get it without killing people, all that sunscreen and they go through, like, twelve pairs of sunglasses a week; it's amazing.

Still, nothing sucks worse than being one of the living dead, which is what stupid Cliff made me, thanks a lot—jerk!

I guess when he snacked on me in the heat of battle he was in full-on zombie mode, so…here I am.

No heartbeat, no pulse, skin roughly the color of freshly-poured cement and, here's a tip: zombies really *do* eat brains.

Which wouldn't be so bad, exactly, if it wasn't *all* zombies ate!

Like right now: zombie smoothie.

Two parts brain, one part smoothie machine, all kinds of disgusting.

Still, we're together, we're alive—technically—and now that we've become monsters ourselves, hunting the bad guys sure is easier.

I guess that's why Ushers, Inc. is so darn popular these days.

Two or three times a week we're fighting off Vampires in Miami or Werewolves in Tallahassee or Zombies in Orlando.

Last week we took our first out-of-state trip; sure, it was only to Atlanta but, hey, it's a start.

It's not very conducive to homework, but ever since we stopped that huge Vampire Invasion last month (you know, the one that started when Mia turned half the volleyball team into vampires and we kind of forgot we'd left them tied to the locker room spigots, d'oh!), well, let's just say we've pretty much got straight-A's for life.

As the previews end and the movie begins, Zach leans over and whispers, "What are you thinking about?"

I shrug and ask, "Why?"

He shrugs back. "You just look…happy…I guess."

I smile. "Good friends, good movie, good boyfriend, what else do the living dead need?"

He snorts and slurps up some more Type-O, settling back for the show.

I look to my left, down the row of beautiful, immortal, young, hungry ushers.

Maybe there are better ways to spend eternity, but until I figure out what they are, I'm fine right where I am.

With who I am.

And who I'm with.

Suddenly the house lights go down and we hear the faint digital flicker from the projection booth above our expectant heads.

In a few seconds we hear the double doors swing open, shut, then Vampire Cliff rounds the corner with a triumphant bow.

He is thinner now, though still large—large in all the right places.

His hair is long, like shoulder length, and straight; his eyes are a cross between chocolate and black—Tracy calls them "dark chocolate," when Cliff's being nice, and "just plain dark" when he's being a jerk.

He's gone down a size or two, and as he takes the steps toward our row two at a time I can't help but think how…confident…he's become since our whole little Monster Battle Royale in the mini-concession stand.

Hey, sure, you could have blown me away, too, the day after the big fight when old Cliff showed up at the Home, wearing a spare usher uniform and acting like nothing had happened.

No fight to the death, no stake through the heart, no Cliff dust scattering all over the concession stand supply room.

Little did we know it's a *lot* harder to kill a Tri-Beast—what Cliff calls himself—than just shoving a measly old stake through the heart.

And don't think he ever lets us forget it, either.

Come a full moon he gets to hunt with Tracy, come a fresh shipment of old blood from the blood bank he gets to feed with Zach and the others and, when he's feeling it, he can even share a brain smoothie with me.

And has it gone to his head?

You bet!

But the ladies are the worst.

Oh yes, Cliff and his ladies; his "harem" he calls it, and there's nothing worse than a reformed geek who suddenly gets a little play.

Cheerleaders, band geeks, chorus stars, shy girls, Math-a-letes, the ROTC girls, stoners, jocks, he's been through them all in the last few weeks.

It's like he's making up for lost time, and as soon as we get to know one, poof, they're gone with the wind.

"Werewolves," he groans distastefully as the credits flicker to life and we hear a howling wolf in the background of the soundtrack.

"Dude," hisses Zach. "You *are* a werewolf, who are you cracking on?"

"I'm only *half*-werewolf," he corrects.

"Make that a third werewolf," whispers Tracy, and we all laugh.

Cliff would blush, but being a third zombie, technically, he *can't.*

Once the laughter has died down he turns to me and whispers, "There's nothing worse than a snobby werewolf, am I right fellow zombie?"

I roll my eyes and offer him a hit off my brain Slushee.

He waves it off distastefully and yanks out a can of potted meat and starts chowing down.

"Gross," I retch. "What *is* that?"

"The third ingredient is brains so, it's good in a pinch. Sometimes I don't like my brains cold in the Slushee machine, you know?"

I shrug and get back to the movie.

It's bad, really bad.

Horribly, deliciously, D-grade bad; just how Ushers, Inc. likes 'em.

I smile, find my straw in the dark and take a big, huge sip.

Ugghh, suddenly my entire head feels like it's in a vice grip.

Brain freeze, what else?

Panty Raid @ Zombie High

by Rusty Fischer

PROLOGUE

"**W**here's Spud?" I ask, seeing Molly waiting alone in our usual spot.

"AP Science Fair, what else?" She sighs and offers me the last of her Sparkz candy bar.

I take it and see if I can taste any of her maroon lipstick on the bitten-off part. No such luck.

Molly has her hair up in a ponytail today. I love it when she has her hair up because I can see the back of her pure white neck, the length of it, the way her soft, long fingers will sometimes fly there in class and scratch it absently.

Now that school is over, she has her State ball cap on, too, the ponytail sticking out the back in that way I also love.

"You gonna hang with us tonight?"

"Waddya mean?" She turns toward me on the stone bench in front of the school, sitting kindergarten style with her long, lean legs crossed in front, her velvety thighs practically caramel in the late afternoon light.

"*Space Vampires 4* opens tonight. Spud said he'd go with me and where Spud goes, Molly goes, so…what? Why are you looking at me like you're going to tell me my new puppy just died?"

Molly's eyes are brown, this deep, chocolaty brown and even darker in the waning sunlight. Now they're sad, like they are a lot lately.

"Didn't…I mean…" she stammers while shaking her head, the end of her raven black ponytail caressing the shoulders of her snug T-shirt. "Why would he *say* that?"

"Uh, because we've seen all the *Space Vampires* movies together, on opening night, and if there's one thing I know about Spud, it's how much he hates to break tradition, so…what? Why are you still giving me the dead puppy dog eyes?"

"Because, Toby, he has to get his tux fitted for the Fall Formal if it's going to be done on time and the only night my seamstress can see him is…What? Now *you're* giving *me* the dead puppy dog eyes."

I shake my head and grab a hand full of quarters from my pocket, shoving them—almost slamming them—into the humming soda machine at my back.

"I'm not giving you dead puppy dog eyes, Molly," I insist, handing her the first sip of my Crank cola despite the fact that she's just torpedoed the only thing I've been looking forward to all week.

She takes it casually, almost expectantly, no *please* or *thank you*. No need for *please* or *thank you*. We've probably shared a thousand sodas and two thousand candy bars in our lifetime, so…why should today be any different?

She hands it back and our fingers linger a little over the cold, already sweaty can.

I pull away first, and she doesn't look hurt.

"Well, how long is that going to take?" I ask after I've had a sip or two to calm my suddenly frazzled nerves.

Yes, I know I'm overreacting, yes I know I'm being a total Mabel about this but…seriously? It's Space Vampires 4, people!

"Long enough to miss the first, second, and third showings, Toby. Just, face it. Dude stood you up."

I snort. Molly's so butch.

"Again," I remind her.

"Yeah, again, well…it's not my fault. If you'd had enough balls to ask me to the dance before Spud did, you'd be standing *him* up tonight instead of the other way around."

I shake my head, ignoring the truth of her statement. "I wouldn't do that to a friend."

She nods, brown eyes soft and moist under the bill of her maroon ball cap. After a few moments, she says, "I know you wouldn't, Toby."

"Wouldn't do what?" barks Spud as he rounds the corner, swinging his new car keys like he's some kind of big man on campus or something.

"Make me go to *Space Vampires 4* alone." I say it straight up, because part of me is hurt but more of me is pissed, and about lots more than just some stupid *Space Vampires* movie, too.

"Oh, *snap*," he says in that way he thinks is so cool in front of Molly. "I've been meaning to tell you all day but—"

"But what?" I grunt and toss the empty soda can into the red wire trashcan without offering Molly another sip. "But those five periods we had together were too hectic to lean over and say, 'Hey listen, I've got to go get my pants hemmed instead of seeing the best movie *ever* with you, I hope you understand'?"

Molly snorts at my obvious sarcasm, pert breasts jiggling in her powder blue baby doll T-shirt, and Spud shoots her a look I'd never want to be on the receiving end of.

"It's not like that," he insists through clenched teeth.

"Whatever." I sigh, grabbing the keys out of my pocket and turning toward the student parking lot. "It's fine. No, really. Seriously, no worries. I'll wear a disguise, sit way in the back, nobody'll notice that I'm completely alone and friendless. I mean, it's not like the entire school is going to be there or anything. I'm sure I'll survive the public ridicule somehow!"

Molly's snug maroon cords rasp as she stands from the stone bench, and her black hi-tops slap against the tile of the school walkway as she follows along.

Spud finally catches up, key ring fixed to his favorite Boy Scouts-style pants jingling.

"Now I feel bad," Molly coos as we walk side-by-side to our cars.

"No you don't." I grin. "You could care less. You never liked *Space Vampires 1*, to say nothing of *2* and *3*."

"No, but I always went just the same."

"You told me you liked them," Spud whines, sounding personally offended.

Molly and I share a look—one of *those* looks. One of those how-can-he-be-so-smart-and-so-dumb-at-the-same-time looks, the ones her new boyfriend never sees or, if he does, never admits he sees.

My car is small and old and parked crooked because I wasn't expecting to drive to school today but Spud called at the last minute and told me he couldn't swing by to pick me up so I was running late and, well…let's just drop it for now.

Spud's car, on the other hand, is new and clean, and he opens the passenger door for Molly before zipping back around to his side.

She is facing me, I'm facing her, and we share another look as Spud frets over some imagined ding on the side of his driver's side door.

It's that not-quite-smoldering, not-quite-lingering look we snatch every chance we get lately, ever since my best friend started dating my other best friend.

I get lost in the look, in those chipper brown eyes and the long, porcelain neck and the budding breasts and the tapered waist and—

"Molly?" says Spud, not quite as cluelessly as we'd both like to imagine. "You getting in?"

And she does, quickly, without another fleeting look in my direction.

I shift my glance from her closed door to Spud's thin face, barely sticking out above the roof of his sleek new sports car.

"Sorry about tonight," he says, again through gritted teeth.

Now it's time to share our look—that slightly smug, triumphant look of his and my own vaguely disappointed, disgusted look.

"There'll be another *Space Vampires* next year, Toby!"

He slides into the car, turns the key in the ignition and zips from the parking lot, not even giving Molly a chance to look back at me as he turns right and guns it toward downtown Tinfoil, Tennessee.

I slide into my own driver's seat, never imagining that would be the last time I'd ever see Molly Sims alive.

CHAPTER ONE

Spud is ticked off at the cafeteria lady for taking so long to open up the new roll of quarters. He isn't saying anything, because that would be rude, but I can see the blush creep up the back of his neck above his blue-on-blue ringer tee. And that's never good.

Ever.

For a small guy, Spud can get pretty loud, pretty quick.

"Chill," I warn him, leaning into his bright pink ear and hoping to derail his building tantrum. "You're making a scene."

He turns and gives me his best ironic face. "Isn't that the point?" He turns back as the cafeteria lady finally squeezes out his three quarters in change.

He storms off in a huff, all five-foot-four of him, but not too far because this is only going to work as a two-man job and if he gets too far ahead of me, well, anything could happen.

And neither of us wants that. But probably, mostly, Spud doesn't.

I shrug and pay for my tray full of extra spaghetti noodles and double cheese sauce, with a side order of the greasiest garlic bread. The garlic bread costs extra, to say nothing of the second bowl of cheese sauce, but it's worth it.

Or will be, I suppose.

If I don't die before I get to use it, that is.

The jocks sit at table three, and the only reason they don't sit at tables one or two is because they're too far off to the side and they like being front and center so the rest of us can sit there and fawn over them all lunch period.

I breathe a sigh of relief because not too many of them are there yet.

Spud starts straight over, jostling on his stumpy legs. I catch a few of our regular table geeks sitting way back in the nosebleed section at table twenty-seven giving us heavy *WTF* faces, but I can't pause now and sign language what we're up to. Operation Rescue Molly is well under way.

And there's no turning back now.

"Are you sure about this?" I ask between clenched teeth, following Spud straight past the subdued stoners at table one and the spazz-tastic Math-a-letes at table two.

"No," he squeezes through a nervous smile that's full of his so-called "invisible" braces. "But…it's Molly, remember?"

Yeah, I remember. How could I forget?

Spud has his tray ready, his bony fingers clearly trembling under the molded orange plastic as the dozen zippers on his khaki Boy Scout pocket pants jingle up and down with his quick, duck walk style.

As I linger a few paces behind, it looks like one of the jocks—of course, it has to be Boner—has his foot ready as well. A big size twelve sneaker all ratty and dotted with ketchup stains, just waiting for us to pass.

Thank God these dimwits are so predictable, because it's pretty hard to "fake trip" when there's not a big jock leg in your direct path to fake trip over in the first place.

The leg goes out and—predictably—Spud takes a tumble, but not without launching his tray straight at Boner's face before he's down and out and winds up splayed across the slick cafeteria floor, wincing from all the germs he must imagine crawling on his face.

There is a moment frozen in time before I follow Spud's lead and do my own fake face plant on the cafeteria floor, where I have the luxury of watching my friend's tray tumble through the air, the white plastic plate sliding off in mid-air and launching itself straight at Boner's big, broad, wide face as if drawn there by a tractor beam emitted from his fat, wide, hairy nostrils.

Before Zack Torres, starting linebacker for the Tinfoil High football team, can react to Boner's spaghetti face and pull his leg back in—'cause no one's *that* fast, not even an All-Stater like Zack—I'm already fake tripping and tossing my cheese and noodles onto his precious letterman's jacket. It lands with an audible *splat* right on the giant T over his cold, gray heart.

Boner and Zack are up out of their seats before we are off the floor, but it's only to reach for a stack of paper napkins in the middle of their table to wipe off their faces and jackets and not to pound us into the cafeteria floor.

At least, not yet anyway.

Spud and I rise slowly, shaky from our face plants as the dull roar of A-

Lunch evaporates like a foggy day at sunset. The back of Spud's neck is blazing red, and I see his bony fingers curled into a miniature fist as he squares off against the much larger Neanderthals.

I join him at his side, our shoulders trembling as Boner literally roars, "What is *wrong* with you two *spazz* asses?"

His words echo high atop the cafeteria ceiling and right back down into every possible nook and cranny as the stillness in the room suddenly becomes deafening.

Forget mouths. Not even a *fork* is moving anymore.

"S-s-s-sorry," Spud mock-sputters, just as we'd rehearsed this morning in his bedroom. Although, I have to say, he sounds *much* more convincing at the moment. "I d-d-didn't see your big foot in my way. Must have b-b-been an accident."

Zack reaches out and shoves my shoulder until I turn around in his direction. "What's *your* excuse, egghead butt?" Spittle flies left and right as emotion gets the best of his spit-controlling capabilities. His shiny caramel face is all hard edges and wiry angles, his close-cropped hair black and stiff like it's been painted onto his big, fat head.

"You've got big feet, too," I bark loudly, feeling Spud's back against mine.

The cafeteria is watching now, and you can almost feel Boner and Zack basking in its worshiping glow. They know they've finally got an audience and the minute they realize it, both their faces…change.

"Who's gonna pay for my new jacket?" Zack asks confidently, shoving me back one step at a time with the tip of his cinnamon-colored index finger, which is about as big as Spud's whole thigh. "Huh, funny guy?"

"Coach *Sprocket*?" I ask, letting him bully me straight into the center of the cafeteria, where a small circle of kids has formed a very neat ring around us, all eager for the first fight of the day.

"You're done for," Boner decrees as he shoves Spud into me and the crowd around us continues to grow by one or two kids per second. You can literally feel the violence in the air, hot and thick and musty—oh wait, that's just Boner's breath—and suddenly both start to suck the wind out of my lungs.

I've never actually been inside one of these gladiator circles before, only on the outside, circling around, in the background, hands in my pockets, head down, wishing I didn't want to look but lingering around just in case something—anything—happened. But I've always wondered what the poor schmuck inside the fight circle felt.

Now I know.

I just hope this works.

"You can pound me into next week," Spud shouts, loud enough so even B-Lunch can hear it. *"Or…"*

I have to give it to Spud; for someone who's not really used to public speaking all that much—or speaking to human beings in general—he really knows how to get the crowd's attention.

"Or…what?" Boner barks, shoving his big, fat finger into Spud's shoulder once more.

"Or…you could be a *real* man and challenge us to a duel!"

The crowd laughs, Boner laughs, Zack laughs. It's such a funny, foreign word—*duel*—that even I can't help snickering. And I've heard that word about a dozen times in the last twenty-four hours.

Then they all stop laughing, at once, as if someone stage left has just slid their finger across their throat in the universal sign language for *cut it out.*

"Or…I could just pound you now and *then* beat you at a duel, 'tardo. How about that?"

Spud nods. I flinch—we hadn't thought of *that* delightful variable in our brilliant little equation—and then he says, "Sure, fine, but then who would let you into Zombie High?"

Suddenly, the angry murmur of violence that's been buzzing around the tight-knit circle surrounding us sounds more like crickets chirping.

"Zombie *High?*" asks Boner uncertainly, and I know he's thinking, *Oooooh, ouch, what have I gotten myself into here?*

"Zombie High?" asks Zack just as cautiously, and I know *he's* thinking, *Oooooh, ouch, what has Boner gotten us into now?*

The crowd is murmuring, too, and if there weren't so many people looking right now, this is the moment when Spud would normally look at me with an *it's working* grin.

Instead, he ratchets up the pressure another notch and says, "Yeah, if you guys were really tough, you'd dare us to a…a…panty raid at Zombie High."

I like how he stammers there in the middle, milking the moment for all the drama he can.

Boner chuckles, "Zombie High," *Beavis & Butthead* style at the same time Zack chuckles, "Panty Raid."

They're so dismissive, so casual, so…wrong. They're so big, so stupid, so…stupidly big!

But the crowd's not chuckling.

They know, even if Boner and Zack don't, the power of Zombie High, the fear it represents, the myth behind the myth, and just as Spud had predicted, they're not going to let it go without a fight.

As if on cue, some clown in the back has picked up on it and starts the chant. "Panty. *Raid*. Zombie. *High*."

Others join in, laughing at first. "Panty. *Raid*. Zombie. *High*."

Then more seriously, more intently.

"Panty. *Raid*."

The crowd is swelling, the volume rising, the vibrating of stamping feet and pumping fists pounding through the cafeteria floor.

"Zombie. *High*."

"Panty. *Raid*."

The volume reaches a fever pitch, girls joining in, guys shoving each other good-naturedly. It's a *bona fide* event, the likes of which Tinfoil, Tennessee, rarely sees, and they've got Spud to thank for giving it to them on a silver platter.

"Fine, fine!" blurts a blustery and red-faced Boner, but not without shoving Spud back a step or two for good measure. "We'll follow you two to Zombie High. What do we care? But you and I both know nobody's made it inside yet."

"Spud's dad works there," I say, loud enough so the whole crowd can hear me over the fizzle of their lackluster chanting. "If anyone can get into Zombie High, it's him."

"Says you," Zack says, shoving me back violently.

Spud looks me up and down, then looks back at Zack and sets the trap. "If you're too *scared* to go to Zombie High with the likes of little old us, that's cool. I mean, like you said, nobody's made it in yet, so why should you two be any diff—"

"Nobody said anything about *scared*," spits Zack—literally—all breathless like, face going pale as the massive crowd *boos* him as one.

"Nobody's scared but you two turds!" Boner adds unnecessarily, making Zack wince.

"Name the date," demands Zack, clearly the brains of the outfit. Which *still* isn't saying much. "We'll be there with—"

"Tonight," interrupts Spud as I hold my breath.

Zack and Boner exchange quick *I-didn't-see*-that-*coming* faces.

Before they can pop off with some big excuse that could derail Operation Rescue Molly for good, Spud plunges ahead. "Meet us at the old graveyard out by Shelter Cove at midnight. *Tonight*. We'll see who shows up on Monday with a pair of zombie panties to prove how brave they are."

"Deal," says Boner, nudging Zack knowingly, as if there's no chance they'll ever actually show up, let alone go anywhere near Zombie High.

Suddenly, it hits me. It worked!

I smile and think to myself, *He's actually done it.* That mad genius Spud has actually shoved spaghetti sauce—and garlic bread—in the jocks' faces and conned Boner and Zack into a real, live panty raid at Zombie High, all without the threat of physical violence.

Jinx coming in four, three, two…one.

Zack's eyes bulge, and he nudges Boner back.

I look over Spud's shoulder to see Dean Crisp wading through the crowd. The vaguely relieved look on Spud's face finds him breathing a sigh of relief because it's almost over now.

Then I turn back, just in time to see Zack's fist flying straight—

At.

My.

Face.

At the last second, just as he pivots to put all his two-hundred-thirty pounds into it and to separate my nose from the rest of my profile, he slips on a dab of cheese sauce and goes down, hard, but not without grazing my jaw with a glancing blow from his ham-sized fist.

It sends me back into the crowd, which is finally cheering now that they've seen some actual violence, and shoves me back in Zack's direction so he can whale on me some more.

Nice, guys. Real nice.

But Zack is already headed for the hills, Boner hot on his trail as Dean Crisp struggles to catch up with one or the other.

Meanwhile Spud drags me into and out the other side of the crowd, yanking me all the way back to table twenty-seven, where the rest of the Chess Club geeks are eager to pat us on the back.

I'd love to celebrate with them, but my jaw feels like it's made of broken glass and my ear's ringing so loudly, I can barely hear what our friends are saying.

Besides, standing up to Boner and Zack was the easy part.

We've still got that panty raid to worry about.

And, you know, the actual *zombies.*

CHAPTER TWO

Spud is neither shaped like a potato nor was that his first nickname. In sixth grade everybody used to call him "Booger," on account of he used to have this habit—what used to? He *still* has it—of picking his nose whenever he's nervous.

Or when he's not nervous. Whatever.

Then one day in eighth grade he did his business, as usual—nervously—and yanked out a piece of crusty, elongated, dried snot so big and round and pitted it looked like a miniature baked potato and, ta-da, "Spud" was born.

And, just like that, "Booger" was out.

"You think they'll show?" I ask as I pace in front of the massive marble headstone Spud is currently sitting on.

"They *have* to," he answers confidently, swinging his new size-eight sneakers as they dangle. "If they don't, the whole school will think they're chicken."

I nod, like maybe I'm actually listening or something, but I'm too distracted by his swinging sneakers to actually focus on his answer.

"You really think you should be doing that?" I look up at him uncomfortably. "I mean, it's a little…disrespectful. Don't you think?"

Spud glares at me like I'm wearing a letterman's jacket and a face full of cheese sauce and garlic bread. "Seriously? We're about to steal a pair of electronic knickers off the living dead, in a building crawling with brain-eaters and bone chewers, and you're calling *me* disrespectful? For what? Sitting on a dead piece of marble?"

I shrug.

"It's not the dead marble I'm worried about," I murmur, turning away.

I suppose he's right, and it's not that he's sitting on a tombstone that makes me nervous so much but the fact that *he* is sitting on a tombstone. You know?

I mean, a week ago, Spud wouldn't even be in this graveyard, or out past midnight without his allergy medicine, let alone shove spaghetti in jocks' faces and acting all cocky four feet off the ground on a piece of granite that's marking the place where a skeleton lies six feet under.

If I'm a chicken, then Spud's a...an...*egg*!

Whatever, just stick with me here.

Spud isn't just afraid of his own shadow; he's afraid of anything that *casts* a shadow, particularly if it's above three-feet-tall and, you know...*breathing*.

And now he's standing up to Boner and Zack in A-Lunch and bouncing his legs all up and down some corpse's final resting place as if he's on some back porch swing, sippin' on gin and juice?

I mean, I know he's messed up over Molly going missing but...this is extreme to the E to the X to the...well, you know the rest of the letters.

Swallowing again, I try to work my jaw back into place as I pace back and forth at his feet.

I don't know how guys in the movies do it. Zack punched me—okay, *half*-punched me—over eleven hours ago and it *still* hurts! And I don't mean just hurts a little and I'm being all wimpy about it. I'm talking like *something's broken in there that's not going to fix itself and might require an ER visit* hurts.

And I keep hearing this little *crick-crack-cracking* noise every time I swallow, like I'm doing it wrong or something's broken or misplaced or bent or twisted out of joint indefinitely, maybe even all the way up to my ear on that side and I don't know. Something might require serious medical attention up in here.

I look up to tell Spud about it—again—but he's rearranging his backpack for the gazillionth time and wasn't all that interested the first few dozen times I told him about my cracking, eroding jaw before we stumbled into the graveyard, let alone after.

I try not to swallow and watch as headlights blaze brightly at the end of the street.

"They're here," I grunt, mouth dry with the cracking and the fear and the dread. "I think. Either that or there are still grave robbers roaming around, and we're probably encroaching on their turf or something."

Spud looks up from his *Iron Man* backpack and nods knowingly.

"I'd recognize Boner's pickup truck anywhere," he says, and I nod.

I'm certainly familiar enough with the front end of it, that being the end I usually see as Boner tries to spook me by pretending to ram my used compact car off the road on the way home from school five days a week.

I expect Spud to slide down off the tombstone and join me on the damp, green earth of the midnight graveyard, but he sits still, watching as the gate creaks open.

Boner and Zack clomp through, as dense and dull as any of the tombstones that suddenly surround them.

Sighing, I turn to greet them.

Why am I not surprised that they're not alone?

CHAPTER THREE

"**N**obody said anything about *guests*," Spud announces haughtily from his perch high atop the moldy grave marker, the one he's apparently turned into his personal throne.

I steal a glance at Haley Mills and her shorter-than-short, white pleather skirt and lick my lips, too speechless to agree.

It's not that I'm a total perv but, come on, you have to see how short this skirt is!

And how Haley...fills...it.

"It's Friday night," says Lilac Forrester, Zack's longtime on-again, off-again girlfriend. "Our boys don't go *anywhere* without us on a Friday night."

"Even...Zombie High?" Spud offers dramatically, like the host of some all-night creature feature fest on the local cable channel, a delicious gleam hiding behind his thick glasses.

"Even Zombie High," Haley sneers, nodding to Lilac with a *you go, girl* smirk while swiping a lock of long, honey blond hair behind her delicate pink ear.

Spud shakes his head in a *these-chicks-just-don't-get-it* kind of way, but still stays put. "Whatever." He sighs, pushing his black glasses up his slight, pug nose. "You all know the rules. Everyone has to bring a pair of panties back or it doesn't count. Even...guests."

"What *rules*?" Boner asks with a crooked-tooth smile, fiddling with the bill of his tattered maroon and gold Tinfoil High ball cap before putting it back on his giant, close-cropped head—backward, of *course*. "No one's ever made it that far into Zombie High to *look* at a pair of panties before, let alone bring back a pair. So how can there be rules for something that's never actually happened?"

Zack nods and shares a quick, slimy, mouthy kiss with Lilac, who I swear only goes out with him because their first names rhyme.

And they're about the same height and their hair is—mostly—the same color. She has brown hair bordering on black, straight to her shoulders but layered to cascade whenever she shakes her head, rolls her eyes, or licks her lips, all of which she does quite often and frequently in combinations of two or three, just to switch things up. She clings to Zack like a hood ornament, one hand always snug in his nearest jeans pocket, the other resting gently between his two, admittedly massive, pecs.

For tonight's festivities she's wearing painted-on pink jeans and a snug black hoodie jacket, zipped down low to reveal the slight swell of her breasts, cupped tenderly in a maroon bra.

That's it. No shirt, just...bra.

You stay classy, Lilac!

I swear if I stare long enough, something you shouldn't really do when Zack's around, BTW, I can see the straps of her lacy black thong between the top of her jeans and the bottom of her too-short jacket which, of course, barely grazes the top of her belly button.

She has one of those squishy stomachs that's not quite flat, which for some reason I've always really dug. Like, really, *really* dug.

Not that I spend a ton of time thinking about it before or after school, but I don't think the chick's covered her midriff outside of school since, like, fourth grade, so it's definitely a preoccupation whenever I'm walking toward her.

"Well, they've never made it that far because they never took *me* along," Spud brags uncharacteristically, avoiding my penetrating glare as I give him major WTF face from ground level.

I know you can't exactly show fear around guys like Zack and Boner but, come on, Spud's taking this bluffing thing to a whole new level.

Haley pouts, juts out her own budding chest beneath her revealing aqua crop top and asks, "Yeah, four eyes, what makes *you* so special?"

For a moment, Spud is speechless. I can't tell if it's because Haley is actually speaking to him, or because of the way her barely-there top moves *when* she speaks to him.

Either way, the silence gets a little too awkward, so I rush to fill it. "His dad's a teacher there," I answer, if only to watch the luscious Haley look in my general direction.

Her eyes are limpid blue and gigantic, just like her thick, puffy peach lips and princess-size ego.

Tonight she has on that too-short white skirt and turquoise sandals with wedge heels to match the crop top that bulges out of her matching white pleather jacket. The fake gold anklet twinkles in the weak streetlight outside the cemetery gate whenever she moves just so.

Even when not speaking, she often brushes an imaginary lock of her straight, honey blonde hair away from those thick, peach-painted lips. She does so now, the movement making the gloss shine in concert with her dangling ankle bracelet.

"He's the *principal* of Zombie High," Spud corrects me tartly, and I whip my head around so fast it takes my half-broken jaw an extra second to catch up, crickle-cracking all the way.

"Since *when*?" I ask, forgetting we have "company."

"Since two weeks ago." He almost sneers.

"Two *weeks* ago?" Lilac's blue eyes flicker between thick, black lashes. "Isn't that when that Sally chick from our school went missing?"

"*Molly!*" Spud and I both correct her at the same time.

"Whatever," says Boner, stepping forward menacingly because, well…that's how he rolls. That's pretty much the *only* way he rolls, him and his stupid practically shaved head and backward ball cap with the big gold "T" for Tinfoil High. "Here's how it's going to happen. You two dweebs are going to take your little map and your little passwords and your little legs and break into Zombie High, and you're going to grab a pair of panties for each of us and bring them back here. In the meantime, the girls and us are gonna have ourselves a little party, dig?"

As if to reinforce what *party* actually means, Boner slips a dented metal flask from his back pocket and wiggles it in the weak moonlight for emphasis. Then he kind of looks at each of us, in turn, maybe, I dunno…waiting for one of us to nod, like we get it?

Spud looks down from his perch. "You guys do whatever you want. Toby and I are breaking into Zombie High and if we make it back, we're going straight to the nearest TV studio and let everybody know that the captains of the Tinsel High football team wussed out on us before the night even began."

"Pretty brave for a pencil-necked geek," Zack says, stiff blue eyes penetrating us both in the pitch black of night.

"Look." Spud sighs, his exasperation clearly showing now that the girls have shown up and…complicated matters. "These aren't like regular panties, okay?"

"So, what *are* they like then?" Lilac twists a dark shock of hair around a black-painted fingernail and looks to Zack for approval, as if she wants him to rate her on how badass she's being.

If she were to ask me, I'd give her an eight out of ten at the moment. Not that she'd ever ask me. Beneath the desperate ache for approval, Lilac's tone indicates she cares but doesn't want to *sound* like she cares.

I nod and give her a reassuring little smile, like I get it, which she promptly ignores.

"For one thing," Spud explains, "the panties are assigned to each zombie. To get them off, we're going to have to reassign them. To us. That means fingerprints, blood types, all kinds of stuff you can't fake. They're like, I dunno, individual shock collars. So you can't just stack them up and drag them home. Each of us gets a pair; each of us brings the pair back. That's how a panty raid works."

I look at Spud and try to send him a message via ESP: *Really? Seriously?*

Because, at this point, in all his gravestone sitting glory, I'm not sure if he's just saying that to make sure that Zack and Boner still come along and bring their muscles with them, like we'd planned all along, or if that's really how the zombie panties work.

But he's barely looked at me since Boner and Zack showed up, and was half-ignoring me before that.

"You know a lot about panty raids do you, Spud?" asks Boner with a *yeah, right* chuckle aimed squarely at Zack and the girls.

Predictably, they swoon.

Well, all except for Zack. He just glowers.

"No," Spud admits. "Do *you*?"

Boner opens his mouth to crack wise, then thinks better of it.

"How does he know so much about those stupid zombie panties anyway?" snarks Lilac, to no one in particular.

I turn back around and do my best to wipe that smirk of her smirky, smirking face.

"'Cause his dad invented 'em, that's why."

CHAPTER FOUR

"**H**e didn't invent the *panties*." Spud sneers as if that's beneath his not-so-beloved father, Dr. Cavendish Krill. "He invented the proprietary electronic grid that's woven *into* the panties."

"What?" Boner nudges Haley as if this might be just the thing to spice up their lackluster love life. "You mean…they're *electric* panties?"

Zack and Lilac—see, I told you they rhymed when put together like that, and don't think Lilac didn't write it that way four thousand times in her journal before deciding to ask him out, either—get all cozy, too, like maybe they wouldn't mind shocking each other's private parts on a boring old Friday night.

In a graveyard, no less!

"Yeah, electric as in an electric fence," Spud explains patiently. "They use them to keep the zombies in line, shock them into submission if they're feeling…frisky…I dunno. It's kind of like a shock collar for their groin-age area. Dad's not allowed to talk about it much."

Spud looks down at his digital watch, sighs dramatically and slides off the tombstone without a hitch, as if it's the kind of thing he does every night, and twice on Sundays. "Look, the guards switch shifts every morning at one a.m., so we don't have a lot of time if we want to slip in under the radar."

"I thought you had the codes," says Zack, but I notice he's reluctantly following Spud out of the cemetery just the same, just like we all are, single file past the little rusty gate at the back.

"I do." Spud doesn't bother to look over his shoulder as his spiffy new sneakers tromp through the waist-high grass. "But there's no code for the guards. We have to slip by them when there's the least of them, which is at shift change. Which is in half an hour. Come on, and look out for cow patties."

We follow Spud in silence, me catching up to walk by his side while Boner and Zack cling to their women, who have stupidly worn heels to a panty raid.

At Zombie High!

"Are there *really* cow patties out here?" I ask nervously, taking big steps just in case.

"Naw." Spud laughs his particular, high-pitched giggle. "I just said that to freak the girls out."

I smile and nudge him with my shoulder but, for once, he doesn't nudge me back. I figure he's just nervous about the panty raid and I focus on trying to keep up with him.

"What's the deal with your dad becoming principal of Zombie High?" I wonder why he never told me.

He shrugs, like it's no big deal. "It's just a promotion."

"Yeah, but…Zombie High? That's like, becoming a general or something. I can't believe you didn't tell me something major like that."

He looks at me funny, like he doesn't know whether I'm making fun of him—or his dad—or not. "Well, with Molly going missing and all, I've had a lot on my mind."

"I guess…" I let my voice trail off as it gets harder and harder to walk and talk in the dark, with the weeds and Spud's frantic pace and the constant threat of cow patties lurking underfoot.

The field behind the cemetery is wide and endless, and the night so dark all we can see in the looming distance are the few lights burning in the guard towers that surround Zombie High. There are four, one at each corner of the wide, high fence that surrounds the giant, five-floor building. It's cold out this time of year, this late, and I'm glad Spud talked me into wearing my black hoodie instead of the zip-up sweater I'd been planning on. Yes, I know how that sounds but it's not like we sat up comparing outfits or anything! I mean, not really.

He's wearing all black, from head to toe, commando style: black Boy Scout pants, black sneakers, black socks, black T-shirt, black jacket, black ski cap; even his thick, rectangular glasses are black.

It's a shift from his usual retro Sci-fi movie T-shirts, knee-high tube socks and a bandage always falling off his elbow, which is always skinned though I don't know how because Spud's not real big on getting dirty or roughhousing or, for that matter, you know, leaving the house.

He walks with ease over the old cow pasture, which hasn't been used for years.

No surprise there. Nothing much in Tinfoil, Tennessee—former tin foil capital of the United States, hence its lame-oid name—has been used in years. Once the aluminum mines shut down and the powers that be realized they could get more out of recycling old cans than drilling new mines, the town of Tinfoil pretty much dried up and withered away.

These days most stores have closed up shop and moved on. We're down to three restaurants—four, if you count the Burger Barn, but that's clear in the next town over—four churches, three convenience stores and one movie theater with two screens, one of which has a really huge, really distracting Gigantor spit wad just left of center.

The high school's about the biggest deal in town, and if it weren't for football and basketball, we wouldn't have to deal with guys like Boner and Zack in the first place. Instead, they're the only excitement this rinky-dink mountain town has, and so they get treated like rock stars, no matter how many black eyes, swirlies, or wedgies they give a day.

The only reason my folks moved here in the first place was for the cheap housing and because, as freelance graphic designers, they could work from anywhere. So why not move to a rustic cabin in the woods, a twelve-year-old A-frame with a fireplace in every room and a wraparound deck featuring a three-hundred-sixty degree view of the famous Crescent Cliffs mountain range?

Which is pretty and all but…did they stop to think how much it might suck for their only son to take a mile hike every morning just to take the trash to the curb?

Dr. Krill moved here because of the local state university, where he conducted his research. At least, until his funding ran out.

He and Spud were actually considering moving away—which would have sucked, major—until the Florida Zombie Outbreak of 2014 changed everything.

When the government got wind of his electric gridding system, and combined that with the fact that only teenage zombies could be rehabilitated, they not only reinstated his funding but quadrupled it—then quadrupled *that*.

From being unemployed to being the government's top-dog in designing zombie underwear, Dr. Krill went from the bottom straight to the top. Spud went along for the ride.

It had all happened so fast.

Now, Spud lives in a new house, behind a big gate, and drives a fancy new car and dates my hot best friend, and although we're still best friends, it's not like it used to be.

Like this thing with his dad being made principal of Zombie High. Without him even telling me? What's that all about?

In the old days if he or his dad stubbed his toe, it's all Spud would talk about on the long ride to Tinfoil High in my beat-up junker. Then again, ever since Spud moved to the big leagues—and away from my neighborhood—we haven't ridden to school together nearly as often.

Used to be I'd drive him to school, but ever since Dr. Krill got him his own car—a fancier car than my folks drive, and they're pretty intense when it comes to new cars—it's like Spud's forgotten my address.

Do you think he could be bothered to drive all the way to the sticks and pick me up with it once in awhile? Not very likely.

Spud says he's afraid he might drive off the side of the mountain, so no luck there.

The only thing that really kept us friends for as long as we've been was Molly, good, old Molly.

And when she went missing, well…if it wasn't for that, no way would Spud and I be hanging out at midnight together, in an old cow pasture or otherwise.

The tree line starts up again about a quarter mile from Zombie High, and Spud pauses to let the leathernecks and their giggling beauties catch up. Lilac is squirming because she felt something squish against her ankle, and Haley is riding on Boner's back, cowgirl style, although neither of them look like they're having any fun.

"How much *longer?*" Boner asks, dumping Haley down unceremoniously. I watch as she totters on those ginormous heels and adjusts her skirt after riding Boner's back all the way here.

And, yes, I know *just* how dirty that sounds.

"Just a little while longer." Spud points to the nearest guard station just across the field. "We'll have to follow the tree line until we get to the back fence, where the guards switch shifts. Follow me."

There is a tone to his voice, a look to his eyes, a spring in his step, and suddenly I think, Spud is actually *enjoying* this! Which strikes me as odd because, wasn't the whole point of this panty raid which isn't really a panty raid to rescue Molly?

And what's to enjoy about *that?*

CHAPTER FIVE

Spud leads us across more brushy land, crouching down between big bushes, the girls complaining about stickers and burrs, the boys grousing because he's not giving them enough time to take sips off Boner's precious flask.

For all Spud's super-duper spy club antics though, we're not very good at being quiet.

The grass is dry and crunches beneath our big, sneakered feet, the girls jingle and jangle with their necklaces and big trampy hoop earrings and bracelets upon plastic bracelets, and the guys aren't much better with their huffing and puffing and the flask clinking every few minutes against their giant class rings.

It's amazing we reach the fence at all with this motley crew but somehow, finally, we do.

There is a keypad midway between the two back guard stations, with a mesh door next to it, the kind you see in baseball fields to let players on and off the diamond.

Spud pushes a button on the side of his watch as we cluster around, faces looking blue and garish in the warm digital glow from his giant watch face. He takes out a to-do list of sorts he's kept carefully folded in his pocket this whole time and squints at the passcode as we hover around, trying to decipher his chicken scratch.

Spud punches six numbers into the keypad and the lock hisses open gently. He grabs the thick mesh door before it can swing open and hit the other side of the fence and alert the guards that we're down here.

We bust through, Spud closes the door and we lean there, against the gate.

Well, Spud does anyway.

The rest of us just kind of linger because, duh. Zombies much?

"I thought you said it was electric," spits Lilac as the rest of us nod slowly. "What gives?"

"The *panties* are electric, like an underground dog fence," he explains, rolling his eyes as if he can't believe we could really be that dumb. "Why would they need electric panties *and* an electric fence, Lilac? That's redundant."

"Call my girl another name, egghead, and I'll turn you over to the guards myself. In two pieces."

Zack's warning is hilarious to everyone *but* Zack.

"He wasn't insulting me, blockhead," snorts Lilac, her wide nostrils flaring as she gives Zack plenty of attitude.

You know, I've ogled Lilac from across one classroom or another for three semesters now, and I have to tell you, up close and in person, Molly's right. She's not that hot.

Lilac's eyes aren't just big; they're dull, and limp, like her brown hair streaked with black, or black hair streaked with brown, or…whatever. Her skin is pale and fleshy, and if she wasn't so tall and leggy she'd be downright…well…dumpy. Her skin is bad and in the garish light spilling from the courtyard we're suddenly standing in, I can tell she's wearing a lot of makeup—tons. And that fleshy stomach of hers keeps threatening to spill over her tight pink jeans every time she bends over to straighten the straps on her stupid high-heeled sandals.

Boner catches me looking and shrugs knowingly, like he'd agree. You know, that is, if we were of the same species.

We follow Spud as close as we dare to just below the nearest guardhouse, then cut across the field toward the building while trying to stay out of sight.

I dunno, as we're zigging and zagging here and there, it all feels pretty anticlimactic. I kind of expected search lights and alarms and field triggers and motion detectors and the like. Alarms going off and trained dogs barking and guards screaming orders and rifles pointing and that kind of stuff. Helicopters hovering, blow horns blaring, walkie-talkies squawking—the full meal deal.

I mean, this place *does* house a few dozen flesh-eating, brain-sucking, virus-carrying zombies, so you'd think it would be the highest security place in town. But so far, not so much. I mean, I've had a harder time sneaking in after curfew—and that's when my folks were *out* of town!

I can't tell whether to be disappointed or…distressed.

Spud seems cool with it, though, and I figure he's been here before with his dad from the way he's all cocky, sprinting across the field in his Jason Bourne gear, so I shrug and sprint to catch up.

We reach a brick overhang and cluster tight, the girls smelling of too much perfume, the boys taking swigs off their dented metal flask and giving off an adrenaline-fueled musk of their own. They are breathing heavy, but not too heavy; their eyes are alive with challenge and bravado, and I think for just a few seconds that we haven't tricked them at all. That they're here because they want to be here, and their girls, too. This is like some alternate keg party for them, complete with girls *and* booze!

And I think we haven't fooled them at all, that maybe they fooled us. But Spud looks so confident, and the guys are acting cool, and the chicks are fairly hot so…am I the *only* fool here? Does no one else care that a rabid, brain-eating zombie could jump out from behind the building at any moment and suck our brains out of our skulls like the last scoop of three-alarm chili from the bottom of the bowl? Looking around, I see that it's all fun and games, so I keep quiet and follow Spud. With Molly inside, and these clowns as my rescue team, what else can I do?

Shadows blanket us, and I use the cover to peer back at the nearest guard tower. It's empty. I strain my neck to look at the second tower in the other direction. It's empty, too.

I nudge Spud with one elbow, and while Zack and Boner are helping Haley pull some stickers out of her hair, I whisper, "Does that seem normal to you?"

He looks up, slightly annoyed that a pitiful mortal like myself might call his judgment into question. I feel kind of stupid, like Zack or Lilac or even Boner, until I see his eyes go wide behind his smudged lenses. His head rapidly moves from guard tower to guard tower. I follow.

It's not just Towers One and Two where the guards have gone AWOL. They're *all* empty.

All four guard towers are empty.

"I mean," I whisper, leaning close so the others can't hear, "I know you said they changed shifts at this time but…shouldn't someone be in at least *one* of them?"

He looks at me, then the jocks and their girls, then back at me. "Look," he whispers. "I may have…overestimated my knowledge of the inner workings of Zombie High a little, okay?"

He's so serious, I have to chuckle. "You think?"

"So, I'm saying, maybe this is…normal?"

"Why are you saying that with a question mark?"

Zack looks up from his girl, watching us, watching him.

"I'm not," he whispers back to me, eyes desperate as he racks his brain for an excuse, any excuse. "Look, we're already here, and the plan is working. Don't tell them I don't know what I'm doing, okay?"

I bite my lip, because if there are no guards, if there's no adult supervision, if we really *are* alone at Zombie High, then no, the plan definitely is *not* working.

Not.

At.

All.

"It's Molly in there, Toby," he pleads. "My girlfriend, my only girlfriend. And she's in there. We just, we're so close. Don't bail on me now, okay? I need you."

I wince, decide, and nod.

"Anything wrong?" Zack asks knowingly, inching our way with a menacing glare in his dark, fiery eyes.

The fence isn't electric, the guard towers are empty, the zombies are just inside and still...still...Zack sends a shiver up my spine when he gets that look in his eyes.

I try not to step back, but the ground beneath our feet is dewy and mushy and once I flinch, well, I just can't help it. He sees it, smiles, but it's nothing he hasn't seen me do a million times before.

"Listen," warns Spud dismissively, glaring in disgust at the flask as Boner slips it into the back pocket of his size XXXL jeans and joins his buddy Zack in towering over us. "I've never been inside before, but Dad says it's pretty hairy. The guards are all on the outside, and the teachers rule by shock therapy, but they go home every night so we'll be on our own."

I wait for Boner or Zack or even one of the girls to look up at the guard towers and see for themselves that nobody's in them, but they're so intent on beating either Spud or me senseless they can't be bothered to look anywhere but down at us.

"What?" asks Lilac, a slight catch to her voice. "You mean the zombies are just going to be...roaming around in there? Free, with no adult supervision or anything?"

"Probably not." I can tell by Spud's quivering tone he's not so sure. "Dad says they have dormitories, more like cells really, but they don't have to sleep anymore, now that they're undead, so getting them to stay put is pretty dicey even when the staff's around during the day."

"So why don't they just break out at night?" Zack's stale bourbon breath splashes all over my face as he leans across me to bark at Spud.

"That's what the panties are for, Zack," Spud whines, and I can tell he just wants to get in, get Molly, get out and get home to his Gamma Man Underoos. *P.S. He's not the only one!* "Each pair of underwear has a sensor in it, so if too many of them cluster together around an exit, or one another, or a cell door, they rush in and break them up with a few quick jolts to the nads, know what I mean?"

"What do you mean 'cluster around one another,' Spud?" Lilac asks, big blue eyes big and blue and *wide*. "You mean there's, like, a zombie social hour or something?"

Spud shrugs. "I dunno, Lilac, they're zombies. Like if maybe they want to eat one of the weaker ones or something they cluster around and…and…well, you know. Come on, we're wasting time. Are we going in, grabbing some panties and coming home heroes, or wimping out and going home losers?"

Boner and Zack stand up straight, as if this is a serious question they actually have to think about before responding. Before they can answer, Spud punches in another key code at the back door. There is a slight hiss and a warm puff of musty, copper-tinged air as the door swings open and…in we go.

CHAPTER SIX

In case you haven't figured it out by now, Zombie High isn't *really* a high school. Although zombies *do* go there.

Zombie High is really a deserted hospital, left in the dust when the aluminum mines shuttered and folks had to start going to the newfangled medical center two towns over in Brighton, Tennessee.

That is, if they wanted anything more than a bandage and a pat on the head from the old coot security guard who manned the wire fence a construction company erected around the entire place shortly after it closed.

It was going to be torn down a dozen or more times over the years, and every time they'd print a big article in the paper and all us kids would get excited about watching the old place blow up. But I guess it's pretty expensive to tear down a whole hospital covering an entire acre of prime Tennessee real estate, and in the end nobody could ever afford it.

So it sat there, year after year, growing rusty and natty and moldy and grody and gradually turning into the place where all the parents—or bullies—told all the kids that the local boogeyman lived.

After the Florida Outbreak last year spread north and cops grew tired of dealing with the occasional local flare-up, the government took the hospital over and staffed it with armed guards and folks like Spud's dad, scientists who could a) keep the zombies in control, b) figure out a way to "cure" them, and c) try to rehabilitate them, if possible—pretty much in that order.

Locals started calling it "Zombie High," on account of so far only teenage zombies have ever had any luck being rehabilitated.

The young ones, the little kids, never seem to survive while the older ones, pretty much anyone over the age of eighteen just generally go brain-dead, shuffle-walk, gnaw-on-each-other zombie.

The teenagers, though, at least according to the news, can actually walk, and talk, and think, so it's Dr. Krill's job to try and figure out why. And even with county funding and a team of nearly a dozen full-time scientists staffing the place, it still has the look, feel—and smell—of a horror movie deserted hospital.

Or something you'd see on an episode of my all-time favorite Scream Channel show, *Spirit Seekers*, on their extra-slimy Super Spooky Halloween Horror Hospital Edition!

Bare bulbs flicker in musty hallways. The walls need a new paint job—or, heck, just new walls—and every few feet is another puddle of standing water that smells like a rat just died there.

Rushing in, Haley steps in one and, suddenly frantic, whispers, "*Please* tell me that's not zombie pee! Please, please, *please* say it's *not* zombie *pee!*"

I chuckle, but for once I'm the only one.

Spud snorts and says derisively, "Zombies *can't* pee, Haley, or cry or bleed or breathe or sleep or eat Happy Meals, for that matter. They're dead, remember?"

She lifts up one of her high-heel sandals, grabs her leg by the ankle, looks at the bottom and asks, "So what *is* it then?"

"Dad says they've been having trouble with the air-conditioning." Spud inches forward foot by foot as our eyes slowly adjust to the dim, slasher-movie lighting inside the dank hallway we've just entered. "The colder it is, the calmer the zombies are so, it's a strain on the system to run it 24/7 like this."

"Phew," says Haley, to no one in particular. She puts her foot down and keeps walking.

Boner is already three steps ahead, making her hurry to catch up, as Lilac clings needily to Zack, whose rippling forearm muscles look even more defined in the dim hallway lighting as he creeps along the wall in his striped rugby shirt with the sleeves rolled up to his elbow.

The side entrance we've just "infiltrated," in Spud's words, is narrow and brief, spilling out into a larger area where we can see several open doors. One is marked "Break Room," another "Spa."

"Look, babe," winks Boner, squeezing Haley's shapely tush and sending a jolt through my zipper as he hikes up her distressed pleather skirt in the process. *Here's why; she's wearing a red thong!* "They even have a spa. Who says I never take you anywhere romantic?"

Haley slaps him playfully on his rigid shoulder while Spud explains, as if anybody besides me is actually listening to him by this point, "Dad says the zombies have a tendency to get a little funky after awhile. The attendants bathe them daily. In there."

He points to the door marked "spa" and I watch with some satisfaction as Haley's fleshy face falls dramatically. Unfortunately, so has her tiny skirt, so no more cheap thrills for Toby!

"Let's try the break room then," suggests Boner, slipping out his dented flask and shaking it so it gleams in the weak hallway light. "I'm tired of drinking this rot gut straight up."

Spud vetoes it as a "majorly, terribly, absolutely epically bad idea," but his words are lost on the would-be partiers as they file through the open door anyway, jingling change and rifling through pockets and purses until they've grabbed up enough coins to pump out two sodas; one diet and the other "leaded," as my dad always calls the "regular" version.

They crack them open casually, as if it's just another day in the locker room. Lilac's fizzes over and she licks her finger, offering it up to Zack to do the same. He grunts and accommodates and they do a little dirty dancing because, you know, it isn't after one in the morning in Zombie High!

Oh God, I think. *This is becoming a really bad late-night Scream Channel B-movie, complete with dancing thugs and trampy skanks in mini-mini-skirts who lick soda off their fingers while zombies prowl the halls!*

Spud paces near the door, ignoring them, as if a guard might show up at any minute. I stand near him, but it's hard to get near him. He's so frantic and turning and pivoting so fast it's like putting your finger too close to the fan blade.

"This is bad," he says, over and over again.

"What's bad?"

He looks at me, startled. Like he hasn't even seen me standing there for the last, I dunno, five *minutes*!

"How long have you been standing there?" he hisses, dragging me to the doorway so the others won't hear.

"This whole time. What, you want I should hang out with the mouth breathers over there and catch third degree dumb or something?"

We both look at the same time to see Boner licking soda off Haley's wrist. She's giggling and blushing and cooing, like it's Valentine's Day and he's just shown up in a rented limo for the night.

"No," Spud says, a little calmer now. "I guess not."

"So, what's with the guards?"

He gives me an odd look, like he can't decide whether to confide in me or not. *A first!* "I dunno, Toby."

His tone is hot and angry, like it's my fault the guards all went AWOL on him or something. Or my fault I noticed is probably more like it.

"I know you know," I say, leaning in closely. "You've been acting fishy this whole time. First, you don't tell me they made your dad principal of Zombie High, which is just plain weird since I'm your best friend—your *only* friend. And suddenly you're telling me it's normal for there to be *no* guards at this creepy joint? That's BS, Spud, and you know it!"

"Trouble in paradise?" giggles Haley, sipping on her can of diet soda and sauntering over in her high-heel sandals, turquoise crop top getting all clingy in all the right places. *Hey, when did she unzip her white jacket? Cha-cha-cha!* "I'm not really sure this is the place, or time, for a lover's spat."

"I don't know," purrs Lilac, oozing into the arms of her Latin lover as if she's somehow able to unhinge her joints and turn her bones to mush. "Spooky places give me the tingles, right *baby*?"

Uggh, I am so hating on this chick right now. And no, it's not just because I'm ten shades of jealous.

Zack nods furiously, like he can't wait to regale us with just *how* tingly she gets in spooky places—wait, that didn't come out right *at all*—but just then there's a sudden clattering at the end of the hall.

In case you haven't been keeping up, everyone who should be out and about at this hour is in this very room, so...clattering = not good.

At all.

"Shhhh!" Spud spits unnecessarily as the clattering switches to clanging.

So, to recap, if clattering = not good, then clanging = *soooooo* not good!

It sounds like a metal door closing, or opening, or locking, or unlocking.

Either way, if it's not a guard and all the scientists have gone home for the night, then who else could it be?

The clanking is long gone now, leaving us with only the clanging. Then, suddenly, the clanging gives way to keys jingling. To me, though, that's pretty reassuring because have you ever seen a zombie jingle a pair of keys?

Me either.

The walls are so high and wet, the floors so slick and tiled, it's like a big echo chamber. So the sounds are like *clank...clank...clank*, then *clang...clang...clang*, followed by *jingle...jingle...* Well, you get the picture.

Unlike *real* echoes, though, this jingling isn't going away. In fact, if anything, it's coming closer and closer. Each jingle gets a little louder, then a little louder still, to the point where I can practically count the number of keys that are jingling.

Twenty-two, give or take a few.

By now Boner and Zack have shambled over, Boner sliding his flask back into his back pocket. He and Zack are elbowing us out of the doorway—and straight into the hall.

"Hey!" Spud warns, but Zack quickly shushes him.

"Sorry," he says, almost sounding like he means it. "Boner takes up a lot of room, you know?"

I whip around frantically, looking for an escape route back into the break room, but by now it's too late to go back inside for cover. Lilac and Haley are quivering in the doorway arm in arm, and it would sound a tad lame to literally break through their linked elbows with a quick, "Excuse me, ladies, I'm just going to use the massive amounts of adrenaline coursing through my body right now to shove this vending machine aside and hide behind it. Don't tell any zombies, k thnx bai!"

So there we huddle, Spud, Boner, Zack, and I, as close to each other as we'll ever be, as the clanging and the key-rattling and the clacking and the clattering turns to…footsteps.

Actual, recognizable footsteps.

"Dude, someone's coming." Boner says, overstating the obvious as his dull, gray eyes grow big and round.

And I'm smiling to myself, thinking if this were a horror movie, Boner would be the perfect guy to say that line.

Then Spud has to go and ruin it by clarifying, for the benefit of *no one*, "Or…*something*."

Now even Zack's caramel face looks more like vanilla ice cream. I can see him peeking back at the doorway to the break room, and it's not to check on Lilac, either.

The ceiling has these old-timey lighting fixtures, like upside down bowls with a light bulb in the middle. The bowls are old and rusty; the light bulbs dusty and weak. Some of the fixtures have mesh webbing over them, bleak and crumbling and cobwebby from years of decay. Others are just gone and it's a bare bulb giving off weak light that looks, somehow, more orange than yellow.

The end result is that the light directly below the lamps pools aggressively for a few short feet but, everywhere else, it's pretty much shadows and rust. Into one of these shadows lurches…a shape. Big and bulky and lumbering along at way too fast a pace.

This time Spud doesn't care who's looking. He reaches out to grab my arm.

Not in a hand-hold-y way, just in a kind of *dude, if I'm going down at this very moment, you're going with me* way. I want to shrug him off, in case the other guys are watching, but I don't. I can't. It's like it's too comforting this way, knowing I'm not going to die alone.

I keep waiting for Boner or Zack—or both—to hack on us, but when I risk a quick peek over, they are totally doing the same thing!

Jocks. They're just like the rest of us.

The lurching and the jingling and the shadows take forever to reveal anything. The hallway is long and narrow, bordered on either side by closed doors and fire extinguishers, half of them missing, but the shadows are so strong, the bulbs so weak, it's going to take a few more steps—maybe more than a few—to see what, or who, is coming our way.

"We should run, you guys," whispers Lilac at our backs, and she's standing so close—or we've crept so far back—I can practically taste the cherry cola and bourbon on her sweet, hot breath.

"Run *where*?" asks Spud without looking over his shoulder at her. His eyes haven't left the large, shadowy shape since it entered the hallway. "The only way out is in his direction, Lilac? Remember?"

Lilac gets a worried look on her face, and Haley doesn't do anything very BFF-worthy to wipe it off. Instead she kind of whimpers and clings to Lilac all the more and this thought runs through my head: *Lilac will live, if things get hairy. Lilac. Will. Live.*

She's just that type of girl, you know? It's not that she's tough, exactly, but she looks like a survivor; someone who'd figure out a way to sell her own grandmother if it meant staying one step ahead of the zombies.

The figure lurches forward, massive in the weak glow from the single bulb overhead.

Big shoes squeak on the damp floor, but we can't squeeze any closer to the walls and with the exit blocked, by him—or her, or it—there's nowhere left to go.

Spud and I had been counting on Zack and Boner to be our muscle, to "man up" and protect Lilac and Haley, but they're practically scratching the brick with broken nails to get away, no matter who they leave behind, girlfriends in short skirts and red thongs and high heels included.

I turn, inch even closer to Spud and hold my house key like a weapon.

Don't hate. Mom saw it on 20/20 or something, and I've never had a chance to try it out until just now.

The shape stumbles another inch forward, silhouetted in the dim light from the old bulb overhead.

Its massive head shifts left, then right, before finally spotting us.

It lurches forward, shambling awkwardly, until its face finally juts into view of the swinging bulb.

Next to me, a tremor passes through Spud's body as he quickly identifies the monster.

"Dad?"

CHAPTER SEVEN

"**W**arren?" croaks Dr. Cavendish Krill, refusing to address Spud—ever—by either of his nicknames. "What on earth are you doing and who—is that you, Toby? How did you two get in here and...who are these other children?"

"You *know* this creep?" Boner's suddenly cocky now that he knows the faceless intruder is just another puny mortal destined to bow down to his superior musculature.

"It's my dad," Spud says, a little more meekly ever since Dr. Krill arrived on the scene. "And he's *not* a creep," he mumbles, almost as an afterthought.

"I'm waiting, Warren." Dr. Krill slides a ring full of keys into a stained lab coat pocket that instantly makes me wonder, "*Where was he going with all those keys in the first place? And at this time of night? And why does the dude look so wrecked?*"

His lab coat looks yellow and faded, at odds with how fussy Dr. Krill has always been about, well...everything, ever since I've known him. I mean, you should see the way this guy organizes his grill tools, to say nothing of the way they gleam and shine as they rest, just so, on special pegs designed specifically for them in his three-car garage.

I cock my head and look a little more closely. The grody lab coat isn't all that's...off...about Spud's dad. His slick white hair, always impeccably groomed and gelled back into place, is now kind of wiry and puffy, sticking way out from his head and looking super Mad Scientist-ish. His round glasses with thin silver rims look smudged and askew. There's a ketchup stain—please, oh *please* let it be a *ketchup* stain!—on his yellow paisley tie, and the front of his starched white collar shirt is sticking out over the braided belt keeping up his pleated khakis.

He ignores me scoping him out and peers deeper into Spud's twitchy eyes. Spud flinches. "Dad we're looking for Molly!"

"Molly? Well, why...what would she be doing here, son?"

I wait for Spud to respond, *That's what we're here to find out* or You *tell* us or something totally snap-worthy like that, but instead he and his dad share this...look.

And I can't be certain, but I swear it's the same kind of look Spud and I have been sharing all night whenever Boner and Zack aren't looking.

It's a very specific look that says, *Keep cool, son. Keep up the charade and everything will be fine. Just fine.*

Then it's gone, and I'm thinking, well, wait...did they even share a look at all? I mean, maybe it's just the spooky setting and Dr. Krill's totally off-putting appearance that has me paranoid and seeing things that aren't there.

Please let them not be there!

"Whoa, whoa, whoa," sputters Haley, quickly squeezing between Boner and Zack—no easy feat, that—and squares off against Spud.

She does everything but poke my best friend in the middle of his pigeon chest. "Who said anything about looking for this Molly chick? We're here for the panties, period!"

"I'm sorry," says Dr. Krill, sounding anything but. "Do we...know each other, young lady?"

"Not likely, pops," sasses Lilac, chewing extra hard on her latest piece of obnoxious neon red gum.

Dr. Krill fixes her with intense, dark brown eyes and inches forward a smidge. "Let me rephrase that." His tone is so cold I could swear the temperature in the hallway just went down ten degrees. "Is there a reason I shouldn't be calling the cops on you right now?"

But Zack isn't letting Dr. Krill diss his woman so easily. "Forget the cops," he huffs, inching forward to stand by Lilac's side. "How about those guards your boy Spud was talking about earlier? Just call them."

Dr. Krill regards Zack icily, but turns to Spud. "Can I see you in the spa for a moment, *son*?"

I watch helplessly as Spud abandons me to chase his father a few steps down the hall. As the two disappear behind the next door over, the one marked "Spa," Lilac blows a bubble with her gum, pops it and says, "What crawled up his ass and grew spikes?"

"Forget him," grunts Boner, reaching out an arm and, with the palm of his hand, sending me halfway across the hall. "What's with this Molly chick we're supposed to be looking for, huh, spazz?"

I'm still whirring around, trying to stay in a standing position, when I come to rest facing away from Boner and the other three clowns. My ears are ringing but my vision is fine when I see a door open up midway down the hall.

I freeze, the sound of Zack and Boner high-fiving each other and the two girls giggling and snapping gum—or maybe that's just thong straps being adjusted—in the background.

Then I see a guard's uniform, a gun belt, squeaky black shoes and pine green pants with a black stripe down the side and think, *Guard! Yes, it's one of the guards! Finally, we're safe!*

Then the door shuts behind him, and the guard turns my way, and he's got…something in his mouth. And it looks, oddly enough, like a chicken leg.

Like…a giant chicken leg.

If a giant chicken leg was wearing the tattered, bloody sleeve of a guard's uniform, that is.

CHAPTER EIGHT

"**G**o!" I shout, turning around and sprinting between Zack and Boner, even between Lilac and Haley—take *that*, self-respect!—screaming behind me as I flee: "Go! Now! Or! You! Will! All! Die!"

Boner has this look on his face, for just a second, like he's ready to pound me into the ground. Not that I'm not used to seeing it all the time or anything but it kind of hurts to see it *this* time because, for once, I'm actually trying to save his stupid life!

Then he turns to see where I was coming from, spots the guard tossing his partner's half-eaten arm down onto the wet, tiled floor and his face changes. It's like some crazy folk punk artist painter dude had a blank canvas and just went spastic on it. His eyes bug out, his mouth grows slack, his jaw drops—even his nose seems to bend!

Suddenly, he's flailing his arms and bending his knees and waving his giant hands and shoving folks aside to get inside. Zack follows, with only slightly more dignity, but even so he nearly tramples Lilac and Haley as they hustle in and slam the door shut behind them.

The room is eerily quiet for a moment or two, all of us looking at each other and, at the same time, no one looking at anybody. Then everyone starts moving, crying, screaming, talking, all at the same time:

"Help me move this over here!"

"Get out of the way, Haley!"

"No, this *way*; turn it *this* way!"

"Yeah, like that!"

"Lilac, swing me a chair over here. Fine, whatever, then grab two…"

As the others slide a break room table up against the door, I find myself standing in front of a vending machine.

Looking at it, with all the chaos in the room, I'm suddenly inspired. I've never done anything like this before. I always figured I'd panic. You know, freeze in the corner with my hands over my head, curl into a fetal position or straight up run for the hills.

No one is more surprised than I am when I don't.

At least, not yet.

But here's the thing. Sodas are—still—fifty cents!

It's like time has forgotten Zombie High altogether and I say, surprisingly calmly, "Does anybody have any quarters left?"

"Get over here!" screams Boner. "We'll buy you a soda after we kill the cannibal guard, okay?"

"The soda is actually to *kill* the cannibal guard, okay?" I insist, double on the surly and not moving an inch from in front of the softly humming soda machine.

"How?" Lilac reaches for her purse as Zack stacks chairs on top of the table.

Why do jocks always *do* that, with the stacking of chairs on top of tables and such? Don't they know they're just going to fall off the minute zombie guard knocks on the door?

"Here!" Lilac shoves a hand full of coins—and lint—only two of which are quarters, and three of which are buttons. "How…how…is a soda going to kill a zombie?"

"It's not." I frown as she hands over another quarter. "I need more."

"Cough it up, Haley!" Lilac reaches for her friend's purse without asking.

Haley manages to snatch it up first, and I see the fire in Lilac's eyes again as she fumes. "Come on, bitch! I know you have more quarters in there."

"No, I don't," says Haley evasively, still taking time to do a mean-girl hair flip as her boyfriend boards up the door against a zombie invader. "Who says I do?"

"I do. I saw your tampon stash in the side pocket. Hand it over, biotch!"

"I'm going to need those," Haley insists, even as she unzips the little black clutch purse.

"I think your period's the least of our worries right now, Haley," Boner implores.

Just then, the flesh of his cheek ripples with the pounding of the door he's leaning against, wide shoulder thumping just a smidge as whatever's on the other side does its best to send Boner flying.

Haley gives a quick squeak and hands over a handful of quarters, several clattering to the floor and—of course—rolling under the machine.

As I'm feeding them into the machine I say, "I need a pillowcase, or a T-shirt or a towel or something."

The first soda slides into the tray at the bottom, followed quickly by the second.

"What for?" Zack shoves his shoulder into the door as the creature on the other side begins to pound more furiously.

Now, even with tables and chairs and Boner *and* Zack putting their all into leaning against it, the door is slowly opening wider and wider with each of the zombie guard's shoves.

"To put these in," I urge, trying to control the panic gurgling inside. "Hurry, anybody! Come on! Off with it!"

Zack doesn't even pause to slip out of his rugby shirt and then slink out of the crisp white V-neck undershirt beneath.

His body is the color of a penny, bronze and hard, with ribs on top of ribs and abs on top of abs.

I'm waiting for one of the girls to "ooh" or "aah" the way they always do in movies when one of those vampire twinks shows up with his shirt off, but they haven't even turned around.

Zack tosses me his shirt and despite me waving my hands to catch it coolly, it totally lands on my shoulder because, well…clearly I have absolutely no athletic ability whatsoever. I yank it down and tie the sleeves together and knot up the top, twice, tightly, before sliding in five of the soda cans I bought before Haley's period stash ran out.

"What's *that* for?" Lilac inches forward and, for the first time, sounds a tad less snarky than usual.

In the background I hear Spud. "Haley, get over here! Zack, put your back into it!"

Lilac rushes over as I'm knotting up the bottom of the shirt, making sure it will hold.

"Hey." Her face lights up, lips glossy and black. "That's pretty cool. Where'd you think of that?"

"I didn't." I heft the shirt full of soda cans and finding it surprisingly heavy. "I saw it in an old Sean Penn movie."

Her pug nose wrinkles and her eyes glaze over. "Who's Sean Penn?"

"He's the guy in those Jason Bourne movies," huffs Zack, miraculously back in his rugby shirt and yanking the makeshift weapon out of my hand. "Everybody knows that."

Lilac pouts and Zack runs to the door just as Boner finally loses his grip and it flies open, letting one angry zombie guard in.

His arms wave and reach for food.

The face above the waving arms is gray and mottled; not rotting, per se, but…definitely dripping.

He growls and roars, teeth bloody and broken from chewing on his partner's arm bone before he saw me out in the hall. Boner tries to slam the door on his arm.

What tries? He *does* slam the door on the guy's arm, but other than making a sickening snap, it doesn't do much good.

The zombie shoves back, pushing Boner a few inches into the wall and wedging the door open a good four inches more. Boner tries shutting it again, the muscles in his red neck straining until they're like the thousand-pound chords that keep the Golden Gate Bridge up, but when it won't budge, we all look down to his gore-splattered sneakers.

There, just inside the doorway, is an obstacle. A pretty big obstacle. The zombie guard has wedged his oozing, broken partner in like a doorstop!

"Ugh," says Haley every time Boner tries to slam the door shut and a rib cracks or a femur busts on the poor doorstop dude.

Lilac has the opposite response. "Crush him, Boner!"

Skin and bone (but surprisingly little blood) spurts onto the wall as Zack hoists his T-shirt full of soda cans—*my* soda cans—and starts swinging.

He's strong, and fast and really, really violent.

Where Boner is like a wrecking ball, I dunno; Zack is like greased lightning.

His arms go up, down, up, down, up, down so fast we don't really know what's happening until zombie body parts splatter and stick and the white T-shirt is littered with gore.

He slams the soda cans down on the zombie guard's arm with a smashing, a breaking and a snapping, and he just…

Never.

Stops.

It's like a cyclone of arm, winding and blinding.

That is, until the T-shirt is gory and saturated, until bits and blobs of the zombie guard's arm are sticking to it; sticking to Zack, and his shirt, and his throat and the top of the table Zack is leaning over while he flails away.

Until the shirt finally flies open and cans go veering off everywhere. They scatter and launch into the air, flying end over end and landing with a thump or a clatter. One zips out into the hall and cracks open, fizzing and fuzzing and spinning around like one of those Whacky Whizzer firecrackers until it's out of foam and juice and comes to an empty, rattling, clattering stop.

By now it doesn't really matter anyway. The zombie is mostly armless, one hanging by a thread, the other so bent and broken and twisted it's just plastered to his side.

Parts of his cheek are missing, leaving a 3-D view inside his jaw line, where his tongue works around miserably as he continues shoving his head through the door as if nothing's happened.

One of the escaped soda cans rolls across the linoleum break room floor and lands at my feet.

I pick it up, staring at it, until Zack reaches over to take it.

His hands are large and veiny and splattered with this kind of black, gooey zombie slime and covered in dripping bits of skin and gore.

"No." I yank it back forcefully.

Zack reaches for it again until Lilac stops him and says, quietly, "Let him, Zack. You already stole his idea once."

He glares at her, and I use the break to aim the soda can at the zombie guard's head and let it rip.

The can sails, twisting, turning, picking up speed, a lethal aluminum bullet that flies right past the zombie's head and straight out the door where it slams into the far wall and tumbles, harmlessly, to the floor.

"Nice," chuckles Zack, picking up another can that's come to a stop between Haley's trembling legs. "Real nice, loser."

And then, as if he's been practicing for this his whole life, Zack lets the can rip and, with a sickening thud-crack-smash-swoosh it lands square in the zombie guard's forehead, cracking his skull and leaking brain splooge all over his forehead and stopping him dead in his tracks.

The zombie guard stops instantly, lets out a burp of dry, moldy air that half-escapes his lips, and half-seeps out of his broken, torn cheek.

Then he sags to the floor like a sack of wet bones, landing on the friend he'd been eating just a few minutes earlier and was all too happy to wedge between the door and the wall.

"Yes!" Zack celebrates, reaching over the bent, crooked, gore-splattered break room table to give Boner a grand high five that's so powerful and explosive it stings *my* fingers—and I'm halfway across the room.

"That's how it's done, son!" Boner squawks, un-wedging himself out of the corner by the door and doing a little victory dance, slap five, handshake, shoulder butt thing with Zack as they both look at me like I'm next.

"Get over yourselves," mumbles Lilac, wiping hair out of Haley's eyes and trying to get her to stop shaking.

"What?" Zack's wide nostrils flare more from the celebration than the actual zombie killing. "We just killed a frickin' zombie, babe! Stopped him, dead in his tracks. What are you talking about?"

"You only killed him because of Einstein here's bright idea," she huffs, blue eyes flashing beneath her black bangs. "Without him, you'd still be trading punches with the living dead!"

I'm blushing, but not as stoked as you might think to have Lilac defend me because, after all this, she still doesn't know my name.

CHAPTER NINE

A knock on the door chills our collective blood, but when I look up through the crack near the doorjamb I see Spud climbing over the two guards on the floor.

He does it so casually, so naturally, it kind of takes me back.

I mean, we've just been through it so we can kind of be all "meh, zombie bodies, big whoop," but Spud was supposedly in the spa room hiding with Dr. Krill so, a few more props, please?

"What's going on in here?" he asks, so blasé and not even grossed out by the zombie corpses littering the gore-splattered break room doorway. Not even a little.

And this is a kid who made me swear not to tell anyone how he cried and cried that time he ran over a squirrel two days after getting his learner's permit!

Boner, still on a zombie-killing high, gets all red-faced and veiny-neck as he spits, "We're taking names and kicking *ass* in here, *that's* what, Numbnuts!"

Spud ignores him, looks me up and down without changing expression and asks, "Toby, you…*okay*?"

"Seriouisly?" I whisper, leaning in close as Boner turns back to Zack for some more male bonding via strange locker room hand-arm-wrist-and-chest-slapping rituals. "Where *were* you guys?"

"Dad said it would be safer in the spa room." He avoids my eyes as he smears a drop of black zombie sludge-blood over the floor tiles with the tip of his sneaker.

"What?" I blurt before I can stop myself from insulting dear old Dad. "While we were keeping him occupied?"

He starts to speak, then stops. His lips are dry and pink. He looks me in the eyes, finally, and says, "Listen, whatever. Dad says..." Then he stops, as if he shouldn't say more.

I grab his arm, hard, the adrenaline of the zombie battle making it more of a pinch than a grip. I'm a few inches taller than Spud and thirty pounds heavier. His forearm in my hand pretty much feels like a matchstick.

"Dad. Says. What. Spud?" I squeeze down on every other syllable.

He yanks his arm free and looks down. Angry red welts show up in a fingerprint pattern. He looks up from them back at me like I just drop-kicked his dog. "Dad says he might know where...Molly...is."

I brighten, but he quickly tosses drain water on my dreams. "That's the good news. The bad news is, well, she's with the other zombies."

CHAPTER TEN

"**W**hat *other zombies*?" I ask as Boner and Zack yank open the break room door and slide the dead zombies out of the way so we can finally squeeze past.

They make a sick, squeaking sound as they squish across the floor, kind of like a mop dipped in mud instead of water. They leave a trail of blood so thick and dark it's almost black.

"The other zombies…on the fifth floor," says Dr. Krill ominously.

His voice is so odd and unexpected, I'd almost forgotten he was here. He turns on unsteady legs. Spud follows closely. So closely I half-expect him to take Dr. Krill's hand, if only to steady the older man's wobbly gait.

"Spud," I say, but he doesn't turn.

"Spud!" I say louder, the sound echoes dark and powerful down the even darker hall.

Finally, he turns.

"You want the other guards to hear you?" Spud whispers, sprinting from his dad's side and racing back to join me. "Come on, Toby. It's Molly, and she's four floors up!"

I yank his arm. "What's going on? This…this…*wasn't* the plan."

He shrugs and watches his father drift out of sight as the shadows swallow him toward the end of the hallway.

"Dad's here now," he insists, chewing his pale, pink lip and staring down the hall. "The plan's changed."

His voice is so quiet it gets sucked down the hallway, so by the end I have to lean in a little to hear him. Spud starts to walk away again, but Boner catches him by the collar of his black pullover and yanks him back so hard I can hear his teeth click together as his head snaps back and forth.

"The plan," reminds Boner, face red with rage and zombie gore splatter, "is to get some zombie panties and get the hell out of here, right?"

"Right," Spud replies accommodatingly, but I can tell his heart's not in it. Then again, that was never the plan to begin with. Not *our* plan, anyway.

"Where are we going?" Haley rubs her hands together as Lilac drags her across the threshold of the break room, her turquoise blue wedges getting that thick, black zombie slime on them—it's a lot more like Jell-O than blood, really—and leaving little prints on the lime green linoleum floor.

"Upstairs," Zack explains, taking Lilac's hand and practically dragging them both into the hall. "That's where the zombies are."

Lilac sounds stressed as she asks, "And...where the zombie panties are?"

Zack nods tensely, but doesn't look back at her.

The stairway is narrow and dank, like in one of those old roadside motels Dad's always dragging us to on the way down to Disney World every summer. An "Exit" sign flickers at the top, revealing more standing water and peeling paint. We hear Dr. Krill's footsteps a floor or two above, thick and steady. He pauses often, the keys on the side of his pants jingling with each step.

"What's with your dad?" I ask as Spud pauses to catch his breath at the top of the third floor landing.

"What do you mean?" He's bent over at the waist, hands on his knees as if he's been running wind sprints all night.

"I dunno. I've never seen his...hair...look like that before."

Spud shrugs. "Well, I'm not exactly...sure."

"What do you mean, you're not sure? He's *your* dad."

"Yeah." He stands and wipes a smear of sweat off his brow with the sleeve of his pullover. "But he hasn't been home lately."

"What's lately, Spud?" The news pinches my chest as if someone was trying to split me in half inside some giant nutcracker.

He shrugs and starts up to the next step. I yank him back down.

"Define 'lately,' Spud."

Another shrug. "Two weeks."

"What?" I wrench him aside as the other four clowns plod up from the second floor.

"Dad hasn't been home for two weeks," he confesses, looking me in the eye. "I figured he's been working hard."

"And you don't think that's weird? Your dad not coming home for two whole weeks?"

"Yeah, I do," he snaps, stomping off as the others catch up.

I chase after him. "So, why didn't you tell me?"

"We're here now, right?" He tries to race ahead, but my legs are longer and, besides, I've always been faster than Spud. Always.

"I thought we were here for Molly, Spud. Wasn't *that* the plan?" I'm ahead of him now, waiting on the fourth floor landing.

When he catches up he says, out of breath again, "Look, I knew you wouldn't come if it was just to see my dad."

So he did lie to me. Just like we lied to *them*, to those vicious cretins still clomping up the stairs.

This was never just about Molly. This was always about his dad, Dr. Krill. My stomach hurts a little, thinking that Spud's been lying this whole time. Suddenly, I'm thinking that if he'll lie about Molly, he'll lie about anything.

And then, just as quickly, this: If he'll lie to me, his best friend, he'll lie to anyone.

"How do you know, Spud?" I keep my voice down as the other four clomp up the stairs like zombies on parade. "How do you know I wouldn't have come just for your dad?"

He looks up at me from one step down, eyes imploring me to understand.

"We *are* here for Molly, Toby, but...I had to make sure Dad was okay first, don't you see?"

"I see." I storm off and wait for him to catch up this time. "I see you're lying to me just like you're lying to *them*!"

The fifth floor landing fills with stomping and noise and clanging bracelets as the others finally catch up.

"Dude," says Haley with a sneer, looking around for Dr. Krill. "Your dad is like, so rude."

Spud shrugs. "He's got a lot on his mind."

I open the door and peer inside the hall, blinking my eyes in wonder and surprise. It's brightly lit, clean and white. "Sterile" is the first word that comes to mind, but also "modern." Like, *CSI* modern.

"It's like it's from a whole other hospital," Lilac wheezes, easing past me. She brushes my shoulder roughly and turns back, smiling. "Sorry."

Zack ploughs past and I'm spun around, knocked aside by Boner as he zips in just behind Zack.

"Uh, *hello*?" asks Haley as the door practically shuts on her face. "A little help here?"

I stop it just in time and she smiles, if only briefly. Her eyes are empty and cold as she flicks past, the pleather of her short skirt making little zip-zip noises as it brushes against her long, muscular thighs.

I don't just mean her eyes are dumb empty, I mean…they're…*lights out* empty. Like there's nothing going on back there. At all. It's like she's not just stupid, she's almost…brain dead. Which, I suppose, would explain her taste in men.

I shiver and let them race forth.

Lilac's right. It *is* like this floor's from another hospital. The walls are white-washed and gleaming. To make sure it's not a mirage, I reach out a hand to touch one, and it's not just painted, it's tiled.

Gone are the upside down, rusty, musty, cobwebby light bulb bowls. In their place are those long, white light bulb tubes like they use in school. They are hidden, four to a row, by frosty white covers as long as most park benches.

There are gleaming white doors with red plates on them that say things like, "Examining Room 1," or "Chem Lab 4." Some of them have no words, just that red biohazard sign like you see in chemistry lab on the bottles and vials you're not supposed to touch.

I reach out to open one and it's locked. So is the one across the hall from it.

Looking up from the doorknob, I see a keypad next to each door, like there was to get in the front gate and the first door we snuck in.

I'm not sure, but I swear in the second one I hear shuffling. This much I know for sure; I don't stick around to find out.

It's cold on this floor, almost chilly, and I zip up my hoodie for the first time all night. I hear a faint whisper and turn around to see Spud a few feet ahead, crouched down, inching forward and calling out, quietly, "Dad? Dad!"

Boner and Zack are a few paces ahead, sleeves and the backs of their necks clotted and clumped with dried zombie sludge. Yeah, that's a good word for it—sludge. They seem eager now, fired up by the blood-sludge and the violence, looking for more.

You know, as if this is just some giant video game to them where they can hit "do over" if one of the zombies actually kills them.

Lilac shrugs and drags Haley forward, giving me a little "sorry" smile as she leaves me in the dust.

I'm standing alone outside door number two when I hear, "Toby?"

The voice is dry and phlegm-moist at the same time.

I turn, though I don't want to, expecting Spud. I see a zombie instead.

A zombie with a *very* familiar face…

CHAPTER ELEVEN

"**M**olly!" I start to scream, but a hand—a cold, dead hand—clamps itself across my lips.

"Shut up, Toby!" she spits, as if she hasn't been missing for the last two weeks, as if she just saw me at A-Lunch today, as if Spud and I haven't risked our lives trying to rescue her! When she's done squawking, she drags me into the stairwell—by my face. "They'll hear."

"*Who* will hear?" I whisper as she drags me down, down, down, step after step.

Her hand is cold and gray and strong, like, Boner or Zack strong. Like, maybe even stronger.

"Dr. Krill, for one." She pauses as I start to tumble on the way back down the steps that I literally just climbed up. She catches me on the second floor landing and, without emotion, adds, "Spud, for another."

"So what if they hear?" I look into her dead, black eyes that are somehow Molly's but somehow not quite Molly's. "You're the whole reason we're here, Molly. We should tell Spud and then get the hell out of he—"

"No," she says urgently in that fall leaf, underwater gurgle of hers, dragging me down even faster as the stairwell door clatters open three floors above and footsteps launch onto the metal landing. "They're why I'm here in the first place, Toby!"

She drags me from the stairwell and out into the hallway on the main floor.

"I don't get it. I don't get any of this. Spud's been lying to me, nothing's going according to plan. Dr. Krill looks like crap warmed up and then freeze-dried. It's like the whole world's upside down or something."

"They're in this together," Molly explains, breath cold and odorless as it spills across my face. "Spud lured me here two weeks ago, Toby. You remember, you were going to go see that *Space Pirates* movie—"

"*Space Vampires*," I correct.

"Really, Toby? Seriously? Whatever, anyway...we were supposed to get fitted for his tux but he said he needed to swing by his house first and pick up his wallet. When we got there, his dad was waiting for us. One of them, I don't remember which, must have knocked me out and...the next thing I knew, I was here!"

The hallway is just as dark and dank and stale as before, but Molly being inside of it somehow makes things better.

If only her news was as good.

"But, I don't get it," I say, literally scratching my head. "He said his dad went missing two weeks ago. He made me feel all bad because I didn't know that."

Molly shakes her head, dark gaze piercing mine. "I'm not surprised that creep hasn't been home in two weeks." Suddenly her face looks fierce and scary, like someone I don't know, like someone I may have never known. "He's been here night and day, taking blood samples, doping me up, testing my language skills."

"H-h-how'd you get out? Just now, I mean."

She looks to her side. Someone—or something—is making clanging noises back in the stairwell.

"Dr. Krill heard something down here while he was in the middle of another test." She grabs my arm and forces me down the hallway toward the break room. "It would have been too much trouble to bring me back to my room, so he told me to stay put. Locked me in and everything. I'd memorized his code and let myself out the minute I heard the door slam down the hall. It's not the first time. I mean, he's a busy guy and this is a pretty big—What? What are you looking at, Toby?"

I stop, just shy of the bloody break room door. The zombie guards are gone. The zombie guards who attacked us, who Boner broke in half with the banging door and Zack pummeled with a T-shirt full of soda cans, are gone.

In their place is a wide black, sludge path, littered with little scabs of flesh, the occasional toenail and/or shoelace. I can see the drag marks deeper into the hallway and around the corner, but it's more like they vanished than were dragged. There's simply nothing of them left.

"The guards," she says with a little nod, following my eyes down the wide, grainy, brackish trail of blood. "They're eating each other."

"But, they're guards. How did the zombies get a hold of them in the first place?"

Her eyes get big and her cold, pale lips twist into a sarcastic sneer. "Hello, Toby, have you *seen* this place?"

She raises a hand and waves it in the general direction of the dripping yellow walls and musty old light fixtures. "It's a dump. And the zombies are smart. They lure one guard in, bite him, he lures the next—it's been going on for the last two days. I think you're the first human I've seen since—"

"Molly," I interrupt, struggling to stop my voice from breaking. "What. Is. Going. On. Here?"

She holds up a hand and sniffs the air, crouching low to the wall and dragging me along with her. We're just outside the door to the "spa" when she stops, ears pricked as if she hears clamoring inside. I hear it, too, moaning and groaning and clunking and clanking, like people—or things—looking for other people, or things.

I drag her in the opposite direction, her gray hand in mine, and she stops hard. It's like trying to drag Boner away from an adult bookstore. She doesn't budge. Try as I might, I can't get her to move. Not an inch.

I look at her, bony and gray, black hair stringy and flat across her marble white forehead. "Molly, please. The front door's right there. I know the code. Spud showed it to us when we broke in here. Two minutes, we can be gone from this place forever. We can make it if we hurry!"

"We can't let them out, Toby," she insists, almost sadly. "The only reason I haven't used Krill's code to run away on one of my little 'field trips' is to stop them from getting out. Stay here, I'll only be—"

Suddenly the door to the spa flies open, banging her on the lip. She falls down in the middle of the hallway floor, sliding a few inches on her now bony butt—and man, did she used to have a nice, round ba-donk-a-donk!—and suddenly a big, gray zombie hand grabs her ankle.

One of her generic purple plastic flip-flops falls off as the zombie hand starts yanking her inside the spa room. I grab her hands and yank in the opposite direction.

The arm holding on to her leg is big and gray and covered in a guard shirt that looks like it's been mauled by a tiger. It's blood-sludge-splattered and covered in veins, like one of those guys who spends *way* too much time at the gym and doesn't quite see what's actually reflected in the locker room mirror.

There's no contest. Not at all.

He drags us both in.

She is up and kicking by the time I untangle myself from a metal cart full of bath towels, stiff and white and smelling of too much bleach.

Suddenly Zombie Molly is on Zombie Guard's back, tugging at his shoulder with her teeth, dragging him toward the giant, gurgling Jacuzzi tub in the middle of the room.

I struggle to stand but I'm swallowed in stiff towels and bent metal rods, the scent of chlorine and bath salts stinging my eyes, the tiled floor slick with humidity and squeaking under my ratty black sneakers.

Zombie Guard is squealing, pivoting around, not from pain it would appear, but intense frustration. With stiff arms he tries to claw at Molly as she yanks off his green and black zombie security guard ball cap and gnaws noisily on the back of his head, and when that doesn't work he tries to flip her off. Once, twice, three times.

She rides him like a bucking bronco, bony legs wrapped around his chest until her stiff blue hospital gown is practically a Brazilian cut bikini and her other flip-flop flips and flops into the Jacuzzi tub, floating on the steaming bubbles like a toy boat in the world's biggest bathtub. Zombie sludge splatters the walls and the sides of the shiny metal Jacuzzi tub, coating it in black goo so thick it barely dribbles down the side.

I scramble to my feet, frantically looking for something to help her with, stopping when I stumble back over the towel cart. It's metal, with wheels, and bars. Lots of bars.

I tip it right side up and jump on top, jumping up, down and up again until it finally clatters to pieces beneath my grungy black sneakers.

Metal bars rattle along the tiled floor with a ricochet of clatters and clangs, and I grab the heaviest one I can find, running back to the zombie and finding Molly still gnawing on its skull.

She's not quite through yet. It sounds like a monkey cracking open a coconut.

His veiny white hands are on the edge of the metal spa tub, water gurgling over and making the floor slippery, his blood-sludge dripping down and making the bubbly water foamy and gray, like dripping ink into a fish bowl.

He's trying to keep his grip *and* still buck Molly off *and* stand his ground and the floor is slick and Molly is losing ground. She falls into the tub, the gurgling white hot tub and he smiles. The zombie smiles.

Do they do that? I didn't know they could do that! I dunno, maybe it's not a smile after all. Maybe it's just...gas.

That is, he's smiling until I shove the bar clear into his ear. He squeals, as if his head's just caught on fire, grabbing for the bar and yanking it free of my hand.

That's okay. There's plenty more where that one came from. I jam my back-up bars into his skull, one after the other, until he looks like an acupuncture patient gone wrong, or that "Pinhead" guy from those *Hellraiser* movies.

One in his neck, one in his eye, one in his other ear, one between his shoulder blades, one in his bicep. He wheels and turns, yanking at the bars but each one he pulls out, I ram one more in.

My arms are tired and the floor is slippery with water and thick, black sludge and, oh yeah, Molly is *still* in the roiling hot water! The jets must be pretty powerful, or maybe zombies can't swim, 'cause she rolls around for awhile and her feet kick up and then her knees and then some side boob—nothing I haven't seen before—but no head.

She finally pops her head up, straight black hair in her dead black eyes, but it doesn't stop her from seeing zombie guard pincushion guy yanking at the bars with bent and sludge-soaked hands.

She smiles, too.

Hmm, this must be some new zombie strain that can smile or something. Wonder how they feel about knock-knock jokes?

She dips down in the water, reaching for bars that have fallen in and, standing back up, shoves two into his head. One through each ear, like those corn-shaped spikes you jam into each end of your corn cob during a Fourth of July picnic.

I can hear them slide in, stiff and gushy, like Dad's electric knife through the turkey skin for that first cut every Thanksgiving. Then the ends of the rods clang together halfway through his brain with an audible "clank" and out go the lights.

Zombie out!

It's like, instant chord pull and the zombie guard goes down, sloshing in water and black, gooey blood and clanging against bent and broken pipes as his big, pale, cold body hits the floor.

Molly reaches for my hand and I grab her and yank her out of the tub. It's not so easy anymore. I remember just a few weeks ago hoisting Molly with one hand into the tree fort behind her house. It was like lifting a bag of potato chips onto the top shelf of the pantry.

Suddenly, hoisting her out of the spa tub feels like I might need a crane and a winch, a gaggle of Teamsters and perhaps a superhero or two.

"It's the muscles," she grunts wetly, tossing my hand away in disgust and hoisting herself out on her own.

Hey, is it *my* fault she's as heavy as a five-hundred pound bag of wet cement? The minute her hot, wet skin hits the cold air steam rises from her gray limbs and flat, saggy black hair.

God, how I used to love to sit behind her in Chem Lab and watch her mess with her hair, her long, pink fingers twirling the ends without even thinking about it or trying to look hot.

Now, her fingers are dead and pale and gray...and her hair. Her hair!

"The muscles," she reminds, as if she's dealing with a particularly slow student. "They get heavier as they harden. Dr. Krill weighs us every two days. I'm over two hundred pounds!"

I'm about to shove her back in the tub and say "No way!" but just then the spa door flies open and Dr. Krill is standing there with a gun.

CHAPTER TWELVE

A stun gun, as it turns out.

He says, "What will I do if you keep killing off all my guards, Molly?"

But his voice is…different now. Cold. Cruel. Not that he's ever been a warm and fuzzy guy to begin with, but this is extreme.

And…the gun?

Seriously?

"Careful, Toby," Molly whispers as we inch toward the spa door, fear creeping into her voice for the first time since she found me on the fifth floor. "Electricity is a zombie's worst enemy."

I'm thinking about how that could possibly be true when there is a disturbance out in the hall. It sounds like sneakers squeaking, like you'd hear on a basketball court during PE.

Then shouting, shouts of "Run! Run!" and "Hey, what are *you* doing there?"

We step slowly outside to see what's the matter. Dr. Krill is still out front a ways, his stun gun at the ready as we creep along behind him out into the hallway. Suddenly a tidal wave of denim and ball cap strikes Dr. Krill just around his middle.

The doorway empties and Molly rushes out into the hall.

I follow her trail of dripping water and steaming skin to see the stun gun lying on the ground, Boner wrestling Dr. Krill against the side of a wall.

Boner should be winning; Boner *always* wins.

He isn't.

Dr. Krill is in his late fifties, early sixties. A little on the beefy side. Not fat, per se, but hefty. Soft, like most of our middle-aged teachers.

Boner is two-hundred-forty pounds of fat-free, brain-free, muscle-bulging, vein-popping, hard-edged slab. He is losing—badly.

Dr. Krill grabs him by the shoulder and tosses him into the nearest wall, Superman style.

Boner lands with a thud.

Molly inches forward to stand in front of the stun gun that has clattered to the floor.

In a movie, Boner would pop back up and get back in the mix with a wink and a snappy one-liner but something has snapped. He stops to rub it, his face a mask of red, veiny pain while Dr. Krill stands on his loafered feet and inches forward.

There is still clattering in the hallway, shoes stumbling down stairs, more sneakers squeaking in the background. Suddenly I think, *Boner's alone? This is a first. Where's his entourage?*

Molly nudges me while Dr. Krill has his back to us and says, "Pick it up."

Her foot indicates the stun gun, though she doesn't quite touch it.

I do, smiling, and start to walk forward.

She yanks me backward. "No, not yet. Slip it in your pants. You'll need it, maybe. Later, probably."

Dr. Krill grabs Boner by the neck and hoists him up and over his shoulder like you would a baby you're about to burp. He turns to confront us just as the stairwell door flies open at the other end of the hall. Zack flies out, stumbling, nearly losing his footing with Haley hot on his trail.

Haley sees Boner's ball cap on the floor, one sneaker lying on its side in a sea of laces, and hurtles herself past Zack. Zack, for all his speed, is still stumbling forward with Lilac just now popping from the stairwell and taking up the rear.

Haley screams and flies at Dr. Krill, fists out, eager to free a dead weight Boner from the older man's shoulders. She does, in a way.

Krill drops Boner to the floor with a sickening thud, turns on a dime and, teeth bared, catches Haley on the most tender part of her young, bare throat. Blood spurts—real, red, human blood—as he tears into her flesh, soaking the walls with a fine, thin spray of deep, rust-colored red.

Zack stops. I can hear his shoes squeaking three yards away.

I turn away from Haley to see him holding Lilac back as he retreats toward the stairwell. His face is a mask of shock and fear and complete and utter hysteria. It's ticking like it doesn't know which way to go.

Molly sees him, too, and grunts, "Looks like a good idea."

CHAPTER THIRTEEN

Molly's hospital gown is clingy and wet as she hustles toward the stairwell. I linger close, 'cause she's going kind of slow, and look through the grimy square window as she shuts the stairwell door behind us.

Krill is still feasting on Haley's neck, Boner looking bent, broken, and ten kinds of expired on the floor at his blood-splattered feet.

"I don't understand," I whimper, even though I'm trying—and failing—to be brave. "What is wrong with Dr. Krill?"

Molly ignores me, looking down at the metal bar that keeps the stairwell closed.

She grips it in the middle with both hands, grunts a little—but not too much—and...bends it. Yes, bends it, like you would a...a...straw! I hear the crinkling of metal and smell the crunch of dust and rust and then the wedge of the door against its hinges as she seals it up tight.

With little more than a grumble she says, "That should keep him. Come on!"

She drags me back up the stairs until we get to the third floor. She yanks me off into a deserted corridor, twice as bad as the main floor, nowhere near as sleek and modern and clean as the fifth floor.

"Come on," she croaks as her bare feet clamor over drywall dust and discarded old soda cans from 1972. "I need to fuel up."

"Fuel up?" I look at the dark, dank floors, the punched-through walls covered with graffiti, the broken light bulbs and dangling cobwebs, and wonder if I'd even eat something out of a vending machine on this floor.

"Where are we?" I ask.

"This used to be the burn unit," she says, idly, creeping along the walls and crouching low to the ground, like maybe she's looking for spare change or something.

I stop her, by the arm, force her to turn around. "Talk to me, Molly!"

"I will." She yanks her arm away. "I will, Toby, I promise. I just…I'm starved, you know?"

"Starved?" I crack, watching her slink away. "You just gnawed on a guy's skull for twenty minutes, Molly? How can you be starved?"

"I didn't do that to eat his brain, clown," she scoffs, as if I still need to catch up on my Zombie 101. "I was trying to slow him down. You can't eat people, Toby. Remember that. Don't ever, ever, ever let me eat a person or…or I'll wind up like that guard."

"Wait," I stumble. "What? You mean—"

Suddenly, a squeak on the floor, then the animal scratching of tiny paws against discarded scrap paper. She stops me with a hiss and chases after it, creakingly, arms and legs stiff as she bends as low to the dirty, dusty floor as she can.

I try to keep up, which isn't all that hard because she runs all kinds of stiff and bent like a crab on crack, but I'm mad when I do because I'm just in time to catch her grabbing a rat from the wet, dirty ground. Its fur is matted and greasy, like Molly's hair, its tail is long and leathery and swirling as Molly's hands grip it around its head and…crunch!

She bites into the back of its skull, like cracking a walnut open with her big, yellow teeth, and starts…sucking…its brain out.

I kid you not. That brain goes right out of that rat's skull and into her mouth, no bigger than a meatball. Smaller, even.

We're talking, olive-on-a-toothpick small.

She chews it, hungrily, with these little "nom, nom, nom" noises like you do when you're exaggerating how much you love the gross, dried out cranberry date nut bread your lab partner just made you in Home Ec.

But she's not being ironic, she's being…prehistoric…nom, nom, nom-ing on that rubber-ball-out-of-a-gumball-machine-size brain like it's going out of style.

She drops the rat corpse to the floor, where it lands limp and lifeless, eyes glassy and black and dull as she scampers forward, on all fours now, as a literal flurry of rats tries to part in her wake.

She grabs two at a time, one in each hand, cracks their skulls with expert teeth, sucks their brains out through the ragged hole, then repeats this process three more times until, at last, she finds a broken desk chair slung out into the lobby and rests against it, legs splayed out like baseball bats and patting her belly like she's just enjoyed the most sumptuous pepperoni and sausage pizza on the planet.

Her skin is a little less gray after that, or maybe it's just that there's so little light on this floor it's harder to see.

My legs are tired and quivery. I'm not used to standing up this long, let alone running and climbing and shoving metal bars into zombie's heads in between all the running and standing. I look for a soft, clean, well-lit, *dry* place to squat and sit but…there is none.

Finally, I just kick a few of her discarded rat carcasses out of the way and slide down the wall to rest my aching rump against the slimy floor. Screw it.

She looks at me and, at last, smiles. "I'm sorry," she says, quietly, almost warmly.

Almost like she means it.

"What happened to you?" I try not to sound as judgmental, grossed out, and ticked off as I feel.

"Dr. *Krill* is what happened to me," she answers with a fire in her deep, black eyes for once.

I start to ask her more but she cuts me off. "Toby, you should have never come here."

"We came here for *you*," I insist.

"How could you?" Molly points to herself, her wet, dripping hospital gown, her clingy black hair, her jointy elbows and knobby knees and concrete complexion and bare feet covered in rat blood and dust. "I'm done for, Tobes. I was done for thirty minutes after I got here. Spud knew that, Toby. He knew it two weeks ago."

"Then why did he tell me we were coming here to get you, Molly? And why did he make us drag Boner and Haley into it? And Zack and Lilac?"

She reaches down, puts a cold hand on my warm shoulder. "He's recruiting zombies for his dad, Toby. Recruiting them the only way he knows how."

I snort and look at her. It's no illusion; her face is definitely less concrete looking now. It's nowhere near normal, but on a dark, rainy day she could almost pass for human again.

"You make Spud sound like some kind of super villain." I snort, shaking my head. "It's Spud, remember?"

"Yeah," she snorts back. "It's the Spud who's always been afraid of his dad, who almost didn't date me because his dad didn't think I was 'refined' enough for his precious boy. That's the Spud who tricked me into coming here, Toby. That's the Spud who's super villain smart enough to trick two dumb jocks and their little tramp girlfriends to follow you two out here all this way."

"But people will find out."

"You think so, huh?" Molly asks, and she's not being ironic. "Has anyone come looking for me, Toby? Besides you, that is? Have the cops shown up at school, wondering where I've been? Trust me, the cops know about this place. Or, at least, know enough to stay away. They're afraid of the zombies, and they're just as afraid of Dr. Krill. No one will find out. No one will care. Not until every young, hot-blooded teenager in this whole town is dead and buried and back from the dead, and by then it will be too late." Her voice is high and shrill, her hands waving, her eyes deep and black and wide. "Tell me," she says when I don't dare answer her, "how did Spud get you and the jocks to show up here tonight?"

"Me? He told me we were coming to rescue you."

She nods, suspiciously; been there, explained that. "And the jocks? They fell for that?"

I blush a little, looking away as I admit, "Well, no. We kind of dared them to come here."

She snorts, cracking her neck and smiling at the sensation. "Dared them?" It's her old Molly voice, with less dry-leaf crackle and saltwater gurgling this time. "That doesn't sound like you, Toby."

"We told them about the zombie panties and called them chicken if they didn't bring home a pair."

She snorts. "Nice one, Toby. Too bad there's no such thing."

CHAPTER FOURTEEN

"**W**haddya mean there's no such thing? They're…they're famous! I saw them on TV! With my own two eyes!"

"Oh, yeah, sure. A couple of prototypes exist, locked up tight in Dr. Krill's office. But in real life? Zombie panties cost, like, a million dollars per pair! No way is the government going to spend that much on a bunch of brain-dead, no-breathers like us."

"But this place? Those panties? That's how Dr. Krill got his job, isn't it?"

"That's how Dr. Krill conned his way into this place. Once the Army found out he couldn't control the zombies, not without million-dollar-per-pair zombie panties, anyway, they just handed him the keys, left a dozen guards behind and walked away. He's been turning this place into his own little science experiment ever since."

I shake my head. All that bragging Spud's been doing, the scientific breakthroughs, the profiles in *Scientific Discoveries* magazine, the awards and plaques all over Krill's office back home…was it all just a sham?

"Did Spud know?" I choke.

She looks down at me and shakes her head. "I have to say…no, Toby."

"But you just said he lured you here."

"He did, but when Dr. Krill bit me that first day, Spud looked genuinely surprised."

"Bit you?"

Molly nods ruefully. "Until Dr. Krill perfects his living dead serum, he still has to create zombies the old-fashioned way—by biting them."

"But, why would he want to create a serum, Molly? I mean, what for?"

"Are you kidding me?" she asks, as if I'm some kind of zombie rube.

"Imagine what a creep like him could do with the power of life, death, and the afterlife. If he could create an army full of zombie soldiers, then the government would set him up someplace a lot better than Zombie High, trust me. But to do that, he needs bodies, lots and lots of *teenage* bodies. And where better to find them than a crummy little town like Tinfoil, Tennessee? That's where we come in. You and me and Boner and Zack and…was that Lilac *Forrester* I saw back there?"

"I don't get it, Molly." I ignore her question, thankful the dim lighting hides my blush at the mere mention of Lilac's name. "Why aren't you trying to gnaw on my brain like those zombie guards downstairs? If you're…one of them, I mean."

"That's just it, Toby. I'm not one of *them*. Krill only cares about the zombies he can control, the zombies who can't think. The Feeders."

"*Feeders?*"

Molly sighs impatiently, like I'm about to flunk Remedial Zombie 101. "The more human flesh you eat, the more human brains, the more like a movie zombie you get. And the less like a human. I don't eat people, so I'm more like a person."

"What about Spud? Is he a…well…you know?"

"A Feeder?" she asks, half-snorting. "I'm not sure, but I don't think so. He looks a tad too healthy to me. Besides, Krill might be two-hundred percent creep, but turning your own son into one of the living dead? That's three-hundred percent creepy, and I'm not sure Krill's there just yet. Speaking of…" She sighs, standing from her chair and yanking me up by my collar with as much effort as it takes to lift a box of tissues off the nightstand by your bed. "We better go check on my friends."

"Friends?" I follow her to a back stairwell marked by a flickering *Exit* sign.

"Yeah, we're going to need them if you're going to get out of here alive."

"Me? What about you?"

"I told you, Dr. Krill might not care if we roam around unaccompanied, but I can't just leave. None of us can. That's the point. What comes to Zombie High, stays at Zombie High. I can't risk infecting anybody else. It's not worth it."

"But you're fine. Look at you. I mean, okay, we may need to get you some gift certificates to a tanning booth and a whole new wardrobe, maybe a makeover—or two, could be three, whatever—but, other than *that*, you're the old Molly. Why can't you leave?"

"I'm fine?" she snorts, looking back at me over her shoulder as her hand hovers near the door to Level Four. "I'm the old Molly? What, you didn't see me scarfing down half-a-dozen rat brains just now? How well is *that* going to go over when I bring a cage of lab rats to B-Lunch instead of a PB & J?"

She opens the door to the fourth floor and I say, "I thought Krill said the zombies were on the fifth floor."

"Yeah," she sighs. "The dead ones, the one's he's trying to turn into super-undead-killing machines. The ones who feed on actual humans. This is where *my* friends live."

Two things spring to mind as I follow her onto the fourth floor. One, there are zombies more dead than...other zombies? Two, I thought *I* was her friend.

Unlike the third floor of Zombie High, the fourth floor is a dizzying maze of tightly-packed hallways, dimly-lit but fairly clean. It's sterile, mostly, so no wonder Molly has to go one floor down for her daily rat fix.

Please, please, *please* say she only eats rat's brains once a day!

I see nothing and nobody, living *or* dead. I see scattered gurneys, and flickering soda machines and overturned laundry baskets and the occasional supply closet.

Then Molly creeps forward and says, softly, "Zombies, oh zombies, come out, come out wherever you are!"

I wait—we wait—and then, there, right...over...*there*. Movement, just a little at first. Then a lot.

Suddenly sheets and crumpled towels fall off of an overturned laundry cart as a young girl rises, giggling, a freckled hand over her pale lips as her faded orange pigtails bounce across her skeletal shoulders. A supply closet with a sticky door bangs open, revealing two skinny twins in matching purple track suits. A soda machine door opens and out walks a tall goof of a kid in pajamas.

They shuffle like Molly. They talk like Molly. They smile. Like Molly.

"Gang, meet Toby." She tugs me into the middle of the floor and shows me off as if I've just arrived at a keg party or something. "He's a friend from my Beforelife."

"*Beforelife?*" I ask as zombie hands reach out and flutter around my collar.

"Yeah," says the tall galoof from the soda machine, shoving my head to the left like the barber does when he's ready to take the clippers around my ear and doesn't want to drown in a bloodbath. "This is Molly's Afterlife. You were her Beforelife. We all have a Beforelife. It just doesn't always pop up in the middle of Zombie High."

I stand still, afraid I'll be devoured as the guy's giant, cold hands probe and pull my hoodie to this side, then the next. The twins join in, lifting up the T-shirt underneath and pressing cold fingers against the small of my back, then the sides of my stomach. Pigtail girl lifts up my sleeves until they won't go any higher, checking my forearms by turning them over and over again, like a chicken over a spit.

"Guys, relax," Molly says with her wry, post-rat-brain smile, using the cover of the still open soda machine door to change behind as she slips into black yoga pants and a pink hoodie she pulls from an overturned laundry cart. "Krill didn't get to him yet, honest."

"Are you sure?" ask the twins as one. They giggle after they ask it, reluctantly stepping away from probing my shoulder blades.

"I'm sure." She slips into pink and black running shoes over a pair of those black socks that only go up to your ankles. "I've been with him the whole time."

"What's with the getup?" I ask her, shrugging my shoulders so creepy tall guy will back.

The.

Hell.

Off!

She says, "I only wear the hospital gown when Krill's around. He doesn't know about this place."

I look at the fourth floor—all six-thousand square feet of it. "He doesn't know about an entire floor of his own hospital?"

"He knows," says the tall guy, shrugging like he's satisfied I'm not a "dead" zombie and finally backing away. "He just doesn't care. The money zombies are upstairs. That's all he really cares about."

I start to open my mouth and ask another dozen questions or so and Molly says, briskly, like she's not in the mood, "Uh-uh, Toby. No more. Thus endeth the lesson for today. For, well, forever. All you need to know is, in Zombie High, these are the only guys you can trust. Period.

"There's Dub here." She tugs on the tall guy's powder blue baggy pajama tops. "And Rosy and Posey," she adds, pointing to the twins, who curtsy as their names are called, "and finally good old Jazz. She's the youngest."

"You look familiar," I say to Jazz, whose red hair is in pigtails and whose freckles stand out against her milk pale nose.

"I should." She giggles. "You probably pass one of my 'Have You Seen This Girl?' billboards on the way to school every morning."

"That's it! You're that girl from Nashville who went missing on her class field trip. You were all over the news a few months back."

She gives me a little nod, sadly. "Yeah, well, that's the thing about getting too close to Zombie High. Sometimes you don't come back."

"Krill?" I ask.

She nods. "Even though he hasn't worked there in awhile, Dr. Krill still keeps an office at the University because of his *research*. Anyway, my AP Chemistry class was on a field trip and he was giving a presentation. He said he'd seen my project win at last year's regional science fair, wanted to talk to me about it after class. I thought I might get early entrance, you know, to the University if I sucked up to him.

"I told my chaperone I needed to use the ladies room, snuck up to Krill's office and he…bit me. Just like that! Sucker was waiting behind his door like some kind of…of…vampire, or something. He shoved me in his duffel bag and walked me right past my chaperone while the poor guy was complaining to a security guard that I wasn't on the bus with the rest of the kids. I stupidly hadn't told anybody I was going to see the good doctor, so nobody ever suspected him. Ever. Not even now, which is why you're still seeing my billboards all over town."

"Dr. Krill carried you in a duffel bag?"

"Hey!" She slugs me, hard. "I'm not *that* fat. At least…not anymore."

"I don't mean that, I mean I used to be neighbors with him for years. Guy could barely lift his car hood to check his oil. He used to ask my dad to do it for him. Suddenly, he's slinging live kids around like a lunch bag, is all. I just think it's weird."

Dub, the tall kid in the pajamas with the haunted eyes and giant, Gorgon hands, says, "He's doing something on the fifth floor, something that's making him stronger. More like us, but not like us. And not like *them*, either."

He says *them* like he's saying *pop quiz* on the last day of school before Christmas break.

"*Them*?" I ask, noting the sour look just mentioning *them* has left on his long, pale face.

Dub nods and, leaning in, like he's afraid to say it too loud, explains, "The *Feeders*."

Molly says, "Gang, listen. The time has come. Krill has turned the guards."

"All of them?" ask the twins at the same time, fiddling with the zippers of their purple track jackets nervously. "Even the cute ones?" they add at the same time.

At first, it seems like an accident, like when you're walking down the hall and someone's in your direct path and you zig to the left at the same time they zig to the left, and then they zag to the right just as you zag to the right and, eventually, one of you just has to say, "No, you go. I mean, you go. No, *you* go…"

But now I can see it's, like, their thing. And I can't tell if it's cute, or annoying, or if they did it in life or they're doing it because they're zombies or what. I suppose it shouldn't matter, but it does.

"Yes." Molly sighs, rolling her eyes at me as if it annoys her as well. "Even the cute ones. Were there even any cute ones? I must have higher standards than you two because they all looked like gross, big, fat rednecks to me."

"Not the one with the sideburns," whine the twins in unison, their voice sing-songy like they're kid actors in some really, really bad TV commercial for grape juice or something. "Or the tall one with the tattoos!"

Yeah, it's official: annoying.

"Any-whatever," Molly moans, "Krill has a bunch of townies downstairs, kids who went to Tinfoil High with me in my Beforelife, and he's picking them off one by one. We need to stop him and get Toby out of here."

"Can't we keep him?" ask the twins in their sing-songy way as they look at me, leaning in to each other like they're at some prepubescent rock concert or something. "He's a cute one!"

Okay, okay, so maybe the sing-songy thing isn't *that* annoying.

CHAPTER FIFTEEN

We split up, the twins going one way, Molly and I going the other, Dub reaching skyward and pulling himself up into the rafters via a moldy old ceiling tile and disappearing like a rat's tail as it slithers into the attic. The last thing I see are his slippers clinging tightly to his bony white ankles.

Jazz stays put, pacing in and out of the fourth floor stairwell just in case Krill or any of the Feeders are still one floor up.

"A cute one, huh?" Molly teases, patting my rear playfully to make sure I still have the sleek, shiny stun gun shoved deep into my back pocket as we walk slowly down the metal staircase.

"Do zombies have bad eyesight or something?" I take her lead as we push open the door to the second floor. "I mean, no one's ever actually called me a 'cute one' before, that's for sure."

"Actually, we have great vision. I can even see in the dark."

A few steps later she realizes that wasn't my point. "Toby, don't you know? You've always been a 'cute one.' You just try so hard to stay off the radar, you don't give any of the girls at school a chance to see the real you."

"I gave *you* a chance," I remind her, blushing slightly and wondering if she can see it with her super duper x-ray zombie vision.

"What, you mean 'after' Spud and I started going out? Real good timing there, Toby. Very nice of you. I can't imagine why I didn't respond once I had, you know, an actual boyfriend."

I snort, but stop her before opening another exam room door. "Molly, I don't care what you say. I'm not leaving here without you."

She looks back at me, eyes fierce with darkness. "Nice try, Toby, but for once, I've got you out-muscled, remember?"

"Say what you want, Molly. I made a promise to myself that I'd bring you home. I'm not breaking it."

"Yes, you are," she says resolutely, kicking in the door to the next examining room. It swings open to reveal a dark, empty cavern. I can't see anything. Suddenly, I hear a sharp intake of breath.

From the look on Molly's face, it's clear she hears it, too. We stand still, but then she smiles, hand reaching toward the light switch.

"Careful," I warn.

"It's not a zombie," she insists.

"How do you know?" I ask just as she flicks on the lights.

"Because zombies don't breathe, silly!"

She's right, and, then again, she's wrong. The "breathers" inside the room may not be official zombies, but they're as close to brain dead as one can get and still have a pulse. That's because Zack and Lilac are crouched in a corner, hiding behind a gurney.

See what I did there?

I say "hiding" but really they've just turned over the gurney and are poking their heads over, as if we can't see them even now when the lights are turned on. Zack looks peeved, like maybe we've caught him trying to get his mack on with his lady friend or something, but then I realize it's not that he's peeved so much as scared.

Scared of Molly.

I follow his intense eyes as he watches her, trying to see what he sees.

It's true, Zombie Molly is a lot more fear-inspiring than Beforelife Molly, who was pretty much afraid of her own shadow, never used anything other than cats as her profile pictures online and stuck mostly to pastel blues and pinks in the wardrobe department.

Her black hair was about the scariest thing on Molly. (Scary hot, that is.)

But Zack wouldn't know any of that about Molly because she wasn't a Lilac or a Haley or a bimbo or a tramp or sleaze or a skeeze. And now she's dead and Zack is looking at her like she's about to tear off his noggin and scoop out his half-brain.

"Relax," I say, but I'm only half-brave because Molly's standing next to me and—I think—she could easily tear Zack in half.

"I'm chill," he lies, looking anything but.

Next to him, Lilac's eyes are open and alert. I haven't seen her in awhile, and she's grimier than she was then but still pretty dang hot. She looks wired and wily and thin and scared and—

"Toby!" Lilac says, and I'm so happy she knows my name I barely hear what she says next.

"Look out!"

I turn just in time to see a hulking zombie in a bloody blue hospital gown, bloody fingers outstretched, white eyes hungry with fever and already licking his dry, cracked lips as he shuffles in from the hallway. Just before he grabs my ears for leverage and opens my skull like a juice box, I feel cold hands shoving me from behind.

I fly toward the gurney, where Zack and Lilac reach out and yank me behind the cold metal bars as if it's the kind of thing we do every day.

There is a pinching in my chest from where I hit the bars, and my ankle is at a funny angle. I know it's going to fall asleep if I don't move it soon, but I can't move it.

We watch, imprisoned, as Molly crouches low and viciously claws at the monster's knees. He swats her left shoulder with giant hands that look—and sound, and most certainly must feel—like they've been made out of concrete. She grunts a quick "ugghh" and flies to the side, landing against the tiled wall where dust from years-old grout puffs out around her head, scattering and smattering in her black hair as several tiles clatter to the floor around her.

I go to help her but Zack holds me back. He's not as strong as Molly, not by a long shot, but he doesn't need to be. "Don't," he says, sweat pouring from his lined forehead as his neck muscles strain to keep me behind the gurney. "You can't beat them."

"It's Molly." I grunt, scrambling through the bars like I saw Dub slip into the ceiling tiles moments earlier. He and Lilac hold me back as best they can, but they're not zombies so it still hurts when my sneaker snaps against their skin.

Grunting, I kick and claw and yank and pull and finally wedge myself through the gurney legs as the zombie stumbles toward Molly.

She is lying face down, but her black eyes are wide open. I see her wink and slide her hand slowly into the pocket of her pink hoodie. She pulls out a scalpel and turns, sitting up and slicing just in time to cut the zombie's thumb clear off.

There is no tearing or second try. There is only a slight "nick" sound and then thumb nothingness. He growls, but not in pain. He just watches, kind of detached, as the thumb bounces and rolls toward us as if it's happening to someone else.

I clatter on the other side of the gurney as the thumb rolls toward Lilac and she screams. The zombie looks her way as I scuttle away, something hard and metallic clattering to the floor behind me. I turn, look, and see the stun gun skittering away where it's fallen out of my back pocket.

I scramble as the zombie lurches, now thumbless, with Molly on his back. He makes a kind of clicking noise with his jaw, like maybe it's broken or twisted or something from Molly's earlier attack, and then tosses her far enough across the room that she lands atop the gurney.

Wow, I did *not* see that coming.

This whole time, I've been expecting Molly to protect me.

I mean, she's the local here. She's the one who understands these "Feeder" things. Heck, she outweighs me by sixty pounds!

Suddenly she is behind me, the zombie in front, the stun gun in my hand.

And.

Now.

I.

Am.

All.

Alone.

The zombie is huge. Seriously; try sewing Zack and Boner together, make them stand on an upperclassman's back as he kneels down before them, and you'll get about half what this dude is like as he towers over me, all big teeth and black eyes and vacant, empty, hungry stare.

He's not fast, but he's got a lot of momentum on his side and I hear Molly scrambling frantically behind me, so frantically I can tell she's not going to have time to save me.

No one is. Not this time.

Now, here's the thing. I've never actually been in a fight in my life. Been pummeled, plenty, been wedgied enough, been swirlied five thousand times but never.

Ever.

Ever.

Fought.

Back.

And now…this?

My first fight is going to be with an eight-foot-tall living dead cage fighter with a thigh for a neck and a tree trunk for a thigh?

I flick the stun gun behind my back, just to make sure it actually works. It does, really well, nearly lighting my butt hair on fire!

Hey, is it my fault these black jeans are all stretched out and droopy from running through Zombie High all night? *Or* that I've got a little hair…you know…back *there*?

The zombie comes, feet pounding on the tile floor like he's wearing

Frankenstein boots, and my heart is pounding, but I have to stop it. Now. Before it gets through me and tears Lilac and Zack, and maybe even Molly, limb from limb.

He reaches down, grabs the shoulder of my shirt, lifts me up and when my hands are in just about the right spot, I shove the stun gun into his throat. I have a lot of adrenaline so it goes deep into his neck, with those little shiny prongs on either side. I can feel them sizzling in his neck blood, or black goo, or whatever it is that runs through their dead, clogged veins.

I can smell the waft of raw hamburger and black charcoal and dead raccoon smell as he gurgles, spits—twice, right onto my forehead—and then drops like a stone.

The stun gun is wedged deep under his chin, and I won't let go of it, so I fall with him, fall *on* him, waiting for him to growl and tear off the left side of my face with his teeth because we're so close together but…nothing.

He's gone. Lights out.

I yank the stun gun prongs out of his throat where two holes, like from a vampire bite, remain in his dead, gray skin. They are singed around the edges, like I shoved giant firecrackers down his throat or something. Black sludge-blood oozes out slowly, like Halloween cookie dough from a tube.

He lays flat out, legs bent at an odd angle, one ankle twisted and blue, his hospital gown crumpled and twisted about his giant thighs. Standing up and looking down at him, I notice his head is shaven, his lips bruised, his nose pug and fat and wide.

He looks…young.

"Skyler," says Molly, not sadly. "He's only been here a week, but Krill's been working him hard. He's a Feeder, see?" She points to his teeth, which I suddenly notice are yellow and cracked and clearly visible through his open, gaping mouth. "His teeth are worn down."

"From what?" asks Lilac, creeping up behind us and smelling like bubble gum and fear.

"Gnawing on bones," Molly says simply, like she'd say "pass the salt" at the dinner table.

I give Lilac a quick side eye and see her shiver, looking behind her with an outstretched hand for Zack, who's still pale and damp with sweat. He doesn't reach back.

"*Whose* bones?" Zack asks, voice slightly trembling but trying not to stammer.

Molly turns, eyeing him skeptically. She's got a look on her face that says, *Oh, what, now that we're at Zombie High you wanna talk to me all of a sudden?*

She answers with a sneer, "Your bones, my bones, anyone's bones he can get his fat zombie hands on. That's what Feeders do; they feed. On anyone, or anything, anytime."

Zack sizes her up pretty quickly and sneers back, "You're one to talk."

I see Molly flinch a little, something only a friend would see because it happens in an instant and then it's gone. "We're different, Zack! He eats people, any people, all people. I don't. Ever!"

I want to defend her, to say something like, *She doesn't, Zack, I swear. I've seen her eat half-a-dozen rat brains in record time*, but somehow I don't think this would sound so good out loud—*or* do anything to help her case.

He looks down at the concrete gray zombie dead again on the tile floor and says, "He's not 'feeding' on anyone anymore."

She huffs in a know-it-all way. "He's just knocked out, for now. He won't stay that way. Unless I do *this*."

With a crunch, without even flinching, she steps square on his throat. Once, twice, three times.

The sound is menacing, like snapping a plastic fork in half; over and over and over again.

Lilac retches, and pukes a clear stream of bourbon and gum juice into the nearest corner. I want to help her, hold her hair, pat her back, do all of those boyfriend things since her actual boyfriend isn't even doing them. He's watching Molly using her scalpel to slice off the rest of Zombie Skyler's head.

There is no blood. Not really.

There just this kind of thick, slow, blackish, goo-ish stuff that oozes rather than gushes, like when you cut into a jelly donut—you know, from *hell*.

How do you cut off a guy's head and there not be blood?

Before Lilac can turn back around and puke some more, I drag the sheet off the hospital gurney and slip it over Skyler's headless, bloodless body.

Molly nods but Zack looks vaguely disappointed. Lilac stumbles over on wobbly legs that are only slightly more flesh-colored than the zombie's sticking out from beneath the too-small sheet.

She says, "Nice being a boyfriend, Zack."

He growls, "Toughen up," without even looking at her and inches toward Molly, asking her, "Where do I get a knife like that?"

CHAPTER SIXTEEN

Zack looks stupid, taking scalpel lessons from Molly. Lilac looks scared but unwilling to take comfort in my arms. The zombie lies, bloodless, headless, at our feet.

I feel anxious, squirrely, claustrophobic, like even as big as Zombie High is, it's not big enough to contain me. "This is stupid," I say.

Zack thinks I'm talking about him—but I only am a little—and gives me a dirty look, waving Molly's scalpel menacingly. "No, *this* is stupid," he scolds. "Hunting these clowns down one by one is stupid. It's amateurish, something they'd do in some B-movie on late-night TV."

Molly kind of nods, and gives me the stink eye. "What would *you* suggest, zombie killer?"

"I would suggest going to the source. I mean, if we find Krill and trap him, then won't his zombies or Feeders or whatever, come to him?"

Molly bites her lip, nodding. "They'd have to. He's the one who feeds them twice a day."

"I don't even want to know," Lilac croaks, fixing her makeup with a fake jewel-covered compact her mom probably gave her as a stocking stuffer two Christmases ago.

"I'm serious," I urge, pacing the room, careful to avoid dead zombie Feeder guy. "If we had Krill, say, tied up somewhere, they'd sniff him out. If he didn't feed them, they'd feed on him. Then, when they all show up, we can kill them, re-kill them, whatever, all at the same time. Right?"

Molly looks smugly satisfied at the thought. Lilac just looks nauseated.

Chapter Seventeen

We split up again. Molly and Zack going one way, Lilac and I the other.

If we were in Chem Lab back at school and I was paired with her, I'd be stoked right about now. Instead, I'm just scared and tired and sweaty and rank and sure she's going to get us killed.

The plan is to sneak up to the fifth floor and sniff Krill out. Molly thinks most of the Feeders should be out on the prowl, looking for us, leaving the fifth floor mostly deserted.

"I can't believe he did that." Lilac fumes as we approach the stairwell. I've been trying to get her to stay quiet this whole time. It's not working.

Then I see a bent and broken gurney, smashed on its side, an empty shoe beside it. "Come here," I say.

"We're supposed to get to the top at the same time as they do."

"I've seen Molly walk. She's slower than we are. We'll catch up, easy."

"She your girlfriend or something?" she asks as I hunker over the gurney, twisting one of the metal bars at the bottom this way and that so it will break off.

"I wish," I blurt.

She says, without thinking, without mercy, "I think she's into Zack."

I say, without filtering, "You think *everyone's* into Zack."

She starts to say something mean, and then snorts. "I guess you're right," she admits. Then, a couple seconds later, "Well, he is the hottest guy in school."

I roll my eyes and grunt as the bar starts to heat up at the joint where I'm hoping it will break any second now. "Molly was never into hot guys," I say.

Now it's Lilac's turn to grunt. "Maybe that's what she told you, Toby, but trust me. All girls are into hot guys."

"Yeah, well, not Molly."

Lilac doesn't miss a trick. "So, maybe there's hope for you two yet."

That's when I finally yank the bar off, feel its weight, deem it suitable and hand it to Lilac.

"What's this for?" she asks.

"If you see any zombies, stick that in their ear."

"Which ear?" She holds the broken bar out away from her body with two fingers like she's carrying a dead fish or something.

"The one that leads to his brain," I joke, forgetting I'm not with Molly or even Spud, who get my humor and who I don't have to explain every second word to. I hear silence and know even before I turn back around that she'll have that blank, soul-dead look on her face. Sure enough, when I do, there it is.

"I'm kidding." I open the stairwell door for her. "Just…any ear. Either one will do."

The stairwell is dark and dank and dripping, just like you'd imagine a stairwell in Zombie High might be.

Every few steps she says, "Gross." Each time she says it, I like her less and less.

I never thought I could hate a girl—any girl, but especially a hot girl—so terribly, horribly, epically much. Her "gross" annoys me, her chomping gum annoys me, the way she won't lift up her feet and just kind of shuffles along like a slug with a maroon bra annoys me.

By the time we reach the fifth floor, I can kind of see why Zack might not have rushed to her aid when she puked in the corner back there in that examining room with the dead Feeder.

Heck, by the time we reach the fifth foor, I'm surprised Zack didn't feed her to Skyler before I could zap him! She steps on something gooey. I hear it even from two stairs up.

This is her worst "Gross" yet!

"Where do you think we are?" I snap just before we reach the top of the stairs, turning around and looking down on her like I might kick out and send her spiraling back to the next level. "It's Zombie High, Lilac. Of course it's *gross!*"

She gives me major stink eye and lip curl and hair twist and bubble gum teeth and sighs. "What's *your* problem?"

"My problem is we could die, at any minute. That huge ass zombie down there? If I didn't have this stupid stun gun, we'd be dead right now. All of us, Molly included. I'm scared, I have a headache, my back hurts, I need to pee like crazy, I could use a double cheeseburger or two and all you can say is 'gross' every five minutes?"

"It *is* gross," she says, missing the point—missing all of it, everything I said—completely.

I inch closer to her half-cute, half-fugly face. "You know who you are, Lilac? You're the girl in the scary movie who dies. Not right away, because you're kind of cute, not in any spectacular way, because you're not the star, but you die. In every horror movie.

"You know why?" I ask before she can stop me. "Because you're clueless. You don't get that there is danger all around us. You don't get that any minute, this door could fly open, a zombie could reach out, bite you and…and…that's that. That's all it takes, Lilac. One bite and—"

"You're wrong." She backs away from me.

I'm being stupid now, and cocky, and half-brave because of the stun gun and what it did to Skyler, and think she's backpedaling because she's scared. Of me.

"I'm not wrong, Lilac!"

She is one step down from me, then two, and I keep coming, ignoring the sound of the door behind me, the shuffling—until it's too late.

"You *are* wrong, Toby," she spits, face full on fugly now and full of rage as she keeps backing down the stairs. "I'm going to live. I'm going to survive." Her voice is shrill, catty and high like I've heard her use when she fights with Zack in the middle of the commons because he tweaked some girl's butt or stared at some girl's rack too long for her taste. "Know why, *Toby*? Because it's *your* turn to die first, smart guy!"

I feel hands on me, on my back, on my shoulders, and I turn just in time to see Haley with her mouth open, jaw cracked, teeth jagged, leering my way with blank, dead eyes as if we'd never met.

I feel her teeth tear into my shoulder, harder than she needs to, and I hear Lilac's dry, remorseless laughter as she stumbles down the steps, running away; from me, from Haley, from danger, from helping me, from…saving me.

Laughing, laughing, and over the sound of Haley crunching, gnawing, on me—on me!—I shout after her, "I'll get you, Lilac. If it's the last thing I do, ever, I will find you. And I will eat you!"

The chewing stops, my shoulder gushes and a voice behind me says, "I doubt that very much, Toby."

Then the lights go out.

CHAPTER EIGHTEEN

I am strapped to a gurney, covered in my own filth. Just…you don't need to know what kind. Just imagine any kind of filth, dry, wet, gooey, caked on, still dripping, whatever…and I'm covered in it.

My head is pounding, my mouth is dry and Spud is talking to his dad, begging with him, "Dad, it's Toby. Please, don't do this!"

"It's already done," says Krill. "If you didn't want this to happen to Toby, then son, why on earth did you bring him here?"

"I thought," stammers Spud, looking down at me with emotionless eyes. "I thought if he saw Molly, if he saw what you're doing here, if you could control yourself, I thought he could…help…somehow."

Krill laughs a chortle so cold, it chills even *my* dead body.

Spud looks at me, helpless now, a boy afraid of his dad, a boy afraid of what he's done; a boy afraid of his own shadow. I know the feeling; or, at least, I did.

Once upon a time.

Krill smiles, fiddling with something around my waist. "Toby?" he asks, in that plastered on smile way phonies always use when they're standing at the front door trying to sell you a vacuum cleaner or set of encyclopedias. "I'm going to take this scalpel and make a small incision near your belly button."

"Please don't," I say, but I'm not begging. I'm just…arguing. Like you would with the traffic cop when you just parked in front of the hydrant to grab a quick coffee and you're too late for school to go around back and find a spot for yourself.

"It won't be a very big one," he goes on, calmly, as if I haven't even spoken. "Maybe an inch, maybe two."

"Why?" I croak, hardly recognizing my own voice. "Why would you do that?"

His phony smile disappears, replaced immediately with one full of snarl, spittle and teeth. "Because I can," he purrs, smile-free.

He grunts a little, like maybe he didn't just make a small incision but stabbed the thing in instead. I hear something, like metal on flesh, but the real proof is in Spud's face. It grows pale. He blanches and looks away.

I can't feel anything.

Nothing. Not even a little.

Is that one of the "perks" Molly forgot to tell me about?

"Say when," I taunt, just because Krill is pissing me off so much. I hear another grunt, but...then nothing else.

"So," he says, almost gleefully, like he's telling me something I don't know from a steady, six-year diet of nonstop zombie movies, "reanimation is complete. No respiration, no pulse, no blood flow and, finally, no feeling."

I nod and mutter, "Awesome."

Spud offers a weak smile as I twitch my fingers beneath the leather straps holding me to the thin gurney.

"Now," Krill offers, and I hear the low whine of some kind of radio feedback, "this is your remote control."

"Awesome," I crack because, hey, I'm dead. Why not? "You made me a robot, too?"

He frowns, starts to lecture, then thinks better and offers instead, "Actually, yes. The electric grid around your waist will—"

"*Hold* on," I sputter. "Hold *up*! Electric grid? Waist? I'm wearing...zombie panties?"

Krill smiles. "Is that what the kids are calling them these days? That's a little...derogatory for my tastes but, if you wish, yes. You have been fitted with a pair of 'zombie panties.' One of only three in existence so, whatever you do, be careful, will you?"

He chuckles, as if his plans for me involve anything *but* being careful.

And I think to myself, *Okay, well, I can't feel anything, so...what's the big deal?*

Then he says, "I can see by the look on your face that you see no threat in these—what did you call them, Toby? Oh, yes, Zombie panties. Well, while you may not have been able to feel my scalpel in your stomach, or when Spud here dropped you on your head when he was trying to strap you to that gurney, you—"

"Spud!" I say, because in addition to having the biggest headache of my life I am in that stage of the Afterlife where you're still more alive than dead.

At least, that's what it feels like to me.

Spud says, as if he's just spilled nacho cheese on my mom's new carpet the first movie into a six-hour mega-Godzilla-marathon, "Sorry, Toby!"

Krill gives his son major WTF? face. "Be that as it may, Toby, I assure you that even the deadest zombie can feel electricity. You might say, other than decapitation, of course, it's their *only* weakness. So, the shock you'll receive will be mild, but I assure you, it *will* be torturous—"

My snort of disbelief interrupts his grand soliloquy. Krill doesn't like that. He stops talking, lifts the little clicker in his hand—it's about the size of Mom's electronic car key—and clicks it. Twice.

There is nothing, for a second. Not even a noise. I don't know what I was expecting. A buzz or something maybe. Then…then…my teeth click together. I *hear* them click together, then watch a piece of one of them ricochet off my bottom lip and veer off in Spud's direction. My body clenches. All of it, every inch of muscle, of flab, of eyelid and kneecap. I go rigid, watching the leather straps strain against my bare, white chest.

I feel a sizzle, yes, I feel it, hot like the scalpel I couldn't feel only it rips open every vein, splits my skin, sizzles my eyeballs and breaks my eardrums. It sizzles and crackles through my body, every inch of it, every cell exploding, ruining them all, ruining me as my body bucks and shivers and shakes, and whatever filth I hadn't been covered in yet, I suddenly expel.

Spud turns his head, Krill smiles and, at last, with steam rising from between my legs, he clicks the remote control twice. "Just so we're clear, Toby. You're mine now, understand?"

I nod, willingly, eagerly. Whatever, just don't shock me anymore! I would do anything for him—anything— not to feel that again.

But it's not enough. He does it again—just to prove he can. Two more clicks and my teeth clamp together, a bit of tongue goes flying and the sizzling starts all over again. It's like flame dipped in gasoline and smeared into every crack and crevice of my spine, like nothing I've ever felt, like the burn and the scarring are instant, at the same time, over and over again. There is nothing to sweat, nothing to pee, nothing to spit or crap out anymore.

I am a dry husk, withering, crackling, spitting, wrenching, like a pig on a spit only…

The.

Fire.

Never.

Ends.

Until it does. And it does, eventually.

My body unclenches itself, the leather strap around my chest quits straining in its leathery, creaky way and, at last, I let my back ease down onto the gurney.

"Just so we're clear," Krill reiterates, "your loyalty is to me now. Not Molly, not to Spud here, certainly not to the brutes you brought in here with you, not even with the other Feeders. You belong to me, and you will tell the zombies you've found me, lead them back here and then your work will be done, yes?"

He's so certain I'm on board, and I am, too. Until…until I look at Spud.

And Spud is looking at me like, *How could you?*

And I shouldn't care, because…I'm dead. And Molly's dead, and Spud brought us both here. To kill us, to offer us up to his dad, I suppose.

But…but…it's still Spud.

And he's still alive and…and…he's all I have.

Krill keeps talking, and I look at Spud and, when Krill's not looking, I wink.

It hurts, to wink, like my eyelids are still burning from the zombie panties but he sees it and smiles.

At least something in this hellish nightmare place smiles!

Krill's voice grates, but I have my eyes on the prize. The stun gun knocked Skyler Zombie out. Why?

Electricity.

Whatever it is about power, volts, it does something to the zombies.

To Skyler. To me.

Whatever Krill has been doing on the fifth floor all these months, he's got some zombie in him. Maybe he's not a Feeder, maybe he's not even as doomed as Molly or me, but a dweeb like him doesn't just toss around high school freshmen in duffel bags and flip dudes like Boner clear across the room if he hasn't been dipping into the zombie Fountain of Youth a little, know what I mean?

CHAPTER NINETEEN

"**I** know where they're going," I grunt as Krill makes final adjustments to the zombie panties.

I prefer "zombie boxers," actually.

"Where?" he growls, and the way he says it—so entitled, so smart, so final—something in me wants to rip his face off right then and there, but I stop myself.

Somehow.

"The spa," I say, suddenly inspired and cobbling together every bad movie plot I can remember in my sizzling zombie brain. "That spa room downstairs. They know it's the closest room to the main exit, that the stairwells aren't safe, that the only place they can hide is in the ceiling. Molly has the blueprints. She found them in the basement, and…and…she's leading them there, so they can all escape."

Krill smiles a generic bad guy smile. "See that, Spud? Your friend here isn't as strong as you thought."

Krill may have bought it, but Spud hasn't. All he has to do is keep his mouth shut until I can get Krill close enough to that Jacuzzi tub to grab him and jump in with him, electrocuting us both and, well, just that. Killing us both.

"Now, then." Krill looks down at me with disgust written all over his plump, shiny face. "Let's let Spud clean you up and I, young man, will ready the Feeders for the feast of all time!"

Krill shuffles away, ambling on the soft soles of his black sneakers while Spud looks down at me and says—aware his Dad is still in the room, at least, for now—"You know you crapped yourself, right?"

I look at Krill. Spud looks at Krill. Krill, at the door, turns back and chuckles, then he walks out of the lab and off to find his precious fifth floor Feeders.

"Can you clean yourself?" Spud asks.

"I should make *you*," I threaten as he unbuckles the leather straps at my neck, my chest, my thighs, then finally my ankles.

"Yeah," Spud says, "you probably should."

I try to sit up, but it's harder than I thought. He smirks and says, "Here, I'll help you anyway."

His hands are warm on my back. Not just clammy, but Jacuzzi-tub hot. It's clear from the pained expression on his face that my back is as cold as his hands are hot. I look down to see a brown and yellow smear midway up the gurney.

"Uggh," I say.

"Gross, huh?" He waves his hand in front of his nose.

"No, I mean…those." And I point at the zombie panties. They are tan, and small, but thick, with thin red stripes running from side to side and no matter how hard I try to yank them off, they stay put; probably that "electric grid" Dr. Krill was talking about. They look antique and painful, like something an astronaut might wear under his shiny silver jumpsuit on his way to the moon circa 1963.

"What are those red stripes?" I ask Spud as he helps slide me off the gurney. My legs are unsteady but strong. I can tell they're strong, just standing there; strong and heavy and solid.

"Electrodes?" Spud says uncertainly. "I guess?"

He shoves the gurney as far away as he can and I say, "How come it didn't short out when I…you know…messed myself?"

Spud shrugs. "Don't you feel that draft on your backside?"

"Spud," I sigh as he leads me to a sink fixed to the far wall. "I don't feel anything. I'm a zombie now, remember?"

"Oh yeah, well, here's the thing. They're not really zombie *panties*, Toby. They're more like a zombie *jock strap*."

CHAPTER TWENTY

Spud has found me a pair of red boxer shorts and a windbreaker to put on over the zombie jock strap. The windbreaker is the kind a volleyball coach might wear. Thin and light blue.

"Spud," I say, looking at my death pallor and ridiculous red boxers in the water stained mirror. "Come on, I know I'm dead but...seriously?"

"They're from the lost and found box, Toby," he whines. "What do you want? An Old Navy gift card?"

"No, but..."

Spud cuts me off, looking over his shoulder as if Krill might already be at the door. "Besides, Dad doesn't want a ton of clothes surrounding your zombie jock strap. He has to make sure there's an unrestricted flow, so...boxers it is."

I nod, but I've got bigger fish to fry. At least he's given me good sneakers from the Lost and Found, even if there were no socks to be had.

Spud is still dressed in black, while my zombie skin is damp with sink water and generic soap from an old school dispenser screwed into the wall, the kind with a bulb on top where you tap the bottom and too much soap always comes out.

It smells good, and I keep sniffing. Spud says, on the way to the lab door, "Dad says the zombies can smell better, even see better, with the rest of their senses turned off. You smelling anything?"

I look at the soiled gurney near the exit and shake my head. It feels like I'm leaving the last of me behind as we walk out into the hall, but I can't feel anything. And I don't just mean a hot scalpel in my belly.

I mean anything; inside or out.

The hall is desolate and empty, and I urge Spud to slow down. "I can't walk so fast." I whine a little, my eyes roving the walls for something sharp, or long, or strong.

"Oh, yeah." He snorts like he hangs out here all the time. "I forgot you zombies can't walk so fast anymore."

He slows down on the last few words, like he suddenly remembers he's *not* talking to the everyday Feeders roaming his dad's halls. "Sorry, Toby." I put a hand on his shoulder and turn him around. "Spud, it's all right. It's not you, dude. It's your dad. You know that right? That he's…evil?"

"He's trying to fix something, Toby," he starts, avoiding my eyes.

I feel strong, in the bones, heavy, in the limbs. I kind of bully him against the wall, where a grimy window lets in the floodlights from the empty guard towers five floors down. "What, Spud? To build some super army of zombies? That's comic book crap, and you and I both know it."

"It's not," Spud fights back, at least with his voice, if not with his eyes. "It's happening, right now. Look at you, Toby. You're a machine, tough and cold, can't feel a scalpel in your belly button. I could dunk you in a pool and leave you at the bottom all night and you wouldn't even make a bubble. You, the rest of the Feeders, you're—"

"I'm *not* a Feeder, Spud." I shove him back against the wall with one pale, cold finger. "Take it back."

"You're *all* Feeders, Toby," he scoffs, looking away even as I inch forward menacingly. "Everyone dad makes is a Feeder."

I cock my head. "You don't get it, do you? While you were helping Daddy clean up his lab, Bones and Haley, Zack and Lilac, Molly and I were fighting off zombies. Not all of us won, okay? Haley did this to me, Spud, not your dad. So…you keep that Feeder talk to yourself. I'll never eat a person. *Never*!"

He scoffs, like maybe he doesn't believe me. "You will when you're hungry, Toby. They all do."

"Molly doesn't," I counter, watching his eyes grow two inches at the mere mention of his ex-girlfriend's name.

"She…doesn't?" he asks suspiciously, like maybe I'm setting some kind of trap.

I shake my head, pushing him again, back into the window until he has nowhere left to go. "Why'd you do it, Spud? To Molly? Why'd you bring her here, knowing what your dad was up to?"

He opens his mouth and I push him again, harder than ever. "If you lie to me, Spud, I'll break my promise in two seconds. I *will* eat someone, starting with *you*!"

I don't think he believes me, not completely, but I think he wants to tell me just the same. "I thought," he sputters, "I thought Dad had figured it out already, a way to make them more human. He kind of has, I mean, he's getting close but…he lied. To me. To Molly."

"*You* lied to Molly," I point out.

"Okay, yeah, I tricked her into coming home with me that day. There was never going to be any Fall Formal for us, but…the real reason was I wanted her to stay with me. To *have* to stay with me. I wanted Dad to bite us both, to turn us both, and that way we could be together forever."

"Spud, she's your first girlfriend. You really want to spend eternity with your first-ever girlfriend?"

He shakes his head. "It's a moot point, anyway, I guess. He wouldn't do it, at least not to me."

"You're not…" I ask, without really asking.

He shakes his head. "I've asked every zombie here, every Feeder, even Molly, and no one will turn me. You know that little experiment Dad did back there with the clicker? He does it to all his 'kids,' as he calls them. Puts the zombie panties on and shocks them until they're afraid of him, Toby, until they're…his. So now they won't bite me, no matter how hard I try."

I nod, and he reaches out a warm hand against my jacket sleeve.

"Will you, Toby? Will you bite me? I hate being the weakest one here. I'm the only human, Toby. The only non-zombie in Zombie High. I can't *stand* it."

"Poor Spud!" I snap, inching away in case I lose it and toss him through the window after all. "Can't stand being human. At least you *have* a choice. Does Molly have a choice? Did I? No. That's why Molly won't bite you. Not because she's scared of your dad's electric jock strap. She *hates* you. She wants you to be weak, and human, and frail and, you know what? So do I!"

I leave him there, alone, on the fifth floor. The Feeder Floor.

He calls after me, twice. Just twice.

Then he gives up, or I stop listening. Either way, the only sound I hear in the stairwell is silence. And breathing, just a little.

But I know it can't be mine.

Chapter Twenty-one

"Zack?"

He is hovering, in a corner, like maybe I can't see him crouched there against the wall, knees pressed tight against his chest, arms crossed tightly over his knees.

"Get up, clown. You look stupid crouched over like that."

He looks around, like maybe he can't see me. "Who is that?"

I step forward, borrowed sneakers crunching on broken glass. "Dude, it's Toby!"

"H-h-how can you see me?" he asks, not budging. "I broke all the bulbs in here, to hide."

"It's, like, bright as the sun in here." I see every dead cockroach on the stairwell, every drop of sweat on Zack's forehead.

And the metal bar in his hand.

He raises it up, in front of him. "She told me you could see in the dark. I didn't believe her, though."

"Who told you?" I ask, sneering. "Lilac?"

"Lilac? What? How would *she* know that? No, Molly."

"Where *is* Molly?"

He stands up, squinting, looking feral and ugly in the bright yellow stairwell light. "She said she wanted to check on her friends," he explains, inching back against the wall.

"And you *let* her?" I ask, raising my voice.

It echoes through the halls and he puts his fingers, his trembling fingers, against his lips. "Shut up! They'll *hear* you."

"Who will hear me?"

"The Feeders, dude. And Haley. She's one of them now."

I look around, behind him, and take a step away. "Where's Lilac?"

He frowns. "That little witch? Who knows? Probably on the fourth floor being chowed on by Haley and the rest of the Feeders, for all I—hey, what are you—"

I pick Zack up, off his feet, and hang on tight. He punches and shoves and kicks but it doesn't hurt. Doesn't even tickle. I shake him, rag-doll style, and toss him down the metal stairs.

He lands on his ankle, and I hear a crunch. He whimpers, and I can smell the fear on him now, thick and musty in this little stairwell. "You suck, Zack. She came with you. You're supposed to protect her."

"Screw her," he says, mock macho. "And screw you. You think you're so tough, a badass zombie who can see in the dark and toss *real* men around? Good luck with Haley, bro. She'll eat you for—"

I kick his face in before he can finish and leave him behind as I trudge to the fourth floor.

I can hear him bleeding the whole way there.

Chapter Twenty-two

Haley has a brick in her hand and is using it to pound one of the Feeders into bone and dust.

She sniffs me the minute I'm out of the stairwell, and drops the brick, running at me with her mouth wide open.It's covered in gore. Her eyes are wild and black and her pleather jacket is torn in three places, jaggedly so. I can see her running the entire way. It's like she's coming in slow motion or something.

I steady myself, stand still and wait until she's just a foot or two away. Then I lift up my foot and kick her square in the stomach.

She stops, doubles over, and I hear her teeth clacking as she tries to tear a chunk out of my knee.

While she's doubled over I take my elbow and crash it down between the back of her shoulder blades. It's something Spud and I used to watch on those wrestling shows, before they got lamer—and faker.

She squats onto the ground, but is feral and wild and keeps clawing at me. No matter what I do, or how hard I hit her, she just…

Keeps.

Coming.

I punch her. She laughs. I kick her. She chuckles.

Her eyes are more alive now than she ever was, but they're only alive with one thing: hunger. She comes at me, face forward, teeth clacking, tongue roving, eyes wide, nostrils wider. Her hair is matted with dirt and sweat and blood, and I yank a big chunk of it to the side. She follows until it falls out, a clump of her scalp coming away with it.

She lunges, and I manage to land a punch square in her throat. Even I can hear her voice box crack. She sputters and coughs, backing away for just a moment. Then she straightens, as if to charge. Instead, she stops, sniffing the darkness like there's someone—or something—there I can't quite sense yet.

As if on cue, Molly steps from the darkness, the flare gun from a first aid kit in her hand and, ignoring Haley and her high-pitched keening, says, "She's eaten, Toby; she's eaten of the flesh. That makes her a Feeder, and she'll never, ever be right again."

She fires and the flare knocks Haley onto the ground as it wedges about two inches into her belly. Her soft, fleshy belly. It sizzles and burns, glowing red inside her stomach until I can see the veins and organs inside catch on fire like a hot dog that's fallen between the grill grates and landed on the hot coals below.

She screams, but only in rage, reaching out to yank Molly down until the end. When she's done and the girl is cinders, the room full of soot, Molly finally has a chance to look me up and down. "What *happened* to you?"

A voice from out of the darkness says, "I happened to him, Molly. And now, I'm happening to you."

Molly hisses—*hisses!*—but before she can lunge Krill is on her, shocking her into submission with some giant cattle prod thingy that sizzles at the end. As she slumps to the floor, I turn and skitter just out of range. Of the cattle prod, that is.

He drops it to the floor and I smile, thinking maybe he's still buying my "goodie-goodie" act. Then he yanks out the clicker.

Before I can say *Please don't sizzle my eyeballs* he clicks it and…out go the lights. Again.

CHAPTER TWENTY-THREE

The minute we come to I know that's it. We're cooked.

There will be no jacuzzi tub retribution, no shocking conclusion, no dramatic finale, no Krill getting electrocuted, no horror movie finale where the good guy—is that still me?—has his day.

Molly and I watch through the downstairs break room window as Krill loads his shiny silver briefcase full of super special zombie serum into a military Jeep.

He straps it in, six ways to Sunday, and only when he's sure it won't fly off at the first hairpin turn, he peels out, punching through one of the joints in the guard fence and tooling down the road.

It's Molly who points out, "What, he didn't have room for Spud?"

I look at her, getting a little side boobage action with the way her hands are chained to the ceiling, arms drawn high over her head so that she stands, like me, mostly on tippy-toe.

She sees me looking and huffs. "Better enjoy it while you can, horn dog. It's the last side boob *you're* going to see for awhile."

The break room is empty, for now, the door locked. But not for long.

Already we can hear the Feeders overhead, clamoring, dozens of feet scrambling as the smell of fresh meat through the thin ceiling tiles above our heads lures them. For zombies, we must be pretty weak. The chains aren't even that thick, but we're still flesh and blood and no amount of twisting and turning or yanking will set us free.

"What'll they do, do you think?" I ask as the clamoring above shifts toward the far stairwell.

"Um, well, they'll start with our feet, like truffle pigs, and eat their way up until there's nothing but wrist bones and chain."

"Nice visual," I say. "At least it won't hurt."

"No." She sighs. "There's that, but…I *was* kind of looking forward to seeing what the Afterlife was all about."

"I'll miss your friends," I say quietly.

"I hope they get out," she says, more quietly.

By now we can hear the horde tumbling down the metal stairwells. Only one or two floors left from the sounds of it.

"I thought you didn't want any of them getting out."

She shrugs. "That was when I still gave a shit about what happens to the world."

I nod, smirking. "I never knew you were such a badass, Molly."

She looks me up and down. "You know, since we're going to die—again—I might as well tell you, I only went out with Spud because he asked me first."

"Really?"

"Yeah, I waited and waited, but you never manned up and took the plunge. I wanted you to, always playing with my hair in class, sassing you, acting all cool and aloof, but…you were too shy."

"I *am* shy."

"Yeah, and, well, now you'll never get with this."

I chuckle, thinking what might have happened if I'd asked Molly to the Fall Formal instead of Spud. But Spud wanted it so bad, and Spud never got anything he wanted and…I hope she understands.

I could tell her about Spud and wanting and never getting and what it's like to be a short guy who wears pants with a dozen pockets and twice as many buttons and weighs less than most third graders but…what's the point now? Better to keep it light, right up until the end.

"Can zombies…you know?" I ask, nudging her side boob with my windbreaker.

She smiles. "What? Get with each other? I don't know. I never had time to try."

"Shame," I say, like I'm some kind of cool or something, and she chuckles, knowing I never will be but kind of liking me anyway.

Now, the door is moving, in and out, as the zombies try to get inside.

"Doesn't sound like many of them," she says.

"Yeah, I thought there'd be more, the way Krill described it."

She winces at Krill's name.

The doors burst open and I wince, but it's only Dub and Jazz.

"Dub!" shouts Molly, twisting in their general direction as her two zombie friends wedge the door shut and slide tables and chairs against it.

"Jazz!"

"Where are the twins?" I ask, figuring at least if they were around someone would call me "cute" before I die.

Dub and Jazz turn, blood-smeared and looking worse for the wear. "They're in the motor pool, trying to hotwire one of those trucks the Army left behind when they bolted out of here last month."

For an instant I feel a flash of hope, then the doors start jangling again.

And if Dub and Jazz are in here, and the twins are trying to hotwire big rigs in the motor pool then…that only leaves the bad guys out in the hall.

"Go!" Molly spits, indicating the windows on either side of us. "Run, now, before it's too late."

"Screw that," says Dub, putting his weight—or lack thereof—into the door. It's like Boner and Zack all over again, and look how well *that* turned out.

"We didn't come here to escape, Molly," says Jazz, pigtails dangling as she crouches low and puts her back into it. "We're here for the rescue!"

CHAPTER TWENTY-FOUR

Some rescue!

The door gives shortly after, cracking open ever so slightly.

Dub and Jazz quickly retreat as the horde swells in size so quickly the Feeders have a hard time elbowing each other out of the way to get first crack at us.

Molly's zombie friends circle around us protectively, Dub hoisting an axe handle—with no top, which I kinda think might have been helpful if he'd left it on for once—and Jazz with a butcher knife she must have gotten from somewhere along the way. I'm thinking, maybe...the kitchen? But what do I know and, frankly, what does it matter now?

Unless it came with a complimentary team of trained zombie killing assassin ninja *sous* chefs, it's not going to do us much good now anyway.

The Feeder arms poke in first, gray and large and angry, shoving aside the break room chairs and reaching for the inside doorknob and, when that fails, shoving through anyway.

The room isn't very big, but it seems to shrink even more as the first of the Feeders finally breaks through, more green than gray, rotted flesh stuck between his yellow chompers.

Molly tenses at my side, arms helplessly over her head with her teeth gritted resolutely, but Dub smacks him down with the axe handle at the last minute. There is a huge thumping "whack" in the middle of his skull and down he goes.

Two more Feeders filter in through the break room door after that, shuffling toward us on bare, gray feet. Dub gets one under the chin with a stomach turning *crack-crunch*.

Jazz gets the other with a butcher knife through the eyeball, but even as they're celebrating, I can see it's a lost cause. I mean, seriously, how long can they keep it up? And how many are out there to make them try?

We're about to get our answer.

The door is sagging inward with the weight of the Feeders outside, like when you're blowing up a balloon and know it's going to pop with your next breath. Dozens of them are out there, hundreds, maybe.

They file in, one by one, shoving each other out of the way to line up single file, but that must be too slow from them. From the spa room next door, we can hear them banging on the wall to try to get in from a different angle.

The cinderblocks shake, dust scatters the floor, and Molly says, "Eager bunch, aren't they?"

She's trying to be tough, but I have a feeling she'd reach out and hold my hand right now if she could reach it. Four Feeders surround us, green and gray, hungry and bloody.

Some wear regular clothes, T-shirts that are too small or denim shorts that are too big. Others wear pajamas, like Dub. The rest wear generic hospital gowns, torn at the hems and covered in gore.

Molly kicks out from the table we're standing on. The Feeders inch back.

I kick, too, but it's no use. One chomps on Dub's shoulder until he can wedge him off with the axe handle, setting free a few teeth in the process.

The tear in Dub's shoulder looks bad, bloodless and raw, clear down to the shoulder blade.

Meanwhile another Feeder tries to drag Jazz out into the hall with her. Jazz manages to fend her off by slicing off her hand with the butcher knife, but by now the hole in the wall next door is getting bigger every second. Any minute now the Feeders on the other side will break through the wall and that will be that. A fresh stream of flesh-hungry zombies will have unrestricted access to our arms and legs—and everything in between.

It will really be Feeder Central then. Feeders from the front, Feeders from the side. The only thing missing is a few Feeders climbing in through the windows at our backs!

A hammer pokes through a falling cinder block, and Dub looks up at us. "Since when did the Feeders start using *tools*?"

"They didn't," I grunt, seeing a familiar face poke through the hole as a fresh chunk of crumbling cinder block tumbles onto our side of the wall.

"Spud!" cries Molly as he finally makes a hole big enough to climb through.

"Dub," he cries, ignoring us and our obvious predicament. "Help me with this Jacuzzi tub!"

I have a glimmer of hope as he retreats, a funny pair of...panties...slipped on over his black pants.

"Are those...?" Molly asks, just as a hungry Feeder launches itself on Jazz's crumpled body and chomps into her arm like Ma Kettle's just rung the dinner bell.

I kick him off—knee him off is more like it—but either way Jazz is getting swallowed whole if something dramatic doesn't happen in the next few seconds.

She grabs my leg like a rock climber reaching out for a lifeline and I yank upward, upward, until she's finally standing on the rickety break room table with me and Molly. From the other room I hear a rush, and a ding like metal on tile, a short, human scream, and then a whoosh. Water fills the break room floor with a sudsy gush as it spills across the lime green tiles.

"They did it!" cheers Molly, feebly putting her hands together above her head in the world's most pitiful golf clap ever.

"Did what?" gasps Jazz, stabbing at random Feeder hands as they clutch and claw at her ankles. She scrambles for better footing on the wobbly break room table that's about to flip over at any minute.

"I'm not sure, exactly," Molly admits.

Dub launches himself into the room through the hole in the wall, cracking skulls and taking names until at last he leaps onto the table to join us. There is hardly room now, not with big old Dub and his long, wobbly legs and wide shoulders and endless dangling arms, but we'll have to make some for Spud if—

"Spud?" I ask as he leans down to walk through the hole in the wall.

His feet are wet. The Feeders' feet are wet.

Suddenly, they're all standing in two inches of water that's quickly receding.

"Trust me," he says, readjusting the second pair of zombie panties that he's pulled on over his black pair of stealth cargo pants.

"But you're not one of us," Molly shouts as a reminder. "The electricity, it will—"

Spud holds up the remote control clicker as the Feeders turn their heads in his direction. There is a moment of mass recognition—of dull, blunt brain power—and then the Feeders scream as one and scramble to get away.

But there is nowhere to hide.

The water has filled the spa room, the break room and the hall outside.

Spud clicks the sleek, black remote—twice—and I sizzle in place. I'd forgotten they were all tuned to the same frequency. Suddenly my boxer shorts are smoking; literally!

I'm not even being cute. The sparks have nearly set them on fire!

I'm vibrating like a live wire, muscles spazzing uncontrollably, bones feeling like they're cracking one by one, my wrists like they're being hammered against the right metal chains around my wrist.

Molly gasps beside me as Dub and Jazz try to scramble away to avoid frying like lobsters in a pot.

But there's nowhere to go but down, where the Feeders are dropping like dead, giant, gray-green flies, the shock from Spud's zombie panties short-circuiting what's left of their greedy, grimy brains.

Spud falls, too.

Unfortunately, he falls flat with his finger still on the clicker, meaning it never goes out.

Until, that is, I do.

CHAPTER TWENTY-FIVE

When I come to—dang, this is starting to become a habit! My hands are free, Molly is sitting next to me, and Spud is lying next to her.

Only one of them is moving.

"Spud," I cry out, shoving him with my free hands, rocking him to and fro.

"He's gone," says Dub.

"Expired," says Jazz.

"But...but...how can that be?"

Dub and Jazz shake their heads, like they can't believe I don't know all the rules by now.

"There's only one way to save him, Toby," Molly explains, winding a towel around a gash in her arm. "You have to bite him."

"*What?*" I ask. "Why *me?*"

"'Cause you're wearing the zombie panties," croaks Dub with a weak smile. "That's why."

"What does *that* have to do with anything?" I snap.

"You bite him," Dub explains.

"I push this," Molly adds, holding up Spud's clicker.

"And you jump start his Afterlife," Jazz finishes.

"What if it doesn't work?" I ask skeptically because this all sounds like some grade-A MacGyver bull crap right here.

"Then he stays dead," Molly accuses, as if somehow this is all *my* fault. "Is that what you want?"

"No," I whine, "but have you ever worn these before? It really, really hurts."

I mean, I hate to sound selfish and all but that's how much they hurt.

You start thinking it's better to let Spud stay dead than feel that pain again.

"Give it to me then," she says, snatching it before I can refuse.

I look down at Spud.

I'd told him I'd never, *ever* bite a human.

But here I am, about to do that very thing.

Will he hate me for it, if this works?

Or thank me?

And will I be able to resist the taste of human flesh, once his blood fills my mouth?

Only one way to find out, I suppose.

I shrug, lean down, and bite Spud on the shoulder where I'm hoping it won't show if he ever has to apply for some kind of zombie job interview or someth—

The sizzling starts the minute I taste Spud's cold, dead flesh between my teeth. (And, yes, it does taste *exactly* as gross as it sounds.)

Immediately, my loins are on fire, then my legs, my stomach, my arms, my hair. All of a sudden it's like glass raking down my body, followed by razor blades sliding across my veins, with a side order of rusty steel rods shoved through my bones and then salt and acid smeared over it all for good measure.

I writhe uncontrollably until it stops.

I'm paralyzed, helpless, sprawled on top of Spud and powerless to move my own body until Molly finally pulls me off.

I'm smiling.

"What?" she asks, looking at a lifeless Spud with eyes full of disappointment and then back to me with a hint of rage.

"I felt his heartbeat," I say, just as Spud's eyes flicker to life.

"The hell?" he spurts, spitting out brackish spa water frothy pink with the blood of his bitten tongue.

He winces a little, looks at the fresh bite mark on his arm and grumbles, "I knew I wouldn't get out of this alive."

A kind of half-chuckle, half-murmur of relief passes through the room; followed by an awkward silence.

Just then, the break room wall bursts open and bricks topple inside, covering us all with a healthy coat of brick dust that sticks to our cold, wet bodies like really gross frosting on an even grosser cake. We hear gears grinding and squealing, panicked voices, and then feet sloshing and, finally, two familiar faces poke through the hole in the wall. The twins!

"Great timing," says Molly.

"Excuse us," say the twins simultaneously—still. "Have you ever hotwired a twenty-year-old Army truck before?"

EPILOGUE

Zombie High is burning in the rearview mirror.

Even over the whine of the mighty engine beneath my feet, I can hear beams crackling and tiles snapping and glass from the blown out windows littering the sidewalks and drive.

I just keep driving.

The truck feels heavy under my hands, but the road is true, and I know just where I'm going. Up, up and then up some more.

I'll have you know that Tinfoil, Tennessee, sits at the base of one of the largest mountain ranges in the south, the Crescent Cliffs. So named because they surround half the county in a kind of crescent-roll shape, the Cliffs are filled with enough nooks, crannies, dips, dives, caves, and caverns to hide a whole city of zombies, not to mention a small truck full.

There are trees for miles, thousands of them, hundreds of thousands, thick enough to tickle each other with their branches and nobody—but nobody—lives there. Well, except the squirrels, and the rabbits and the foxes and the field mice and the moles and the possums and the raccoons.

Even if you figure one squirrel per tree, there are enough fresh, tiny, bubble gum-size brains to last us the next few years, at least. By then, I suppose, things will have died down enough for us to sneak out and maybe, just maybe, go home one day.

Maybe.

For now, though, we escape.

We'll never get to go home, period, if the Army catches us.

We'll only be able to use the truck for the next nine miles or so, and half of that will be tough, gnarly back roads in case the giant bonfire that used to be Zombie High alerts the cops.

Still, walking into the Crescent Cliffs is the least of our worries.

"They'll all think we're dead, you know?" says Molly, looking at me pointedly from the shotgun seat.

Her hair is almost dry, lying flat and straight in thick black bangs against her forehead. There's a smudge from the charcoal we used to start the fire on her left cheek.

"I know that," I agree solemnly, thinking of Mom and Dad and what they'll think when they knock on my bedroom door in a few hours and find my bed still made and me nowhere to be found. "But...that's okay, for now. We'll tell them, one day, what really happened. Why we had to run away without saying anything. Or telling anybody."

"How?" asks Jazz, orange hair damp from the spa water and flecks of black Feeder blood sludge on her throat. "When?"

"A letter, a postcard, something real, in our own handwriting, so they know that only we could write it. And sometime soon, so they don't have to worry too long."

"You don't mean that," says Molly hopefully.

"I sure do," I growl. "Krill may have ruined our lives, but he's not going to ruin our parents' lives as—"

"What!" gasps Molly, bumping her head on the giant truck's dashboard as I slam on the brakes and the back tires, four to an axle, skitter to the left just a little in the wet, dewy gravel of dawn's early light. "What the hell, Toby? What are you stopping for?"

I shove the great big truck into park and unclick my seatbelt violently.

"Who is that?" asks Dub from over my shoulder.

"Is that..." breathes Molly, blinking her eyes.

"Yeah," I grunt, switching the engine off with a clattering thud.

It's Lilac, all right, limping along the brush line, looking over her shoulder, dragging an axe handle in the mud like she's getting tired of holding it over her shoulder.

"Forget her," says Jazz, looking over her shoulder.

"Yeah," agrees Dub anxiously, leaning down to talk some sense into me. "Let's get out of here before the cops show. Or someone even smarter."

"Can't," I say, pocketing the keys so they won't get any ideas and peel off without me. "I made her a promise. And I intend to keep it."

"Toby," Spud rasps from the backseat, skin so pale he might as well be a ghost as the zombie blood–MY zombie blood–gurgles sluggishly through his veins. "You. Don't. Have. To. Do. This."

Even though it takes whatever little energy he has left to choke out each word, I know he doesn't really mean it. And even if he does, at this point, I just don't care.

I open the truck door and step down onto the ground. It feels different, somehow, the fresh air, the soft earth, the blanket of leaves beneath my soggy shoes.

Everything from now on, I suppose, will feel different.

After all, I'm dead.

I wonder if the killing will feel different, too.

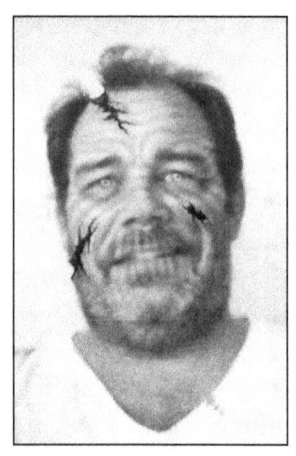

~ABOUT THE AUTHOR~

Rusty Fischer is the author of several YA supernatural novels, including *Zombies Don't Cry* (Medallion Press, 2011), *Ushers, Inc.* (Decadent Publishing, 2011), *Detention of the Living Dead* (Quake Books, 2012) and *Vamplayers* (Medallion Press, 2012).

Visit his blog, www.zombiesdontblog.blogspot.com, for news, reviews, cover leaks, writing and publishing advice, book excerpts and more! And if you can't wait for his next release, download his complete YA novel *Vampires Drool!* *Zombies Rule!* absolutely FREE at www.scribd.com/doc/38953974/Vampires-Drool-Zombies-Rule-by-Rusty-Fischer.

www.ingramcontent.com/pod-product-compliance
Lightning Source LLC
Chambersburg PA
CBHW071856220626
47052CB00002B/143

* 9 7 8 1 6 1 3 3 3 1 5 9 0 *